THE CHEEKY TIKI

BANG GANG

in

The Case of the Creepy Christian Camp

Cherry Zonkowski

Cherry Squared Press, 2016

CONTENTS

The Case of the Creepy Christian Camp

CONTENTS (Contd.)

Preface

Six years ago, I did a well-reviewed, well-received one-woman show in San Francisco called *Reading my Dad's Porn and French Kissing the Dog*. And then my life exploded with horribleness, and my money situation changed and I wasn't able to work on a second show—which totally sucked. My hard-earned reputation as a performer dissipated. People forget. To keep myself sane, and because I always have to have a project to work on, I started writing this book.

One thing writers will tell you sometimes is that you should write the book you want to read. So I did. That's how I produced an extremely unusual, genre-defying piece of trash (which, by the way, is also how I describe myself).

The book you're about to read, or maybe the book you've just read, or are thinking about reading, is about a group of people who represent a diverse panoply of different sexual, racial, and gender identities coming together to rescue gay and transgendered teenagers from abusive Christian religious households. They do it while codenamed after Gilligan's Island characters and drinking tiki cocktails. But they do it! As I write this preface, it is three days after the shooting in Orlando, and it has never been clearer to me how much we need to educate and fight against homophobia, how very far we are from winning that fight.

I started this book as a NANOWRIMO (NAtional NOvember WRiting MOnth) project which I didn't finish at the time, but I am stubborn. I keep going with projects--and relationships--way way past when any sane person would stop. I was reacting at the time to two other novels:

I had been reading Fifty Shades of Disgusting Narcissistic Abuse and Heterosexual Bourgeois Monogamous Propaganda Bullshit, and I cannot even tell you on how many many levels I hated it. And I even actually have sexual fantasies about sadistic bad boy billionaires! My friend Dixie says the book will help open people's minds to kink and a more satisfying sex life. Maybe so. Personally, I worry that het men will use it to coerce their female partners into feeling like they are uptight if they don't like being sexually abused. But the real problem to me is not the book itself, but the vacuum around it. Kink that goes mainstream is always male dominant, unless the woman is evil. WHERE is the femdom pop culture equivalent to this book? WHERE is the detective novel where an English teacher solves mysteries by analyzing grammar while a slave licks her feet? (Answer—it's my next book). WHERE are the books that show non-monogamy as viable sexual options? They are out there, but we need so many more, and we need them to be fun. I wanted to write a book and read a book that showed a variety of people who find sexual fulfillment in all different ways and configurations, and I wanted to celebrate sexual and other diversity.

I also read The Girl with the Dragon Tattoo, which I liked a lot better. But there's that kickboxing lesbian, Miriam Wu, who gets her ass handed to her by a bad guy? I wanted to read a book where kickboxing lesbians don't get their asses handed to them. Where they prevail.

I have come a long way personally since I started writing this book, and I have learned a lot. One of the things I want to say in this preface though is that I know I always have more to learn about how to truly fight for the rights of LGBTQIA people and sex-positive feminists. If something here offends you, know that I am ready to listen, and I am ready to change my mind in the face of compelling arguments. This book is sex positive, pro ethically made porn, pro kink and pro sex work. If you have problems with any of that, this book may not be for you. But feel free to read it and see what you think. Just please register all complaints kindly, okay? I'm freaking sensitive.

This book also takes on some weighty subjects for a light book, and it was researched heavily one way or another. Some of that research came from listening to people's stories about their sexuality all my life, and listening to the stories that Dixie De La Tour presents at Bawdy Storytelling. If you read a particularly wild story in here and think that THAT could not have happened, please know that it almost certainly did. The wilder the story, the more likely it is that I borrowed it from life.

I relied on other kinds of research so that I could accurately depict the state of sexism and homophobia currently infecting the evangelical Christian movement. And I hate to say it, but the situation is so much worse than I wrote here. There are Christian-run "reform schools" where being gay/transgender is just one of the possible offenses—and there are a lot of such schools. The one in this book was inspired by--but not in any way based on--one such school in the Dominican Republic, and I highly recommend the documentary Kidnapped by Christ if you want to know more. At one point I sat down and talked to a survivor of another one of these hell holes. That survivor is severely traumatized by what they went through (they identify as genderqueer)—and who wouldn't be? And who can understand what they went through? But I feel like it's part of my mission to help people understand what's out there while offering narratives of hope, survivor fantasies of power. When I told the survivor I know that the young trans boy in my story is not in need of rescue but the rescuer, tears came to their eyes. We need to fight to empower our youth against hatred. This book comes out of that conviction.

I was hit hard by Orlando, like everyone I know and love. Since I have been working on this book about rescuing gay and transgender teens from abusive religious households, the relationship of religion/authoritarianism to abuse is an obsession with me. As I get the book ready for final publication, a question I never thought of until now occurred to me and hit me hard: am I queer? Am I queer enough to have written this book? The only person who called into question my right to post my opinions was a straight white cisgender male, and I went off so hard our friendship might be over. I feel on a deep and personal level that these are my issues. But why?

I started thinking about Sam. Sam was my stepsister. She was ten years younger than me and I was out of the house when our parents married, and they lived in Nebraska. My mother still does. I remember scolding Sam at age eight for saying homophobic things that she learned from her brothers. I was home from college in California and had gay friends I loved, so I snapped at her and told her those things were hurtful and untrue. When she was ten I visited Nebraska for about a month, and a few friends, a lesbian couple, came to visit. We spent an afternoon with Sam, and I saw her watch my friends in fascination and ask them indirect questions and afterwards they said, "You know you have a baby dyke there, right?" and I said, "I do now."

I made a mental note that if she ever needed somewhere to go to get out of Nebraska, I would help her. but I never made that offer out loud, and years went by. I visited Nebraska as little as possible because that place is a FUCKING SHITHOLE of conservatism and it makes me gag to step foot on its rancid soil. I'm sorry, I know there are some decent people there. But they all know exactly what I mean. Words cannot convey how much I hate that place. Anyway, Sam grew up and I didn't see much of her: we didn't connect. I remember once walking into her room when she was a teenager and seeing a bookcase that used to be mine. It was full of sports trophies and stuffed animals. When it was mine it was full of books. So we weren't much alike. She grew up, became a soccer star in high school, went into the military and then...she killed herself. With a gun.

It was the days of Don't Ask, Don't Tell, and she had broken up with her girlfriend--who intended to tell. I remember talking to another military lesbian years earlier, and she said this was a common pattern--the more out, obvious lesbian would have a relationship with someone straight-passing, and when the relationship was over, the straight passing woman would have an attack of guilt/shame/disgust/homophobia and report the relationship, throwing all "blame" on the less straight-passing partner. Hell, this used to be the plot of lesbian pulp fiction too: the evil dyke seductress and the young innocent who would eventually find dick and be "saved" while the other one died, often of suicide. My stepsister had untreated mental health issues, anger from her parents' divorce, but ultimately she killed herself because of the rampant homophobia and authoritarianism atmosphere of hate that told her she was worthless because of who and how she loved.

My mother called me in tears. "We knew," she said, about herself and her husband, Sam's father. "But we were waiting for her to tell us. We accepted her and she never knew it. Was

The Case of the Creepy Christian Camp

I wrong? Should I have brought it up? Could that have saved her?" And what could I say to my mother? Yes, and no, and you did the best you could. and it should never have been something she had to bring up, and I failed her too, and she's dead. So in the wake of Orlando I have been crying for all the gay teenagers out there who will be a little more afraid to come out, a little more likely to kill themselves, when we've lost way way too many of them already. This is just one of the many reasons why I see this as my fight. This is one of the reasons why I wrote this book. I don't come from a Christian evangelical background. I come out of the toxic masculine authoritarian structures of the military, and I see the relationship between them clearly. I grew up fighting against a hateful patriarchy that made my father feel he had the license to bully and tyrannize over us relentlessly—because he was the man. The same bullshit that evangelicals, like the Quiverfull movement, still preach. I feel the connection at a visceral level.

In this book you will meet characters, many of whom are committed to doing what they do because they have seen close loved ones and friends killed or hurt by homophobia and patriarchy—but always lurking behind them is Sam.

Acknowledgements:

This book would not have been possible without the unswerving faith in me shown by so many people. I want to thank:

My mother, who always has my back.

Lisa Pimental, my rock, who helped me every step of the way. She is the best person I know or could hope to know.

My team: Dave Cherry, the best older brother, designer, and illustrator a girl could hope for, and Stephanie Pascal for your dedicated work.

Dixie De La Tour, whose Bawdy Storytelling is my constant inspiration in the power of stories to change lives.

Steven Black, Eva Konig, and Aaron Seeman for believing in me and turning out for me year after year.

Bryan Loop and Angela Gunn, my lifelong friends, whose support for me has spanned long decades of amazement.

Marc Mitchell and Robin Cunningham, whose enthusiasm for this project kept me going when I might have thrown in the towel.

Don and Carla McCasland who helped me through dark, rough times and celebrated with me in better ones.

Larry Edelstein, who saw my show FOUR times, and supported this book too with his generosity.

The Case of the Creepy Christian Camp

Phil Venton and Nichole Stockman, who show me that new friends can be as kick ass and down for me as my old ones.

To Xandir, who survived hell and lived to tell the tale, and whose insights and criticism saved me from making many blunders.

And to Sarah Kayler and Jonathan Gilbert for your generous support.

This book is dedicated to the memory of Samantha Hill.

"Joy is our birthright."
Billie Bertan

The Case of the Creepy Christian Camp

The Case of the Creepy Christian Camp

The Case of the Creepy Christian Camp

Prologue

Lindsay listened at the door. The house was quiet, but she knew he was still awake. She heard the distinct clink of ice against the side of the glass, the deep and labored sound of a drunk struggling for breath. She hoped this would be a quiet night.

The sound of glass smashing against a wall told her it wasn't going to be.

The Case of the Creepy Christian Camp

Not Very Far Away

A woman struggled against her bonds, black rope biting into her wrists. A luscious woman, glorious red hair spilling across cream-colored sheets, face down, her body curved like soft-serve ice cream. She gave a tortured moan and pulled against the ropes, but they were secure, cutting slightly into her pale skin. She wore nothing but a wisp of cloth—not panties but the transparent ghost of panties, a white lace accent barely visible against the ample curve of her ass, pale as cream except for three angry red welts.

Another woman stood with her back to the woman on the bed, her outfit a stark contrast to the erotic picture presented. She stood in low heels in a pink suit, skirt and blazer with a conservative white blouse: an outfit that sang Sunday school songs and organized church raffles. But she gripped in her hand a slim black cane, flashing it through the air to hear its swish. Her dark, sleek hair was swept up into a bun beneath a pink pillbox hat, white gloves immaculate against the black sheen of her cane.

The room around the pair seemed incongruous: drab, dingy, dull. Plain furniture from decidedly unhip thrift stores. The slotted headboard that the redhead was tied to had been painted yellow a long time ago, and it looked like it might come crashing down with one big pull. On the pressboard nightstand stood a reading lamp, which took a halfhearted stab at lighting the room but settled for dim gloom. An ugly pressboard bureau slouched drunkenly across one wall, one leg shorter than the others; on its top lay an organized selection of instruments for causing pain, or, for people who are bent that way, pleasure. One dusty, stained armchair lurked in the corner, with two expensive suitcases sitting beside it.

"Stop squirming!" The pink-suited woman whirled and brought the cane down again on the redhead's vulnerable, quivering flesh. The redhead gasped and writhed, then stilled her body and its responses.

"Sometimes you like it when I squirm," came her breathy soft voice, a feminine voice that sounded like silk and candy and wet dreams.

"Oh ho. So you can talk? I didn't ask you to talk. You have a beautiful mouth, but it's not meant for talking." The dark-haired woman picked up a leather paddle and brought it crashing down, striking a rapid tattoo on the red and white ass, crisscrossed with evidence of pain. The redhead steeled herself against the onslaught, letting nothing but the faintest whimper escape.

"Oh, yes my pretty. (SMACK) Show me how strong you are. (SMACK) Show me how willing you are to take this pain—for Jesus. (SMACK) I will beat the sin out of you and take it away from you and leave you pure." The paddle smacked again, hard.

Both were breathing hard after this barrage of blows, and the dark-haired woman stepped back.. An observer would have seen an Asian woman in her late twenties, beautiful in her own right, in her perfect pink wool suit, looking breathless with triumph as she surveyed her handiwork.

She ran her hand against the reddening ass, cupping it,

6

feeling the heat generated by her blows. She purred the next words: "Tell Jesus that you love him. Tell him you take this pain willingly…for him."

"I don't love Jesus! Fuck Jesus! Jesus can drink my piss!" the redhead snarled.

The Asian woman's mouth quirked up in a smile. "Oh what a bad bad bad little slut you are! What a filthy-mouthed whore! The devil is in you, and this is the only way to beat him out of you!" She placed the cane down on the table then picked up a wooden paddle and sent it sailing down; the sweet thwack of the paddle against pale creamy flesh rang out hard, and the redhead gasped.

A loud banging sounded against the door and a cry rang out, "Open up in there! GINGER! MARY ANN! Enough already, you crazy dykes!"

The Case of the Creepy Christian Camp

Chapter 1: Get Ready to Go

"Shit!" said Isobel "Ginger" Jensen, struggling against her bonds for real this time. She knew it had been a bad idea to start this scene so close to a rescue, but it was the best way she knew to relieve her stress.

"What do you fucktards WANT? We are BUSY!" yelled her partner.

The door flew open, and a slight Latino man, graceful and slender, stepped inside and surveyed the bed. Both women glared at him. "Shit, Mary Ann, might as well untie me. Fun's over for tonight."

"Oh my sweet sweet Jesus! You girls do not stop! Keith! Come and see! Mary Ann has Ginger tied up again!"

"Dammit, Gilligan, when we're on the job, call me Skipper! How many times do I have to tell you?!?! A tall black man appeared scowling in the door, but his expression turned to a smile as he took in the scene appreciatively. "Damn. I never get tired of this."

"Can you girls keep your hands out of each other's coochies for even one hour? We're here to do a job!"

"Get OUT of here!" yelled Felicity "Mary Ann" Wong, reaching down and untying Isobel's hands. Isobel sat up and rubbed her chafed wrists, smiling at Felicity's bad temper. "This

is a fucking private moment, assholes! This is a beautiful expression of our fucking love! And the job's tomorrow night!"

Keith "Skipper" Davis shook his head sadly. "No, the job
got moved. We need to do this tonight. You guys need to towel
off quick, get dressed, and meet us out front ASAP."

Chapter 2: A Rescue

I sobel and Felicity took three minutes flat to get untied and end the scene; then Isobel shot a look at Felicity that she instantly understood. Felicity gathered her up, whispering words of reassurance. Aftercare might be quick, but it is still necessary. They scrambled into their action gear. Ten minutes later the four members of the team assembled in front of the small rented house that was their temporary base of operation.

Isobel envied Felicity: when it was time for a job she just changed into plain black sweats, but Isobel had to find a way cover all the glowing white of her skin and her flame-red hair without looking like Catwoman. Her first time, giddy with excitement, she had actually dressed in skintight leather, but never again. It was way too hot and hard to move in, and it had scared their rescue almost to death.

Felicity said, "Okay, Skipper, what's the deal? We had everything set for tomorrow and this is going to screw up our travel plans, all our arrangements." From here on out until the job was done they would use only code names. Safety—anyone overhearing them wouldn't know their real identities.

"We got a call. Shit went down tonight, bad, and sounds like it might go on tomorrow night. This kid needs help. And we're it," Keith Davis, code- looked like what he was: a club bouncer. He wore a dark T-shirt with a bulletproof vest under a light windbreaker, on top of dark black jeans cut for mobility and not fashion. He had an arm slung loosely around Margarita Rimsalt aka Gilligan aka Beto Ramirez. Margarita preferred to dress in drag for jobs. She claimed it was a kind of disguise, but Isobel remembered her saying once, when tipsy, that she always felt more ballsy in drag. Ironic but true.

Isobel heard the news about the change of plans with a sinking heart.

"Does the girl know we're coming in tonight? Does she know we're coming at all?"

"You know, communication on this one has been bad from the start. This girl's parents have her on lockdown, communication blackout. They yanked her out of school. She goes to church and back—nowhere else. But this is what we do, right? We rescue gay teens, genderqueer teens, from intolerable oppression," Keith sounded calm and steady, no doubts about the mission.

"If they want to be rescued. If they ASK to be rescued," Isobel said. "If they don't ask, we don't know how much of this bullshit they've internalized. She could scream."

Felicity put an arm around her. "Yeah, but we have the word of the girlfriend, Jess, that Lindsay wants to be rescued. There's a risk, relying on secondhand intel. But I've talked to Jess; I've told her how important it is that we be sure. She's a levelheaded girl, and I trust her. *We* trusted her. Remember? Okay?"

Isobel did remember. A sixteen-year-old girl, sobbing in a coffee shop, frightened because her first love was immured in an evangelical hell. But when she said Lindsay had told her she wanted out, they sensed she was telling the truth. And given the level of abuse—isolation, physical abuse, and food deprivation—they felt they had to try. Isobel looked down and nodded, summoning up her courage. Too often she felt like the weak link. Keith and Felicity both were fearless in their own way: Keith calm and smiling, Felicity gleeful, ready for a fight. Isobel felt damaged and broken next to them—but being damaged and broken turned out to be her very own strength. She was needed.

Felicity nodded. "Okay, then. Travel plans?" she asked.

"I called the Professor and had him update all arrangements. We got lucky; it's not a heavy travel weekend. We still got the ID so we're good there. After we pick up the girls, Little Buddy and I will drive to the Dallas airport. We have a car rental there so we ditch this van in the airport parking lot. We'll fly out with Lindsay, and you two will take the other car and drive north with Jess. Gilligan here will do just a quick makeover on them both just in case before the flight, light disguise. Wigs, makeup, change of clothes. Flight's scheduled for 5:30 so that gives us two and a half hours to grab the girl, do the makeovers, and fly."

"Okay, then," Isobel gave a bright smile. "I think we best go get this girl."

It was a half-hour drive, and as they piled in Keith said, "Okay, Gilligan, remind us of what we're facing, security-wise."

Beto had slipped behind the wheel and started the car. He glared at the road and told them, "I fucking hate that code name. I want to be Margarita."

"Margarita's not a code name. It's a drag name. Which you *perform* under. This is supposed to be a security measure."

"Fuck that. Then I want to be Ginger." Everyone but Margarita smiled. Isobel was five foot eleven of pure movie star beauty with naturally red hair: Ginger to the bone.

"We can argue about this later, okay?" said Felicity. Her brisk tones restored order in the car. Isobel smiled at her in the dark. She loved when Felicity sounded like a schoolteacher you didn't dare disobey. She reached her hand up to her neck and felt for the leather collar she wore. It comforted her, the physical proof that she was owned.

"Okay, well, this job should be simple. We go there and enter the code. Unless they changed it in the last 24 hours we're in like motherfucking Flynn." Beto drummed his hands on the steering wheel. Isobel could see the sparkle of glitter and silver on his nails. A small smudge of oil marred the effect: being a drag queen mechanic is not easy on the hands.

"How do we know the code?" asked Felicity. "Are we relying on the girlfriend?" Information offered by those close to the targets had been unreliable in the past. They each silently remembered the last job, a trap, with fake information. Word was slowly leaking out about their operation, making the job harder all the time.

"We put a very small camera on the neighbor's roof and got a gorgeous shot of the security panel. Want to hear something hilarious? It's 6666. Like somewhere in their minds they know they're fucking evil. Anyway, there you go: easy peasy cock teasy."

"Oh, God!" Felicity laughed. "That's horrible. Stop with the catchphrases. No catchphrases!"

"And can you curse a little less when you get the girl?" Isobel's voice, rarely heard before these capers, was suddenly sharp and insistent. "This girl got beaten for wearing nail polish. You swear like a sailor and you're going to freak her out. We *don't* want her freaked out." Her job was to keep the girl as calm and safe as possible. It wasn't easy at the best of times to convince a sheltered, abused kid to gather up all her courage and leave her family. A smack-talking foul-mouthed drag queen didn't always make the job easier.

"Okay, okay, I'll talk like a perfect fucking lady. When

the time comes. Okay? Anyway, Skipper types in the code. I wait in the car. Mary Ann waits outside the door to provide backup if needed. Skipper and Ginger go in, Ginger grabs the girl, everyone runs out, and we all go get margaritas."

"I want to go in with Ginger," said Felicity mulishly.

"Well, you know why you can't, okay? You can either go in with Ginger for the job or travel with her later. Christ, you girls are joined at the hip. No, at the coochie!"

Isobel nodded in the dark. "It makes sense, honey, you know it does. This way Skipper is the most likely person to be seen and ID'd. They will freak out so hard when they see their girl being stolen by a six-foot-three black man that they won't think rationally. And they'll look for *him*, not us. He'll be long gone, and we'll have the girl."

"But that's it! This guy is a gun nut! He sees Skipper, he's going to shoot first and ask questions later."

"I'm wearing a vest, girl. I'll be okay." Keith's voice sounded as sure and solid as rock. No one had ever seen him flapped or flustered. He moved in his own pool of calm.

Felicity, on the other hand, ran on adrenaline, addicted to high-octane stress: "Vests don't protect your head, your knees, your feet. And you're the person hardest to carry if we need to get you out of there."

"My love, we can't change the plan now. We agreed. Knock it off," Isobel whispered, lightly kissing Felicity's neck to take the sting out of her words. "Anyway, if shit went down tonight hopefully he'll be so dead drunk he won't wake up. No one will wake up; we'll get the girl; everything will be fine."

"Did we manage to get any word to her? Does she know we're coming?" asked Felicity.

"No," answered Keith. "Her family has had her locked down with no outside communication for the past two weeks. Daily beatings, but last night's was out of control, the girlfriend

15

said when she called. She only knows about it because she hides in the backyard with binoculars. That's rough."

"She was crying her heart out, Jess said. Asshole fucking Christians!" added Beto/Margarita. "She has no idea she's being rescued tonight. It will be your job to get her to agree to come with us. We'll give you as much time as we can," he grinned. "It's a good thing you can talk the stink off a goat, girl."

Isobel smiled in the dark of the car and everyone's eyes squinted a little from the sudden brilliance.

"Anything else we need to know?" she asked.

"Dog," said Beto. "According to the girlfriend, the dog is an old, fat, lazy, friendly pug with asthma. So she shouldn't be able to bark loud. Name of Honeypie. Shouldn't be a problem, but you never know with vermin."

"Dogs aren't vermin!" Felicity yelled, smacking Beto in the back of the head.

"Where I come from, they're lunch!"

"You're from Highland Park, idiot. No one eats dogs in East LA."

"Honey, you don't know half the things I have put in my mouth! Anyway—here we are."

Parker, Texas, three a.m. The minivan pulled around a corner in a middle-class housing development. Beto swore.

"This place is so fucking ugly. The architect took too much Xanax; that's what I think. These houses are lazy ugly. He was like, la la la, let's design ugly houses for breeders because I don't give a fuck about them and when people see it everyone who sees it will say, 'eeeew.'" He sang out the words to the tune of "Girl from Ipanema." Isobel stifled a giggle in the backseat. Beto always defused the tension, thankfully. Isobel had neither Keith's calm nor Felicity's love of danger. She hated the way her heart was in her throat and her hands shook. But no one else could do the job she did.

The houses looked like miniature Southfork ranches, recalling the home of Parker's most famous fictional family, the Ewings. The buildings sprawled on enormous lawns front to back but almost touched side to side. They weren't identical but close, with subtly altered superfluous architectural features: little stained glass windows like orange slices on top of the door, doodads over the windows. Though the team could not see the colors, the windows gleamed enough in the dark to show that they were painted in pale pastels and whites. Isobel felt her gorge rise. She hated suburban neighborhoods, always had; they reminded her of beatings and rape and really crappy Christmases. So there she already had something in common with the target.

They pulled up in front of a particularly large, ugly example of Texas McMansion ranch-style housing. The lawn was expansive, and the three of them hustled across it quickly. The street was utterly deserted.

The plan went smoothly: door opened thanks to a skeleton key, code entered. Isobel grabbed Felicity and kissed her passionately before slipping inside the door, right behind Keith. Felicity grimaced and slipped into a shadow on the porch so as not to be seen by unlikely passersby or curious insomniac neighbors. She turned on the walkie-talkie to listen to the progress of the other two, on the alert for signs of trouble.

Inside the door, Ginger and the Skipper went directly up the stairs; they had memorized the floor plan. On her dog bed in the living room, Honeypie cocked an ear and raised her head off her pillow for a second, before settling back down into a complicated dream where slow cats turned into giant bones when you chased them, and life was bliss. At the door of Lindsay's room, Keith turned and faced the hallway, easy and relaxed but very alert. He picked the second key off a key chain and opened the locked door. Isobel slipped inside the room, steeling herself for what she would face. This was her moment. This was when she had to get everything right, say all the right things, and be very, very strong.

The room was decorated in late Texas Christian princess: everything was pink and white, and ruffled and lacy, with inspirational bible verses framed on the walls, surrounded by soft pink flowers. Isobel was relieved to see that the bedside light was still on, thank God. The first step was always to try to get a low light in the room—if the target was asleep, having a stranger wake her up in the dark could terrify her into a scream. Here was a girl who had been beaten and terrified, on a short fuse. The very first rule of rescue: *absolutely* no screaming.

A figure on the bed lay huddled, making noises somewhere between sobs and snores. Isobel walked over to the bed and looked down. The girl was asleep, but making small choking, whimpering sounds, as if she had fallen asleep crying and had not stopped. Looking down, Isobel saw in horror that Lindsay had a black eye and bruises around her neck, indicating choking, strangling. Her head had rolled off the Christian pillowcase that promised angelic protection. Isobel felt a wave of nausea and sat down on the bed. The gentle movement of the bed would alert the girl to her presence and sitting would bring her face closer to her level. She took a deep breath, reached down, and whispered, "Lindsay? Lindsay, honey, wake up." Her voice was its very softest, sweet and breathy, the voice of a kitten drifting on a cloud of rainbows.

Lindsay came awake, blinked, eyes wide for a second in shock.

Isobel pressed a finger to her lips. "Shhhhh, honey. Jess sent me. Jess? Nod if you understand."

Lindsay nodded.

"I used to lie awake after a beating like this, wishing someone would just come and take me away." Her beautiful voice was very calm, and she gently took one of Lindsay's hands. They were cold, and she held them, just letting the girl feel the gentle warmth for a beat or two. Gentle physical contact enhanced trust. Thanks to Sequoia—"Lovey"—she knew everything there was to know about creating trust quickly. "After my dad beat me, I would sob and sob and wish someone could just take me away from all of it…did you ever wish that?"

The girl hunched over in the bed, curled into a defensive fetal position and pulled her arm away. A sob like a spasm rocked her body. Isobel put her hand on her shoulder.

"Don't cry right now, Lindsay. Later, all the crying you need. But right now I need to know, honey. You can leave right now, honey. I can take you somewhere safe where you won't be beaten. And Jess will be there with you. But it has to be your decision, honey."

Lindsay turned and stared at her. Her eyes were filling with tears and she saw that Isobel's eyes, too, had filled with tears and that one had spilled over and was rolling down her face. She sat up and nodded and spoke her first words.

"You'll take me away?"

"Far away."

"What about Jess?"

"Her too. She wants to come with us, honey. She loves you so much."

"Now?"

"Right now. It has to be right now. Don't stop for a single thing. Just come with me, walk out the door and down the stairs and out."

"Will I have to come back? Will they make me come back?"

This was a tricky question. Some targets needed to be reassured they could still be in touch with the life they knew; some needed reassurance they would be safe away from this nightmare. Isobel looked into the scared, brown eyes looking up at her and said what she hoped she needed to hear.

"No one will ever *make* you come back, honey. I promise. Not ever."

Lindsay looked up with wide-eyed terror, but then a look of anger and determination crossed her face, and she gave a jerky nod. Isobel felt a wave of relief.

Ten minutes later, the girl was bundled into the back of the car, and they were off, stopping briefly around the next corner to pick up Jess. Isobel felt another wave of relief when she saw the girl on the corner. Lindsay was going to feel a hell of a lot safer now with her girlfriend in the car and a lot less likely to back out. Those were the absolute worst—the two times they had gone in for a rescue and the kid backed out. Too afraid of the team to accept help, too afraid to run off into the blue with total strangers. The last one had two black eyes, but they couldn't get her to leave the only world she knew.

But Jess and Lindsay sat still and silent, gripping each other's hands with white knuckles, frightened but determined looks on their faces. The car glided swiftly out of the housing development and onto the freeway…and then right back on the shoulder as a loud pop and the sudden listing of the car announced they had an unexpected flat.

All eyes went to Beto, who yelled back, "Don't you even say it! Don't you even fucking say it! This shit—sorry, honey—this is not my fault. This is a rental car. Those tires are new! This is not supposed to happen! I checked the tread! This is bullfuckingshit! Sorry, honey."

Isobel leaned over to Jess and Lindsay, who looked panicked at this turn of events. "Don't worry. Now they will fight over who has to change the tire, they'll end up doing it together, and we'll be back on the road in ten minutes. We build 'Gilligan time' into our plans now." She smiled at the girls warmly, and they gave her nervous tentative smiles in return.

"I'm not changing your stupid tire! Do you see these? I got them done especial!" He brandished his long fingernails at Keith, who just laughed. Margarita always exaggerated her Chicano accent in times of stress.

"Well, maybe, Little Buddy, a mechanic shouldn't have long fingernails. Now this is officially *your job*, so come on, let's go do it."

"Oh, you're coming after all?"

"Well, I assume you need someone to crank your jack," he smiled.

"Baby, I love it when you crank my jack!" Margarita batted her eyes at Keith, and the two climbed outside to fix the flat.

Isobel looked over to see how the girls were taking this raunchy byplay. Something loosened in her chest when she saw them smiling at each other. They weren't paying much attention to what was around them. They would be okay, these girls. This was going to be a clean rescue.

Chapter 3: Beach House

Two days later, Sequoia "Lovey" Jones was taking one last glance around the room made ready for their new guest. She enjoyed fussing over guests, even more so when the guests were scared teens who hadn't known a lot of nurturing fussing in their lives.

"What do you think?" she asked Jess. "Did we miss anything?"

"It's amazing, it's perfect, I can't believe…oh, God, when will they be here? I keep getting scared they won't come, that they'll be caught."

The girl launched herself into Sequoia's arms, and she gathered her up into a warm, reassuring hug.

"They're on their way, sweetie. It's going to be.…" She paused, hearing a whooping yell from downstairs. "Honey, I think they're here."

She said the last words to thin air: Jess was already racing down the steps like her ass was on fire. Sequoia shook her head in amused sympathy for young love and followed her more sedately down the stairs.

Out front, a sturdy ATV pulled up in front of a lush compound carved from the east end of the island of Molokai. Jess, a slim, young girl with dark hair, catapulted herself from the lanai and raced up to it, and Lindsay tumbled out of the car and threw her arms around her girlfriend. The girls let go, backed up, and looked at each other for a long moment, nose to nose, and then the floodgates opened: tears started streaming down both their faces as they hugged again. Sequoia arrived outdoors to see them in each other's arms and she smiled—she didn't go out on rescues, didn't do the legwork before the rescue, so this was her first chance to meet the kids. She waited a minute while they cried and held each other and then swooped down on them, arms spread wide with welcome. She loved this part of her chosen work.

"Lindsay. Welcome to our island of sanity," she said, and she reached out and squeezed their arms gently and let go. "I know Jess is dying to show you your room, but I want you to know that I am both hostess and therapist here, and you come to me for absolutely anything you need. Complete confidentiality. You understand?"

The girls nodded and babbled for a minute about how grateful they were. Sequoia watched them as they hesitated and then threw their arms around her neck and sobbed. She returned the hug with zest and followed them up to the house. She was a big, black woman who looked a little like Oprah at her heaviest (plus fifty more). She secretly thought this helped people trust her faster and decided that was okay. Whatever worked.

Jess had Lindsay by the arm and was tugging her up the stairs. "They gave us this *amazing* room, Linds. It looks out on the ocean and has a little balcony and its own bathroom and—"

"OUR room?" squealed Lindsay. "For real? Even though we're—"

Lindsay whirled around to look at Sequoia on the stairway, who laughed. "We didn't rescue you to keep you apart.

23

Look, you girls have been through hell. You're thousands of miles from home and among strangers, though hopefully we won't feel like strangers for long. You need each other, you need to be good to each other, and what you do when you're alone in your room is no one's business but your own. Unless you're mean to each other. Are you going to be mean? Call each other names? Hurt each other?"

The two girls, hands clasped tight, shook their heads emphatically no.

"Okay, then. You've both been through a lot. If you need privacy, there's a room that opens on the other side of your bathroom, feel free to use it if you need alone time." The girls' hands clenched each other's tighter, and they edged closer together, their bodies saying emphatically that alone time was not what they wanted. They set off, Jess a step ahead and dragging Lindsay to the house, to the big, comfortable room where they put all the new arrivals. It was painted in serene blues and lilac, welcoming flowers bloomed in vases, and the room was fully loaded with amenities. A big bowl of tropical fruit. A stereo stocked with a wide range of MP3s for all tastes. A small fridge stuffed with mineral water, juice, and soda. Sequoia saw to all of it: making the rescued feel taken care of, deeply welcome, was the first step in her job. Everything a teen could want was here—except booze. Isobel, who'd been a tough punk rocker in her teens, had argued for a six-pack, saying teens need to start feeling trusted, but when the first "trusted" teen drank the six-pack in ten minutes and spent her first night puking, Isobel conceded the point. Sometimes freedom has to come gradually. Sequoia spent time researching each rescue and his or her tastes, so that each arrival would feel at home and safe. But for Lindsay, the most important thing in the house was Jess and her smiling face.

The next day, Sequoia sat down to a meeting of the team

at the secret tropical island compound of Leo Andropoulos, aka Warren Muffet, aka Mr. Howell. The meeting room was designed for elegance in the tropics—opulent comfort. When she arrived, Keith and Margarita, dressed in a lushly flowered tropical sarong, had already made themselves comfortable around the antique Brazilian rosewood table. One of Margarita's hands was drumming on the exquisite finish of the tabletop; the other snaked down and sideways. Sequoia suspected that whatever it was doing was responsible for the smug look on Keith's face. Across the table, Sequoia's heart warmed to see her own adopted child, Max "the Professor" McEntire, oblivious to everything but the contents of his laptop. He hunched forward, elbows on the tabletop, lost in a world only he could see, occasionally blowing wisps of hair out of his mouth. Sequoia gently rode him from time to time, suggesting he cut his long front bangs off to match the back, which he kept shaved down to almost nothing. But when he dressed up, he liked to spike the front with ten tons of product. So on weekdays, he could be seen constantly blowing it and shaking it and pushing it out of his eyes.

Very much aware of the increasingly energetic play across and under the table, Sequoia smiled indulgently and shuffled her notes. In a few minutes she would be leading the meeting, but Isobel and Felicity had not yet put in an appearance. Keith and Margarita might as well enjoy themselves, and she knew they got an extra kick out of the slightly public, slightly hidden love play. Exhibitionists, she thought fondly to herself. And she could hardly claim not to be one herself. Sequoia approved of enjoyment. And she emphatically approved of sex. Hot, steamy, delightful sex, releaser of tensions and endorphins. She looked forward to the time when she would be getting some for herself. But that would come later. When the job of the others was over, hers began.

25

The Case of the Creepy Christian Camp

Yesterday, she had spent two hours with Lindsay, one alone and one with Jess. Delightful girls—which could actually be a problem. They had run away from their small Texas town, fine and good, but running away caused even more problems than it solved. Running away was only the first step. Both girls were loving, which meant they had attachments, relationships, friends, family, even pets they were reluctant to leave behind. Jess was dizzyingly IN LOVE with Lindsay, but she was a teenager. Did she really, could she really, give up her whole life just to be with her girlfriend? Right now, sure. But teenage love could evaporate like morning fog on the beach. Sequoia frowned down at the file, foreseeing problems.

Sequoia Dill-Jones was an impressive woman. Of only medium height, she somehow seemed as tall and as solid as the tree she was named for and was much the same color as rich redwood furniture. She was a big woman: big laugh, big ass, big brain, big breasts, big appetite. And a huge heart. She did not go out on the rescues with the commando team because stealth and deceit were not among her talents. She could lose a fight against a one-armed five year old and had never, ever, won against ice cream or chocolate. She shrieked when she was startled, and she was almost completely incapable of lying. But despite all that, these rescues were her idea in the first place, and her job was ultimately the most important one, at least to her thinking. The others took kids out of tough situations, running through the night and courting danger, dressing in black and braving arrests. And then they dashed off to find the next kid, the next rescue. They liked the high of waiting in the dark to see if it would come off—well, Keith and Felicity did. Isobel was more complicated. But Sequoia oversaw the care of the traumatized. A research psychiatrist and therapist, she had made it her life's work to understand how people could heal from terrible situations, how they could put themselves back together and be better than before, wiser, more compassionate, and more loving. Terrible things happened, and unless the world could figure out how to heal the trauma, terrible things would keep happening, with each traumatic injury begetting more injury down the road. So it was Sequoia who kept tabs on the research and sat with the injured: therapy, meditation, yoga, drugs, art? What was the path to a healed heart? And for each gay or transgender teen they rescued, she worked with them to make a path.

The door opened, and Sequoia looked up to see Leo enter, holding a tray of ridiculously carved tiki mugs: ceramic coconuts, hula girls, tiki idols. Felicity and Isobel stumbled in directly after, still holding each other, gave each other a clinging kiss, and slipped into their chairs.

"Welcome, my tired triumphant lovelies! Excellent job! Have a cocktail! My own concoction!" Leo offered them a tiki mug from the tray, and they each hesitated.

"No coconut in the blue ones," he said. Felicity and Isobel reached out and grabbed the blue coconut and tiki idol and slumped into their seats.

Margarita's hand reappeared above the tabletop, and she yanked her purse onto her lap, extracting a package of wet wipes, wiped off her hands, and crumpling the wipe, left it on the table.

"Brazilian rosewood, my dear! Throw your cumrags elsewhere," Leo said, smiling to take any sting out of his words. Each tiki mug was carefully placed on a coaster from one of the world's most famous tiki bars as he took his own place at one end of the table. He and Sequoia sat at opposite ends with the Professor and the women on one side, Keith and Margarita on the other. Keith's large frame filled out his side—there wasn't room for another chair.

"To another rousing success!" Leo said, and they toasted.

The Case of the Creepy Christian Camp

Sequoia was not surprised to find that the drink was delicious, fruity but suffused with the complex sugars of rum. She tasted a hint of lucuma and hibiscus, and hibiscus syrup was one of her personal favorites, like cherries with more complexity—she knew he was having a love affair with the stuff right now. That was Leo's way—he wanted, he needed the best and a wide variety of it. The best rum, the best fruit, the best tiki mugs, and the finest commando team to conduct his pet project.

"Lovey, please," he said, nodding to her and bringing the meeting to its official beginning, reaching to his right and gently angling the laptop screen down, bringing the Professor blinking into the room. Max looked around, smiled, and reached for his drink. Leo didn't need to call her Lovey in this setting, but he reveled in the code names, sometimes going so far as to imitate Jim Bacchus's legendary rich man's drawl. The code names went hand in hand with his legendary passion for all things tiki.

Sequoia looked around the table at the most deeply loved faces in her life, the family she had built. "Right, well, congratulations on a job that went smooth as silk. Couldn't have gone better. Lindsay is doing well, but of course we have problems. The biggest of the problems is that, well, she loves her mother."

The team groaned. Margarita muttered curses in Spanish under her breath. Sequoia completely understood. In the long run, loving her mother was a good thing; it meant that Lindsay had not been damaged beyond the capacity to love—but it complicated things. Teens had been known to return to the worst situations because they couldn't stand to leave a family member behind. Admirable, loving, human—and really fucking dangerous. If Lindsay went home, she put them all at risk. Even if she promised up and down not to say a word about them, those promises would melt like sugar under a rain of blows. That's why the girls knew nothing but the team's code names and weren't told where they were or how to get there. But that didn't mean they were safe.

"I haven't had time to build trust with her, but I think there was more going on here than physical violence. I think... sexual abuse too—when I asked a few probing questions, she denied it, but, well...." Making statements like this raised ticklish ethical questions. She had asked Lindsay this morning for permission to share a few things with the team—only what they needed to know to help her. Lindsay had looked at her with big, scared eyes. She didn't trust anyone yet; how could she?

But the team needed to proceed to help her as a group; in a very real way, they had just adopted her. Lindsay may have loved her mother, but her mother had not protected her. The group was going to have to usher her into healing and so would need to know as much as they could, especially so they could avoid hurting her more, hitting her raw spots. Sequoia had gently explained this, and the girl had nodded tightly that she had understood, but after that she had clammed up.

Sequoia sighed and continued: "So we have this situation in front of us. We just kidnapped an underage minor girl and transported her over state lines. As for Jess, luckily, very luckily, her parents trust her and are completely supportive of her sexuality. So...things could be worse. They probably won't be trouble. Right now Lindsay doesn't want to go back, but if she decides to go, you know we can't stop her. Then we would really be kidnapping her—that's not what we do. She doesn't know where she is or any of our real names—right, 'Ginger'? Right, 'Mary Ann'?"

"Yes," Felicity replied emphatically. "We were very careful."

"Okay, then. So Jess also has ties. She loves her family,

and she left a note so that they wouldn't call the cops to report her absence. But clearly they aren't going to be thrilled that Jess ran away."

"She left a note?" gasped Margarita. "What did she say? 'Dear Mom and Dad, off with a bunch of freaky perverts and weirdos to rescue my girlfriend, don't wait up! Kisses!'"

"Max was in communication with her and helped her craft the letter. She didn't give any info we didn't pre-approve. And she doesn't know where we are either. They both know we're somewhere near or in Hawaii, but after we arrived at the airport in Honolulu we traveled by boat and arrived by beach with Jess. Lindsay was so traumatized that she wasn't paying much attention to where she was, and she slept a good part of the time."

"Thank God for Ambien," muttered Felicity.

"So for Jess, she needs to understand how much she's willing to give up for her love and how much she isn't. We need to get in touch with her family and assess how much we can trust them. If they're willing to move away from Parker, maybe Jess can go back to them. But if she goes back the police will question her about Lindsay, about where she is. It's a terrible position for the poor girl: give up either her family or her girlfriend. And moving away from Parker won't stop the police: wherever they move the police will question them. It's the disappearance of a child, after all—legally."

"What's your assessment of Jess and Lindsay? Will they make it, or is this just the lure of forbidden love and teenage drama?"

Sequoia smiled. "That Jess is impressive. A good head on her shoulders and a lot of determination. Reminds me of you a little," she smiled at Felicity. "But I'm not sure they have enough in common underneath the drama. I just don't know what Lindsay is made of—she doesn't trust me yet. But we *need* to convince her that there's no going back. We need to convince her that her mother is an adult and will have to fend for herself. Lindsay cannot protect her any more than she was protecting Lindsay. Someday when she is an adult and can stand on her own feet she can go back and confront her father. But unless she's an adult, he would have the power to keep her. We wouldn't be able to rescue her again."

"You don't think there's any way to protect her legally?"

"Her father is a minister. A generous supporter of the police. And this is *Texas*, where rape is the second most popular team sport, right after football. She CAN'T go back. And she needs to hear that from someone she trusts. That isn't me—not yet."

All eyes turned to Isobel. As good as Sequoia was in these situations, she wasn't a chronic abuse survivor. Isobel had made an instant connection with Lindsay, strong enough for Lindsay to trust her and walk away from her whole life. Now Isobel had to keep going, even though it stirred her own terrible memories. But it was necessary. She knew that. If you rescue someone and then abandon her, that's no rescue at all. She nodded.

"Yeah," she said. "I'll talk to her. She won't go back."

Chapter 4:
The Wrong Kind of Camp

Isobel nodded while Felicity squeezed her fingers under the table. This was harder than midnight rescues. But they all knew why it was necessary.

"All right, team, end of work, time for play. Our drinks are fruity, and so are we! Oh! Except! Lovey has something she wants to say...." His Jim Bacchus impression intensified for a moment as he gestured with his coconut to Sequoia. She grinned affectionately at him. *My man*, she thought. *Such a showboat.*

"Okay, well.... When I talked to Lindsay she told me something I didn't like the sound of one bit. Her father threatened to send her somewhere, somewhere *bad*, somewhere where they were going to burn the gay out of her. Those words."

Keith leaned forward. "A conversion camp. I thought those were gone, discredited.... Anyway, we know all about them, know how to deal with them. Rescued a kid from one once. Never understood why we didn't just take all of them."

"Now, you know why, you know exactly why. That kid got a hold of our card. He called us. He wanted rescue. Those other kids did not—he left the card behind to a few who might, but those kids turned it in to the authorities, and we almost got tracked down. And we can't just switch out phone numbers because kids out there need help. They can't call our card and get a 'sorry, wrong number' message. You know gay kids have sky-high suicide rates, worse than any other group except veterans." She looked around the table and saw their faces, calmed down some. Keith knew this. He was just grumbling. The rescue team had to go right into those places and take kids away. It twisted them up inside to leave kids behind. It would. Of course it would, and she knew it.

"Anyway, from what she said, this place is off the radar somehow, out of the country...her dad said it was where 'stinking liberals and commies and fags' couldn't even find them."

"Nice mouth for a Christian," Beto snapped.

"How bad could it be, Sequoia? They are still their children, right?" Felicity's own parents wouldn't speak to her, but they had never lifted a hand to her. She still sometimes had trouble wrapping her head around how much viciousness there was in the world.

"Well if it *is* completely off the radar, we just don't know. If it was just the usual bullshit 'therapy' and conversion pep talks, fine. Even that weird stuff where men cuddle to make up for a father's lack of touch and that's supposed to make them less gay—well, weird, creepy, but doesn't need to be 'far far away.' If it's off the radar they could be back to aversion therapy, electric shock, nausea drugs, physical violence. Even—corrective rape." Her mouth screwed up as she said the words as if she could barely spit them out, and she reached for her drink to wash out the taste of them.

The group sat, sobered despite their potent drinks. "Corrective rape": rape, usually for the girls, to convince them that they wanted men. Yeah, thought Sequoia, that's sure to do it. Sickest shit she could imagine.

"Well," said Leo. "I'll put some of our better spies on it. Until we know more, let's not ruin our day. There are assholes

33

out there; we can't save everyone; that sucks. But right now there are two girls making out on the beach in the sunshine instead of one sad girl worrying outside while the other gets trapped and abused in her own home.

"That's right," Sequoia nodded. "We don't know too much about this, but we will start looking at who her father has been talking to lately, asking a question here and there. We'll find it. We will find it."

Leo nodded and brought out the voice again, "And now—I absolutely *demand* that you drink these cocktails with the full attention that they deserve, while I make another round. We'll have another meeting about Jess and Lindsay in a week, and you all know what you need to do until then. To sex, cocktails, and the beach!" He toasted them, and they raised their glasses in unison, drained them, and filed out of the room to play and frolic.

Except for Isobel. She changed into a white bikini and headed down to the beach, but play was not on her mind. Felicity changed to a red flowered cover-up and went with her to meet up with the girls. Sure enough, Lindsay and Jess were in the warm water, frolicking.

Felicity and Isobel sat down side by side in a double-wide chaise longue. Their hands crept toward each other, touched, and intertwined.

"I don't know if I can do this," Isobel whispered.

"Honey, it's hard. I know it's hard. But you're strong. I have known you a long time, and you are so so strong."

"Yeah, okay. Time to be strong." She stared down at her white foot in the sand, willing the strength.

"Okay, the girls are about to come out. Who are we?"

"We're Ginger and Mary Ann!" This was a reminder not to let their real names slip. The chances of it coming back to bite them were small, but they were there. Safety third, after all. Sex. Compassion. Safety.

"You're damn right we are." Isobel reached up and touched her collar, white to match her bikini, vinyl for the water, for luck.

The two girls caught sight of them, waved, and then ran out of the water to join the women who sat on the beach. A sea turtle sat beside the *chaise longue,* taking in the splendor of the sea and sky, making everything seem serene through its stolid charm. As they came near they saw Mary Ann generously slathering Ginger's pale skin with sunblock, everywhere she could reach. She removed the white collar from Ginger's pale neck, slathered the screen underneath it, and then snapped it back into place.

Lindsay had come up and sat down in a chair beside Isobel, gazing at her with hungry adoration in her eyes. Isobel knew that look. The whole team did the rescue but Isobel got the gratitude—because she made the connection. Isobel reached over and grabbed her hand for a second, smiling at her and then letting go.

"Why do you wear a collar?" Lindsay asked.

"Because I'm her slave," Isobel smiled. "It's a kind of game, but it's also serious. I like it."

Lindsay tried to take this in and her gaze fell—to Isobel's legs, where some of the marks of the cane were still visible from the other night, along with a few stray bruises.

"She hurts you?! Why would you let her hurt you?!" she yelped. She edged her body a little farther away. Jess came up and held her—abuse was only one day in her past.

Isobel spoke, picking her words carefully. "Oh, honey. Well, first, I hurt her so much before she *ever* hurt me. It's weird, sweetheart, and Lovey can probably explain it to you better than I can, but I'll have a go. You've been beaten. Well,

35

I was beaten too—a lot. And raped. Incest." She looked away and then back.

She looked into Lindsay's eyes, and the look she saw confirmed what they had suspected. The abuse had been more than beatings.

"So bad sh—stuff happened to me, and once bad stuff happens, it's a part of you. Me. It's in there, and your mind starts to work to protect yourself from how horrible this stuff was. There are two basic ways to do it from what I understand. The first is to say, 'Okay, that happened, it's over and I will NEVER talk about it again, and I'm fine, really, thanks for asking, let's just drop it, okay?'"

Lindsay nodded vigorously. That was what she wanted to do. Forget it ever happened. Move on.

"Okay, that's *totally* understandable except for one little thing: it doesn't work. Wish it did, but it doesn't. You'll have nightmares. The memories will come back when you don't want them. You'll get anxious; you'll get depressed. You'll strain and split and break. So the other thing to do is to talk about it, work with it. Make it part of you. No, it's already a part of you, always will be. So you accept that."

Lindsay looked confused and uncomfortable.

Isobel sighed, "Okay, it's hard to explain but let's get concrete. One day you're going to be reading something, maybe a novel or a news account, and it will have something sick, terrible in it. And maybe you feel nauseated. Maybe you throw up. Fine, understandable. But maybe some other time—similar story—but you might find yourself...suddenly really turned on. Because some part of our crazy brains doesn't know past from future, and it tries to make what happened to you *retroactively* okay—by making it sexy. Sex is this big *amazing* force. It's life. And it can make us take what we're scared of, where we didn't feel powerful before, where we even felt dead inside—

36

and we can own it, play with it, make it ours. So in that moment when you get aroused by something sick and twisted and you feel so so gross, you have a choice to make. Are you going to hate yourself, or love yourself?"

"And, mind you, by 'love yourself,' she's being literal. She means masturbate," chimed Felicity.

The girls shrieked. Jess giggled, and Lindsay goggled.

"And that's what *you* do?" Some shock in her voice. "All that stuff is still inside *you*?"

"You're forgetting the other possibility—Ginger's such a sweetheart that she does. You can become the abuse. You can pass it on to someone else," Felicity explained.

"Yeah, and if I were a slightly different, more aggressive person, maybe I would have gone off, had a kid, and started doing it to them like was done to me. Because that stuff is in me. Or maybe I let myself be torn apart by guilt and depression and bad feelings—and okay, sometimes that does happen to me. Sometimes what happened to me hurts so bad I can't get out of bed. But eventually I do, and I keep trying to live. These are the choices we have. You got violence in you: do you turn it in to destroy yourself, turn it out to abuse another—or do you try to find a way to get it out safely? You gotta choose a road. I thank whatever god or goddess there might be that I fell into the hands of this one." As Isobel said the words, Felicity reached up and patted her face. It was a gesture of comfort.

"You met in high school, right?" said Lindsay. "You ran away from home together?"

"Oh, you want to hear our story?! Well, okay, but I'm going to need another cocktail for this. Hold up."

Isobel ran back to the lanai and made cocktails at the wet bar. Then she strolled back down to the beach, thinking furiously. She had told this story many times, but every time was hard, and every time she shifted things around a little: what

37

does *this* girl need to know, to hear?

Felicity waited for her to come back, graciously accepted a cocktail, and murmured "good girl" under her breath. Isobel smiled. Then Felicity turned and faced the girls: "Okay so you just heard some of Ginger's story. You'll hear more later—but there's not much more to it. Rape, yada yada, beatings, incest, blowjobs for daddy on Christmas."

"Oh you *bitch*!" Isobel said. She noticed Lindsay's slight flinch and reminded herself—no swearing. "That's *my* horrible life you're talking about," but she laughed, and the girls laughed too—nervously, uncomfortably, but they laughed.

"So," said Felicity. "I'm going to tell it, okay? How we ran away together."

Isobel leaned back in her chaise in relief. Felicity had sensed she wasn't up to it today, to tell the story and go through it all. She was right. And hearing the story through Felicity's eyes always made it less grim. More of an adventure. The story of their love. And it was easier for Felicity—who had grown up with strict parents—to censor out the parts that teenagers didn't need to hear. No one had protected Isobel that way, and sometimes Isobel thought she never would know what was appropriate. And maybe she didn't want to know.

Chapter 5: Ginger and Mary Ann

"Right, well, I was born into one of those super-focused Chinese immigrant families. My parents went and opened a Chinese restaurant in Nebraska, on the grounds that there weren't as many of them there, and my father loved old Marlon Brando movies, from back when he was sexy. I think my father was closeted, actually. Anyway. I'm the oldest of four girls, and my parents raised me very strictly, and you know, I didn't mind it. I was the oldest sister, and my mother trusted me with my sisters a lot because she was working very hard, and I have always liked being in charge."

"She was little Miss Bossy Perfect Pants," Isobel said.

"Oh, yes, very much so," Felicity grinned. "But the strange thing is I really liked my life, my childhood. You would think that couldn't be true: how many teen runaways had a happy childhood? My parents expected me to get straight As and be good at everything I did, sure, but I *liked* getting straight As and being good at everything I did. I played violin too—technically well, but with no real feel for music. I didn't *care* about music; I cared about being excellent. And then when I was in high school, I had a few friends, overachievers. I was in the band. I ran the school newspaper. I did model UN. My parents were thrilled. They told me, 'Don't screw it up by dating boys!' I said, okay! No problem! I never even thought about *why* it wasn't a problem.

"Anyway, then one day in my junior year in high school, the door opens and we get this student, this transfer student, and she stumbles in and she looks as slutty as you could get away with looking in high school. Ginger! And I'm sitting there and I hear the whooooosh...of every boy in that class, um, 'coming to attention' at the same time."

Jess grinned. Lindsay looked confused. Jess leaned over and whispered in her ear and Lindsay squealed, made a face. Isobel watched her carefully and thought, "Yes!" It was a good, healthy squeal, girlish. Not horrified.

"She had too much makeup on, and it was smudged. She had on this black vinyl skirt and a pink mesh top with a T-shirt underneath it that was ripped, and I looked at her and it was love at first sight."

"You remember what I was wearing? Awww..." Isobel squeezed her hand.

"So I'm an overachiever, right? Super-competitive. So I looked at her and all these boys with their mouths open, drooling, and I think, 'No, she will be *mine*! She will be all mine!' And I was staring at her. Staring at her and wondering what her pussy tasted like, whether it would taste like a Red Hot because of all that bright red hair. I had never *ever* had a thought like that before." She reached up and pulled Isobel's hair, pulling her back to meet her lips and kissing her. Then Isobel picked up the story.

"It wasn't love at first sight for *me*; it was hate! I hated her. I saw all the girls in class looking at me the way girls did, like they hated me and despised me, and there she was with this look I couldn't read. So I thought she was extra-shocked, shell-shocked by what a whore I was. I sat down next to her just to piss her off; this perfect, pretty, prim little girl with her pink sweater and her Hello Kitty notebook, and I wanted to slap her. I wanted to slap the prim right out of her."

"But despite that we fell in love. Crazy ridiculous love. And we ran away," Felicity said.

She paused. It was always hard to decide what to tell about that, the way they got together. She picked her way through the story, editing a little here, gliding over some stuff there. She was damn sure these girls weren't quite ready for the whole story, but as she picked her way through the details, she remembered.

Felicity's Story

I took one look, and my heart fell at Isobel's feet. And my sense of achievement, of wanting to solve a tough puzzle took over—I had never set myself a challenge and failed. I was a champion tennis player, straight-A student, all that stuff. But if I achieved all these things, I thought as I walked home from school that day after first meeting Isobel, it was because I wanted them, because I never doubted myself, and I pursued my goals like a bulldog. But now all I could think of was this tall redhead and the way I wanted to kiss her, wanted to let my hands rove all around those curves, wanted to grab her ass and pull her toward me and feast.

And I had no idea even how to start. I had never flirted before. Once in gym class I kind of stared at this girl's really perfect ass for a minute, and I realize now what that was about, but at the time I just thought, "Damn!" But with Isobel there was no hiding what this was. So I watched her. I watched the way boys laughed about her when they were together and called her names with lust in their voices and girls put their noses in the air and called her the same names with pure contempt and disgust. And then I watched when boys, trying not to be seen, passed her notes in class or came up to her. They all

41

got bounced back by Isobel's enormous force field of hostility, just a giant thick wall of "go *fuck* yourself" that she emitted all day during school. It was weird…why did she dress like a slut and then push everyone who was attracted to her away as if she hated them? And how was I going to make friends with someone who burned with such pure anger? And friendship wasn't what I wanted anyway.

In the end Isobel made the first move, if you could call it that. In a quiet hallway before school, with no one else around, she stalked up to me and said, "Hey! BITCH! Stop staring at me all the time! I see you! I'm not blind! Why are you *always* staring at me?!!"

And I looked up into her eyes and said, "Because you're beautiful." And I just looked at her and I don't know, later she said I let everything I felt just shine in my face. She looked at me. Anger, rage snapped back into her eyes, and she looked at me like she wanted to skewer me, and she said, "52 Morris Lane. My house. Meet me there after school. Three thirty. Unless you're a chickenshit. I think you're a chickenshit!" And she whirled and turned away.

Well, I was no chickenshit! She thought I was all prim and proper? Well, she didn't know I was a tiger in a pink sweater set. So I was going. What would I do when I got there? No clue. What did Isobel have in mind? Did she want to fight? The idea of fighting her made my heart beat faster. I wanted to touch her, I wanted her to touch me, and I didn't really care how it happened. I was fit from sports, and fierce, so I could probably give her a run for her money even though she was eight inches taller—five nine to my puny five one. But I realized I wouldn't fight her. I fantasized about her hitting me, feeling the shock and pain and impact of her fists on my body. I would goad her and let her hit me and love the blows. It got me hot to think about it. It flashed through my mind right then that something might be *very* wrong with me, but I did not care.

So I got to the house, and it was in a pretty clean, modest neighborhood. On the outside it was a nice enough middle-class house, blue with white trim. I knocked and waited, and Isobel threw the door open without a word, and I walked in. On the inside, it was chaos. Insanity. Isobel stepped aside and the stink hit me, and it was dark. I had to pick my way through bottles of beer on the floor. Cigarette butts piled amongst the ash. The place smelled like a men's room in a bar that never got cleaned. I wasn't smart enough to try to look like this was normal; my mouth dropped open, I looked up at Isobel, and she had this look: rage, defiance, the sneer of a queen. And she grabbed my hand and took me to the basement, where the smell and the booze and the cigarettes were *worse*. The room had an enormous TV and a huge, leather three-piece couch, black with little white spots where cigarettes had burned through to the upholstery.

She pulled me to the middle of the room and turned to me. We stood there facing each other, my heart racing, I had no idea what was going to happen next.

"Say I'm beautiful again. I *fucking* dare you," Isobel said.

Isobel slapped me. My ears rang. Her chest was heaving. Mine too.

"If you think I'm so beautiful, you prove it," she said. "Do you like pussy? Eat my pussy. Eat it!"

She pushed me down on my knees and pulled up her dress, and she wasn't wearing underwear. Her hand on my head was hard and rough. I was so much in love, it was crazy. I smelled that pussy smell and it went to my head like a drug; I wanted to crawl into her. I licked her pussy before I even had my first kiss and I breathed it in, smelled it, licked it, I had no idea what to do and I really didn't worry about it, I was just doing what I wanted to do. I knew I never wanted to be anywhere else but here, licking fire-red pussy. Isobel grabbed my head and pushed against me, grinding on my nose and lips. I couldn't breathe. I tried to pull back just a bit just so I could breathe, but she wouldn't let me. Then for a second she did; she threw my head backward and collapsed down on the ground with this look on her face. She looked…broken. Then she looked at me and I reached up to touch my face, and her face went all raged again and she yelled.

"Did you LIKE that? Was that *beautiful*? Do you want MORE?" She was ferocious and angry and so, just, gorgeous.

So I looked at her from where I was still kneeling, and licked my lips, her juices still on my face, and I said, "Yes."

"WHAT?!! What the FUCK is wrong with you?" she was near screaming.

"Yes," I said. I wouldn't back down. I do not back down. "*Yes*, I liked it. *Yes*, I want more! And YES, it was beautiful!" Isobel went berserk. She jumped up, yanked me off my feet, slapped me again, and then pushed me on the couch and started spanking me, her hand just slamming into my ass. And it hurt! She wasn't playing; this wasn't slap and tickle, and I yelled, "Ow!" and grunted, but I would not ask her to stop and I would not cry, and after while she stopped and just put her hand on my ass then she threw herself down on top of me and she was so big. She was all around me, and I could feel the fur from her pussy as she ground into me and her smell and she made this cry—and I know now that she came, but I didn't really know it at the time—and she shuddered and then she rolled off me right onto the floor and curled up into a ball and started sobbing. Her chest was jerking, and she was sobbing out, "I'm sorry! I'm sorry! I'm sorry!"

I stared crying too. We were both a mess. She had mascara all over her face, and I grabbed her and pulled her to me and she was getting mascara all over my sweater and I was crying, and she kept saying, "I'm sorry."

And I managed to get the tears under control and swallowed hard and said, "I'm not sorry! Don't be sorry! Don't be sorry! Please!"

And I pulled her to me and kissed her on the mouth. And do you know, I was afraid to? She flinched away like I had hit her, and she yelled "Are you CRAZY? I raped you. I RAPED you."

"No! You didn't! I wanted you to…do those things. I did!" I looked away from her then—it was hard to say that and look her in the eyes. My parents didn't teach me *anything* about sex. "I could have stopped you."

"No you couldn't! You're *little*. Weak. I'm huge! You couldn't have stopped me."

"Four years karate. Brown belt. I could have beaten the *hell* out of you, trust me. I didn't even try. And you would have stopped if I had wanted you to. I know it." It wasn't even true. I never took karate! I just wanted to! My parents wouldn't let me. I had to play tennis because it was a girl sport. But she needed to feel I wasn't helpless, and I wasn't, so, okay, I lied.

"You think?" And she smiled at me for the first time, this little scared half-smile, and my heart just flipped over. I saw she wanted to believe me, and that was that. I knew right then it wasn't love before; it was just raging lust. And now? Now it was love, and it was so big and deep it was terrifying. And then we really kissed, just holding each other and kissing and kissing, and we started crying again and her makeup got everywhere. I had to sneak into my house and lie to my parents. My clothes were wrecked, my ass was bruised, and God did I smell like sex! Just thank God she didn't bruise my face!

Before school I waited for her and walked to school with her and she looked puzzled. "What are you doing? You're a good kid. You don't want to be seen with me?! What will your friends say?"

"My friends? Fuck those guys," I said. I think that was the first time I ever used language like that. And I meant it! I was suddenly completely bored of grades and band practice and all that bullshit. What did it matter? I had my Isobel.

So after that we were inseparable, and everyone stared. They stared when we walked in the halls together and when we ate together in the cafeteria. They stared when she came to my tennis matches and cheered for me. My superbrainy journalist and band friends pulled me aside and asked me why I was hanging out with such a freak, but I just smiled. "She's more on the ball than you could imagine," I answered. And we might have gotten in big trouble eventually because it was really hard to hide that kind of love, but no one could even begin to think that a red-hot punk goddess and the little Asian dweeb were in love.

Four weeks later Isobel stopped me on the way to school. She had a black eye and something wrong with her arm. I felt a flash of rage that someone had hurt her and then fear and nausea, almost dizzy, because I knew who had done it. She hadn't told me much about her family, but come on. Anyone could have figured out how fucked up the stuff that was going on in that house must have been. So I sat with her on a park bench while she just told me all of it. All of it. The school bell rang, and we let it and we didn't budge, and she told me. You know. You can guess. Rape. Incest. Beatings. And now... she was pregnant. When she told her father he went ballistic, accused her of being a whore, and beat her harder when she said it was his, saying that was a filthy lie. She even thought he believed it. She swiped fifty bucks from his wallet and was going to run away. Right that day. Immediately.

"I shouldn't even have told you," she said. Her hands were twisting in her lap, and she's sixteen and trying to be brave and protect me. ME! "I should have just disappeared from your life. I'm fucking poison. But I wasn't strong enough to go without saying goodbye. I don't want anything from you, okay?" she said. "I don't even want your pity. I just want to get away from you before the whole stinking mess of my life drags you down with it. But if you could loan me the money for an abortion…I'll pay you back when I get work…I will." Her lips tightened, and she looked away.

"I have $3,000 in my college account from my summer jobs. We'll empty it out, get you an abortion, and run away."

"That's crazy. That's *crazy*. You're a straight-A student! You're going to college and law school and probably going to sit on the Supreme Court after that. You have to let me go—I'm *nothing*, toxic waste, okay?"

"I'm not going to do *any* of that. I'm not letting you out of my sight from now on. I'm sticking to you. You won't be able to get rid of me," and Isobel heard that I was determined, and she knew she needed me, and she just gave in. She felt guilty about it, but she couldn't do it alone, and I wouldn't let her. We planned out what we were going to do and how to do it, while I held her hand there on that bench.

The story Felicity told omitted the scene in Isobel's basement, focusing more on the love, the commitment, the sense of rightness.

"And ten years later, here we still are," she said. "Holding hands. And that's our story."

"And did you ever regret it?" Lindsay asked Felicity. She was looking at her feet and raised a glance over at Jess.

"Me? No. Not for a moment. But that's me, and what's true for me may not be true for anyone else, understand? I didn't tell you this story to tell you what to do. Just to let you guys know you aren't the first girls to run away because you loved each other."

47

"So…" Lindsay was looking out at the horizon, with a thoughtful look on her face. "So that's how you guys ran away together, but what's the rest of the story?"

"What rest of the story? We ran away with each other, and here we freaking are. Ta-daa!"

"No, I mean like: who are you? Whose idea was this? How did you end up rescuing teenage lesbians, anyway?

"Oh, that. Well, that's what we're not supposed to tell you—security, you know."

"Yeah—and it's just not our story to tell."

Chapter 6: Mr. Howell's Story

Why have I become who I became? Good question. Not an easy question, but let me give it a whirl.

My father wanted to know when I was sixteen or so why I wasn't a lady-killer. He felt I should be "out there," as he put it, swinging my giant cock around. And I wanted to, God I wanted to, but I had no "game," as they call it now. And no money, which didn't help. My dad had money—but he was cheap, oh, that man was cheap. We had some money, and he drove a nice car, but he was a Greek immigrant, and some of these immigrant dads think you work harder if you never have money of your own. In 975, I was getting a $3-a-week allowance, at the age of sixteen. And, mind you, I was working my tail off for it. We owned apartment buildings, rental property. Basically, my father was just a notch above a slumlord. I was installing things I had no business installing, taking care of all the wiring and plumbing for the apartments. I was illegally doing all kinds of things I wasn't trained to do properly, and getting paid a quarter an hour to do them. Anyway, we would go around about it: Why no girls? Why no girls? And I would tell him because I had no money. And he would make this noise, this incredible, snorting harrumph and say, "If the girls want you, you don't

49

need money." And I would say, okay, but they DON'T want me so I DO need money.

So one day he tells me, "Get in the car. Get in the car. I was about sixteen and a half. He had been asking me around that time if I was gay, was I gay, was I gay? Half teasing, half scared—I don't know why he was so *afraid* of it. Anyway, asking when I would get a girl, and so forth. So I get in the car, and I ask, okay, where are we going? Come on, tell me. And he says, Reno. And we had never taken any kind of father-son trip before. My dad's idea of a father-son activity was fixing a toilet. So I naturally ask, *why* are we going to Reno? I'm too young to gamble. I'm too young to drink. Tell me what's up

He wouldn't tell me. He just tells me to shut up and wait till we get there. So I just say, all right then; time for a nap. I fall asleep, and we drive to Reno. We were living in Sacramento at the time, so it wasn't too long a drive, and we pull up at this place, and I wake up and we get out, and I say, this isn't Reno. I had never been to Reno, but Reno is a city, I knew that much. This is a weird place out in the country, with a big, pink door. And we go in this door, and there's a bar to one side. My dad goes over to the bartender, and this was still the seventies so kids were in bars all the time and no one cared. My father used to take me to bars and have them give me a Rob Roy when I was five. So my father said, "Give my son here a Coke." And he turned to me and he says, I have to go talk to someone. You stay here. And I STILL don't get it. I look around, and there are maybe a handful of old codgers smoking away and drinking at the bar, and behind the bar there are pictures, like places have pictures of celebrities. The pictures are all autographed, except they're all women, and I've never heard of any of them. There are pictures of Sandy and April and Bambi, and they all have little hearts over the i's, and they all are wearing bikinis and little flirty dresses—and I *still* didn't get it.

And then my dad comes back and he grabs me by the arm. He pulls me along this hallway that smells like cheap perfume and sweat and says, "Here, have a good time, don't say I never gave you nothing," and he shoves me in this room, and there are two women in there. Two! I had no idea what to do with one! But that's Greek pride for you. My son—he gets two! Anyway, that is when it sinks in. Then I get it. Not before. I almost piss myself; I want to run right away except I know my *dad's* out there and God knows what he's going to say if I reappear right away. And I have my own Greek pride. So I just stand there, and they stand there. There was a blonde and one who looked Latina, caramel skin and big doe eyes. She's *cute,* and that makes it even *worse.* Then she smiles at me, not a sexy smile but…impish. She winks at me, and I relax just a little. Then she goes to the door and throws it open—and there's my dad. Standing there eavesdropping. And she says, "You don't have to worry, Papi. We will take such good care of him. Why don't you go get a girl for yourself?"

And my dad looks really embarrassed and says, "No, no, I'm married…okay…I'll go wait in the bar. You take your time, okay?"

He looks at me, and I give him this embarrassed nod, so he leaves. When he's good and gone—and they leave the door open for a long minute to make sure he is—they come back and close the door. And they turn to me, and they *are* sexy; did I mention that? They were wearing little short peignoirs—there's a word I didn't know then—and the blonde was wearing pink and the Latin girl with dark hair and eyes was wearing blue. I can picture them clear as day even now. And the blonde says, "I'm Barbie and this is Rita, and we're *not* going to have sex with you, okay? So just sit down and relax."

I was so relieved, I stumbled over to a chair and just collapsed into it. Then I thought about my father, and it's like they could read it on my face. So Rita says, "Don't worry. We'll tell your dad *whatever* you want us to, so you relax. Let's just get comfortable and talk."

They were great women; they really were. They talked to me for a long time. They poured me a glass of champagne and told me they would tell my dad that I did him proud and refuse to say another word about it. So we talked. They asked me why my dad brought me here and I told them I was a little shy with girls. And they asked why that was, when I was so good-looking—you know, they were so kind to me. They saw I was a terrified sixteen-year-old and they knew the best way to make him a man wasn't to terrify him or shame him.

And God, the questions they asked me. They asked me if I liked girls, okay, yes, yes, I like girls. And they said, which one of us do you like better? And I was shy and wouldn't say—they were both really cute, but the Latin one was a little younger and had this truly amazing butt, and big brown eyes. The blonde, Barbie—she had big blue eyes and was trying to look like a Barbie doll and that's never done much for me. She looked like what the stuck-up girls at my school were going to look like in ten years. But Barbie saw where my eyes went when she asked and said, honey, to each his own you know? Plenty of guys love the way I look. I'm not upset if you like her…I like her too." And she hugged Rita and kissed her cheek, and the way she did it made the first little spark of lust go through me.

Rita came over and sat by me. They told me some things about how to kiss girls and how to touch them and what girls like. They asked me what I liked, and teased me sweetly, and got me talking. I told them what I fantasized about—things I never told anyone before and wouldn't tell anyone else for years. I told them that sometimes I fantasized about tying a girl up and then licking her pussy, that sometimes I fantasized about having two girl slaves that I would make kiss each other.

52

They asked me if I wanted to watch them kiss and I said, of course! So they did. I sat there with my head swimming thinking that *later* I was going to masturbate like hell to this. It's funny how I knew they would let me masturbate right there and then—but no. I couldn't do that. But it was just so easy: they asked if I wanted to see them kiss and then they did, and they seemed to like it. I think they honestly did like it.

After a long time of talking to me, finding out what I liked, they gave me some advice. They said, "Well, we have to tell you, we think you're going to be a little, um, unusual."

"Like a really horny little freak!" laughed Rita.

"I would not have put it that way," Barbie said, glaring at her a little bit. "But yeah. So it's really important that you, you know, take the time to find girls out there who are adventurous themselves. There *are* girls out there who like to be spanked and tied up and do, well, all kinds of things."

"Girls like you!" Rita laughed.

Barbie smiled a naughty smile, and she suddenly seemed a lot sexier to me. But she kept talking. "So don't let the wrong girl tell you that what you want is wrong, because there are girls who will tell you that. But you have to remember that the *only* way sex can be fun is if you are who you are, do the things that turn you on. Do you understand?"

I did. I really did. So they each gave me a big, long kiss and messed my hair up and took my glasses off and fogged them up, and marched me back to my dad and told him that he had a big lusty straight son to be proud of. My dad slapped me on the back and paid them, and that was that.

I thought about them a lot after that. That started me off thinking of whores, prostitutes, sex workers, whatever...as just really nice people. Which of course is not always true but you would be surprised. I dated girls at my school and then my college, and they just seemed uptight, or...well, I know now that they just were…girls. They were confused and innocent and didn't know what they were doing. They were nervous about sex and curious, but they often didn't know what they were doing. They would grab my cock like it was a pump handle and give me bruises. Or they would kiss like being hit with a wet mop. I had a girlfriend who reached her hand in my shirt and pinched my nipples so hard I almost cried. So I started hanging out in strip clubs, started dating a stripper. She knew what she was doing. Well, I was taking a filmmaking class in college at the time, so I asked her if she would make a little porno for me with one of the girls at the club. Whew! My first porn shoot followed by my first threesome. That was a *good* day. It turned out I was really *good* at making porn because I could find the girls who liked it. A man doesn't need a woman with huge breasts and a perfect ass in his porn as people think, but men need smiles—naughty, hot little smiles. Not just moans and groans. The truth is, porn stars aren't usually good actresses. They just really like sex. So there I was, in my twenties and I stumbled into this. I took out a few credit cards and maxed them out to get a little capital, then made enough money to pay them off in two years. I made porn, and I fucked porn stars. Because of Barbie and Rita. I did it as a sideline and then went on and got an MBA, doing this part-time, thinking about how I could do it bigger and better.

I had a great life. Money and tail—that's all man needs to be happy, right? I had a talent for it, you understand, not just for making the porn, and eventually I hired other people to direct and make the porn. but it was money I had a talent for. I didn't tell my father what business I was going into. To this day the man thinks I'm in "plastics." Well, the breasts on the porn stars are plastic enough. I'm not even sure he would be against it, my dad; I just don't want to talk about it with him. Ever.

After my MBA I moved to Reno—I wasn't ready for Vegas yet, you understand, and I bought a small strip club/casino of my own. I tried, for a porn maker and strip club owner, to keep it what they would today call "sex-positive." I like ladies; I don't want to exploit them. I know I did when I was just getting started. I couldn't afford to pay them very much. But they all knew if they really needed something or got in trouble, I would do my best to help them. Anyway, I tried to get the rep as "nicest guy in porn." I was good to the girls, sometimes like a creepy uncle, but good to them. Girls would throw themselves at me, stunning, hot girls, but I could always tell which ones were hot for me and which were making a career move.

I branched out a little more. Right from the start I was doing a lot of girl-on-girl, and sometimes girl-on-girl-on-girl. And I realized, well, there was a hell of a lot of money in gay porn. This was the mid-to-late eighties by then, the AIDS era. Gays were simultaneously more visible and less interested in risky sex. Nothing safer than jacking off to porn. So why not gay porn? Well, why not? I started looking for someone who could make good gay porn and needed a backer. I found a gay club owner who hooked me up with some possible guys, I met with them, and then I was making money off gay men too. I tried making porn for lesbians, but that's a trickier market, let me tell you. I know some women liked my girl-on-girl porn, but it was mostly for men. The girls who made it, they were enjoying themselves, but most of them were straight and they all were sex workers—they were used to performing for what Lovey says is called the "male gaze." Anyway, I was so interested in doing this at the time, that I got some lesbians in from a club as a focus group—there's my MBA at work—and had them tell me how my girl-on-girl action might appeal to them more. Ha! That was fun. I pre-screened my group until I had a nice group of women, all of whom were at least open to the idea of porn, though some of them said what they had seen so far they hated. I set them up with champagne and beer in a very comfy lounge, and watched. They knew I was going to watch. What I didn't know is that it would turn them on so much they wouldn't care! They started "playing along," so to speak. That was AMAZING. I got to see what they really were doing with each other, and my girl-on-girl porn got more realistic. I paid those girls a lot, but it was worth every penny.

But sometimes I would sit in my extremely nice apartment, and I would think, "I should really do something good for people with all this money." But then I would think, "Who wants money from a porn freak? I can't give it to a politician, that's for sure." I didn't want to give it away to a cause I didn't care about. Some part of me still felt that what I was doing, no matter how much I enjoyed it or how much I tried to be good to people, was sleazy and wrong and disgusting. I wanted to atone, redeem myself. Also, I was bored.

About eight years ago, you understand, I was in a rut. I could have all the hot girls I wanted. My life was all about hot girls all the time. And as it happens, when you get too much of something you get desensitized. Known fact. When guys get too much porn—and nowadays with the Internet people can have unlimited porn—they want weirder and weirder…thrills. I went to the Netherlands and fucked transgender sex workers and went to all the European sex shows and watched every single kind of porn known to man, part research and part just trying to reignite that kinkiness. I made some weird porn in those days. Terrible arty porn. Dream hospital porn with buckets of eyeballs in the corner of the shot. Horrendous and ridiculous. I defy you to make a bucket of eyeballs sexy. It cannot be done.

Around that time I was passing through San Francisco and saw a Craigslist ad for a hotel scene. In the ad she just called herself "woman." The ad started, "Do you want to fuck?" So like a lot of guys I thought, well, hell yes! The woman prescreens the guys, they show up, and there's a gang bang. Well, that sounded like a thing to do. I hadn't done *that* before, so I sent the woman the info she wanted, but she didn't even send a picture, nothing, so I had no idea, and then when I got there, there was this woman. This overweight black woman—a beautiful woman, luscious curves. And she was fucking these guys, just tearing it up, and she was LOVING it. I never saw anybody have so much fun having sex, and I have seen *a lot* of sex. And when one guy was done, she would lie still and look around the room and then yell, "You!" and she pointed and when she would do that, in that half-second before she pointed, all the guys would lean in and there was so much tension, and then afterward, after the guy had fucked her, the deal was he had to leave. He just left, and then she picked the next one and that's the way it went.

It was amazing. She was passionate—and so real. I guess the thing is I have mostly had girls who were good at it because they worked at pleasing a man. And they loved pleasing men. But this woman was eating men like candy, she fucked you for *herself* and she had the dirtiest mouth. She would yell, "Oh yes fuck me *daddy*, fuck my cunt you cocksucking bastard, harder, and I *mean* it now." Sometimes she would taunt them and yell, "Is that all you've got?" And when she did that to *me*, it made me angry, and it was meant to make me angry and I grabbed her, grabbed her head and pushed her down while I fucked her and she said, "Oh GOD that's the way to FUCK! That's how I fucking LIKE it!" And I came hard and rolled off and thought, well, that's it, she's got to be done now. And she did pant for just a minute or two, but then her eyes lit up and she pointed to the next guy and she yelled, "You!"

I went into the bathroom and cleaned myself up and went home. But I thought about her. I thought about her and masturbated thinking about her and that was weird. I mean, I had had tons of sex workers who really worked on their bodies, and they were all skinny and had perfect tits, often surgically enhanced, and had soft skin; they waxed and exfoliated and buffed and worked out and polished and dyed and enameled. And she wasn't that at all; she was something else. She was just so real. I don't mean her body was real. I mean, a body that has been worked on is as real as any other. This was more about real passion, about sincerity. She was getting gang banged, and yet she was totally in control. She was *topping* a whole room full of guys at once. That is a powerful woman.

I found myself checking for her next Craigslist ad two months later. I flew into San Francisco just for the occasion.

I wanted to see it again. I wanted to see her again. I went again and she took me earlier, sent me home sooner, and it was amazing, like last time; she was strong and knew exactly what she wanted and she pulled it out of me. She made me fuck like a bull, and her pussy was amazing. It just felt right. But of course that wasn't the main thing for me; it was the whole experience, and it was just…strange. The feelings I had about this woman. I don't know what it was drawing the rest of the guys. I know what it was for me.

Anyway, the fourth time I went, she met my eye early, and smiled, giving me this great hot eye contact, and then… picked someone else. And she did that every time. She kept picking the guys next to me, on either side, and there were about eight guys there, and I thought, she's saving me for last. And that felt like an honor, watching each guy stumble home, stumble away—she fucked them under the table. And then it was my turn, and she waited until the last guy had already left and I took her in my arms and felt myself slide into this big juicy delicious woman, this real woman. I had been being teased by her all night; I'd had a hard-on for hours, and I just— she clenched her muscles around me once, and I groaned and came and I felt a little guilty but I couldn't feel too bad about it because it felt so fucking good.

I said, "Okay, that never happens to me," and laughed.

She laughed too and said, "Happens to me *all* the time."

"Do you mind if I rest here for just a minute?"

She said it was okay, so I cuddled up to her, and the next thing we knew it was morning. I woke up still holding her tight. She had, has, this wonderful smell, like vanilla and bourbon and sex. I asked if I could treat her to breakfast and she said yes.

And that's how I got to know her, my Lovey, Sequoia. The great love of my life. She told me she was a *doctor*, a psychiatrist doing postgraduate research as well as logging therapy hours and getting a master's in family counseling at the same time. That's not even possible. She said she didn't have time for a sex life so she just did this every once in a while and "got it all out." She told me she wanted to specialize in bringing new drugs and therapy modalities together to heal people from dysfunctional abusive homes. She's talking about this over ham and eggs, gesturing wildly, and I realize, my god, she's also brilliant. I have never met a woman this smart. I mean, I know lots of smart women—never discount the intelligence of a sex worker—but she was amazing. And passionate about everything she talked about. Jesus, she was the single smartest person I had ever talked to. I wanted to sit at her feet and learn everything I could from her.

We talked a lot about sex, and that was blowing my mind. She had a lot of thoughts about the healing nature of sex and the way sex could work therapeutically to help people who were abused.

So I asked her if she had been abused. It seemed like the obvious question to ask: isn't that what people do? They want to heal themselves and the self they see in others? And I felt so close to her somehow.

She told me she couldn't tell me about that just yet, so she asked me what I did. When I told her, her eyes lit up. She wanted to know *everything* about making porn and owning strip clubs. I told her she should come to Las Vegas and I would take her to a strip club, and she said, "Okay. Let's go." It happened to be the beginning of summer break and she miraculously had time off. We swung by her house, grabbed a few clothes, and went that night.

We ended up spending the week together. I am so glad because we just found that we didn't want to be apart. We needed to tell each other everything, everything about our lives, everything we had been holding back from telling anyone else because at some deep-down level we both felt like we were the weirdest freaks in existence. I told her about my dad taking me to the whorehouse, and I *never* tell that story. I took her to my strip clubs and she got lap dances—it was hilarious. She told me she was a feminist, and she talked to the strippers—really talked to them and asked them about their work. She has this sincerity, this deep, grounded, wholesome lovingness that it's really hard to lie to. She was just interested in what they had to say and sat and talked with them and bought them "drinks" just to hear them tell her what they thought of their jobs. Which was all over the place. I had never even done this—I knew some strippers were better than others but to hear them talk—to hear about those who did it because it was the best pay possible and some who just loved it. For some a job and others a vocation. And when she found a few who really really loved it, she got a lap dance and that was something to see. She was laughing and a little turned on—despite being "straight."

My fellow club owners thought I was insane. They had never seen me with a woman who wasn't a porn star or a stripper or just looked like one, and here was this woman, a fat woman, no makeup. Some laughed. I felt one moment of shame as their judgments hit me, but it was immediately replaced by a feeling that I cared much more what she thought than what they did. So I kept right on bringing her everywhere. And if they had any spark of heart or soul—and okay, a lot of them don't—but those that did, she won them over. Because you have to love her. I do. She's the best thing that ever happened to me. And the sex is…amazing.

Those first few weeks I told her that I wanted to do something better, that I worried that I was doing harm, doing something so sleazy. I had fits where I worried that I was exploiting girls even though I had gone very high end and paid well for good stars. Sequoia helped me with that. And then she told me her idea, the little fantasy she had because she read a lot about abuse and where and how it happens, and there were cases, she said, cases where she couldn't help.

She told me a story about this family, and they had a daughter—a Filipino family, and the girl was seventeen and a half, and they caught her kissing her girlfriend. They hit her a few times, they yelled abuse at her, and then they pulled her out of school and wouldn't let her leave the house. They denied her phone privileges. every once in a while they would relax, or it was late at night and she managed a phone call out, but the house was locked tight and there was nothing her friends could do; it's not illegal to ground your child. They stopped hitting her so no one could call child protective services. They fed her; they didn't hit her; she was under eighteen. They just yelled at her and threatened to send her back to the Philippines to marry a nice boy. But for some reason they didn't. Money troubles, maybe.

On her eighteenth birthday she got ahold of the phone after they were asleep and made a call to 911. The parents caught her and interrupted the call, but it was too late; the police were on their way. When they got there she told them she was eighteen years old, an adult, and her parents were holding her against her will. The police walked her past her parents while they cried and begged her and berated her not to go.

And Sequoia said sometimes she hears stories like that and wants to DO something, to rescue the gay kids who need more than just therapy, but need rescue—abused kids. She told me if only there was someone who would just risk it, just go in there and get those kids out. Abused kids. Ones who wanted rescuing. And could we do something like that? My heart started racing, and I thought, well, why the hell not? So I told her, we are going to need a team. Her smile was so big it almost blinded me.

Chapter 7:

Lovey and Mr. Howell Converse

Sequoia came into Leo's office in a stew. She wore a long print maxi dress in a shade of calm light blue, at odds with the rage on her face. Her earrings were jingling as she literally shook with anger.

"You know Lindsay's story? That her parents were going to send her someplace—someplace where she could get straightened out but good?" She flung herself into a leather chair across from his expensive desk and looked at him. And just looking at him, calm and collected in his white linen suit, with a tall fizzy drink in front of him, calmed her down.

"Oh, yes. *Terrifying* possibility. Do you have something?"

"I think so. Kid emailed me a video, talking about it. It's in the Dominican Republic. All the things we're scared of: electric shock aversion therapy, beatings. Maybe rape. Maybe RAPE! 'Corrective' rape, scary brainwashing tactics. He's eighteen and out of his house now, but still so scared of these fuckers he begged me not to let anyone know who he was. He says they have ex-military with guns who will come after him if he talked."

"Shit. That's bad. What do we do? You have any ideas?"

"None. NONE! It's killing me. It's outside of U.S. legal jurisdiction. The kid wasn't too clear where it was—a long jeep ride from the airport, that's all he knows. They blindfolded him for the first part of the drive, until he was in the jungle, so he couldn't tell east, west, nothing. And we don't have anyone *asking* to be rescued from it anyway."

"Is that so important? This place is clearly fucked up beyond repair. Surely the kids will welcome their liberators," Leo leaned forward, but sipped from his frosty drink.

Occasionally his obtuse calm made her seethe. "No, it's *very* important. It's fucking crucial. You know, those conservative assholes—just this week—are claiming there should be an 'underground railroad' to rescue kids from gay parents. I was eating corn on the cob and I shot corn out of my NOSE I was so angry. They just shat on the whole idea of the Underground Railroad. I hope the ghost of Harriet Tubman kills them in their sleep! They want to kidnap children! And I'll bet they do it, and they won't stop to ask if the children want to be kidnapped, because they think THEY know best. They always think they know best."

"I see. Yes, I get it. So if we go in there and rescue children who haven't asked for it..."

"We'll be no better than they are. Right. And we have to be better, we have to be, or there's no fucking point to any of it!" she crossed her arms.

"So what, my darling love, do you want to do about it?"

"Well, it won't hurt to try to find out more."

"Eve."

"Yes. Absolutely. Eve."

Eve, Sequoia thought. A force to be reckoned with, a tireless crusader in the evangelical movement, stamping out the sin of homosexuality wherever she found it—and a mole. Sneaking their cards to trapped kids on the sly, nosing out abuses, "therapies," and camps. Only Sequoia knew her legal name; to the rest of the team she was always just...Eve.

Sequoia nodded. That was all they could do: gather information. Put out cards. Get Eve on the trail. Go fishing and hope they could land the whole abusive school.

Chapter 8: Lovey's Story

Some people, their religion drives them crazy, and some people use religion to hide their crazy: my father was one of the latter. My mother died in a car crash when I was little. I think now that my dad might even have done that on purpose; he was driving. That left me and my older brother in his care. My brother, Jerrod, was seven years older than me; I was six. My father was the scariest thing in the world to me. Before my mother died, he would go to work and then come home and take a belt to us in the name of Jesus, and then Mama would sneak into our rooms later and cry and hold us. And I loved it when my mom came into the room and held us, and she would whisper that she was sorry. But then she died.

My brother got it much worse than me. I know now he was protecting me but I didn't understand at the time why he would sass my dad and get his ass beat so hard. I loved my brother so much. Jerrod and I used to dress up in my mom's old clothes and dance to Donna Summer. I followed him like a puppy. I hated hearing him cry.

When my mom died, my father got worse, and Jerrod would keep trying to protect me from him. He was in junior high by then, and my father was disappointed in him. Wanted him to go out for sports, date girls. Instead Jerrod kept getting more and more…swishy. Then my dad found him one day when he was fifteen wearing makeup and our dead mother's clothes, and beat him so hard he…well, he died. Our neighbors called the cops, and there were lights flashing everywhere, and then we were at the hospital and the next thing I remember my grandmamma was clutching me tight and telling me she was never going to let me go, not ever, and I was going home with her. My dad went to jail, and I started living with Grandma.

Now my grandmother was a great woman. One of the world's really great women. Okay, she had one of those grandma things where she had to show you she loved you by feeding you. Once we got home from the hospital and she told me my brother died, I didn't eat or talk for weeks. My grandmother would hold me and beg me to just have a few bites, "baby, just take a bite," and mostly I lived on milkshakes and soup. Whenever I tried to eat solid foods they made me choke. But my grandmother cooked like her ass was on fire, turning out all my favorite foods. She cooked me biscuits and chili, sweet potato pie, mac and cheese—everything I used to love. Before. But I couldn't eat it. Then one day she made me some sweet lemonade with fresh squeezed lemons and some fried fish and hush puppies, chocolate chip cookies and pecan sandies, and then just left me alone in the room with this pile of food and suddenly I was so hungry. I *loved* pecan sandies, and my grandmother's were tremendous. The cookie had this buttery crispness, but each of the pecans had been dipped in a bourbon praline sauce, and my mouth started watering. I started eating and eating them, and when I looked up she was standing in the doorway watching me with tears streaming down her cheeks. I knew she loved me so much. She said it too, but it was the food that made me feel it. I still feel loved when I eat really good food, especially soul food, the best food on earth—even when

I cook it, I feel the love.

My grandmother loved her family, food, and learning, in about that order. She believed that I was brilliant and when I got good grades, she would cook me whatever I wanted. My grandfather had died about five years before I was born, and my grandmother had this big run-down house, and all her children were in and out of it all the time.

One day when I was about one2, she said it was time for us to talk about these things. She was my mama's mama, and when Mama died she said she wanted to take me and Jerrod. "Your daddy was crazy," she said. "I *hated* what he did to my baby girl, and then to you and Jerrod. I wanted to come get you but I was scared of him. I'm so sorry. I'm so sorry." She cried. I cried. We both cried so damn much for a while.

My grandmamma cooked huge Sunday meals, and all of Mama's three brothers would come. Two of them were married and had wives and children, and me and my cousins would roam all around the neighborhood playing games and causing trouble. They were the first ones to call me bookworm and tease me because I needed glasses. My grandma would scold them for it, but that just made them tease me all the more. I know now they were jealous because everyone loved Grandma, and all the kids wanted to live there and have her make them pecan pies whenever they wanted. But during the week I lived there all alone with her. They thought I got spoiled all week long like they did on Sundays, but my grandmamma was too smart to do that. I did homework and read to her while she was cooking and went to bed on time. I did get to eat her cooking though. They were right about that. Their mamas couldn't cook a lick compared to Grandma.

Anyway, after a while I needed glasses and started putting on weight so then I was a fat girl with glasses, but Grandmamma would go to library book sales and yard sales and keep buying me more and more books. I stopped hanging out with my cousins because they called me a "poindexter," so on Sundays I started to hang out with my Uncle Ray. Uncle Ray didn't like to watch sports with Uncles Freddie and Marcus. Ray was my *cool* uncle, the one who wasn't married and would go out dancing on weekends. Grandmamma said weird things about Ray sometimes that I didn't really understand, like, "It takes all kinds to make a world," and, "It isn't anyone's business what he does as long as he wasn't hurting anybody." So eventually I asked her, so, what does he do? And she told me it wasn't my business either.

But I figured it out in time, that Ray was like Jerrod and that people thought there was something wrong with how they were because they weren't like other men. But I thought it was great they weren't like other men, because I *hated* the other men. I hated the men who hung out on street corners and would holla at you as you went by, and I hated my dad, who was in prison for killing my brother. I didn't even like my other uncles, who would get uncomfortable when Ray was around and make excuses not to talk to him one on one. So I loved Ray even more and he loved me back, and it was like he sort of took Jerrod's place in my mind and became my big brother. He was great, like having a brother and an auntie in the same person. He took me out shopping for my school clothes, helped me do my makeup in high school, tried to talk to me about boys. But I didn't want to talk about boys. I was closed up tight for a long time. The best, though, was in high school when he finally told me what I had already figured out and introduced me to all his friends and they would come over and laugh and drink cocktails and make me feel beautiful and important. That was how I wanted the world to be; that was freedom.

Because I kept reading, I did really badly at school socially. No one wants to hang around with a girl with glasses and a big bag of books. I didn't have boyfriends, and I thought I didn't want them, but sometimes I would have these fantasies, fantasies that were just over the top. They scared me. Fantasies about having dicks, so many dicks, men surrounding me. Cock in my mouth and in my pussy and in both my hands and rubbing against me, all at the same time. And there wasn't really anyone I could talk to about sex. That was something I really couldn't ask Grandma about. On this subject she did not encourage curiosity.

She lectured my uncles, even now, when they would come over on Saturday, about treating their women right. She had drilled into them that they had to respect women, but all she said to me was to watch out and not get pregnant because she wanted me to school out more, so I shouldn't be fussing with that since there would be plenty of time later. I said no one would ever want me and she said, "Oh yes they will. They will because the sexiest thing a person can be is smart."

She told me if I just hung on and went to college it would be filled with great, smart, nice boys who would be thrilled to date me. Well she wasn't right about that, but she was on the right track. I got so curious about sex that I started reading about it, going to the library and reading the Kinsey report, the Hite report; I must have been fifteen years old, and that's when the penny dropped and I first realized my uncle was gay, and his roommate was not just his roommate. And maybe my brother had been too, and that's what my dad meant when he yelled "Be a man!" as he hit him. I sat there in the library and started to cry, silently, tears running down my face, because it just seemed so, so stupid. I wanted my brother back.

I was trying to figure out what I wanted to do; I knew I wanted to go to college, but sometimes it seemed so hard to get there. We had really shitty schools, but my grandmamma managed to get me a place at Berkeley High when I got into high school and she read up on what I needed to do to go to college. That was hard, too, because Berkeley was a good school—if you were white. The college prep classes were great, but most of the black kids weren't in them, and they didn't want to be. It wasn't the teachers; teachers in Berkeley were as progressive as you can get. They were always trying to get more black kids into the college prep classes. They loved me. But the kids, they were cruel. "Oreo" was my nickname all through and kids telling me I needed to "talk more black." Made me cry sometimes.

But my grandmother told me not to mind them. My life was going to take me places they couldn't imagine, she said. She even tried to go to school with me, so we could study together—she went to the community college. That was hard. She was brilliant, she *was*, but she left traditional schooling a little too late, and she couldn't hold a train of thought steady. Her thoughts were like brilliant butterflies flitting in and out—lots of color and movement—and to do well in school your thoughts have to be like a well-trained dog that goes where it's told and performs what it needs to. I told her, when she was crying once because she got a low grade on an English paper, that she was smarter than any of them and that what she was writing was a kind of poetry when what they were looking for was boring old regular writing. That cheered her up and she clung to me and asked if I would please be a teacher, like she always wanted to be. That was about as big a dream as she could dream.

But I knew even then better than that. I had read *Their Eyes Were Watching God,* and I knew you can't let your grandmother make your life choices, no matter how much she might love you. I didn't want to be a teacher. I was aiming higher. I wanted to have the answers to the problems that had shaped my life, or at least work on them. I wanted to know why people couldn't get along and why my mom had let my dad beat her and then Jerrod and me and hadn't left him; what was wrong with her? What was wrong with my dad? I wanted to know why people couldn't love people as wonderful as Jerrod and Ray and why anyone thought there was something wrong with them. And I wanted to know about sex and how this fit into the equation. Of my other two uncles, Freddie and Marcus, I wanted to know why Uncle Freddie and Aunt May always looked like smug, like they had some great secret they didn't want to share with the rest of us, and Uncle Marcus and Aunt Sondra would always snipe at each other. What's the secret to how people learn to be happy? How was I going to help make people happy?

In high school I started reading Freud. To get into UC Berkeley, I wrote an entry essay about wanting to help make people happier. I was a shoo-in: great grades, school theater and newspaper and choir, and SAT scores that made the other kids go "wow" and say racist things to me. White kids would say things like, "I thought you people didn't do well on standard-ized tests," which was bad enough, and black people would say shit like, "I knew you weren't really black." Dammit! If there's one thing I hate, it's internalized racism. I went home and told Grandma and she told me, "Secretly, they don't think they're as good as white people, and that is the saddest thing in the world." She was brilliant like that—she hit the nail on the head and made you sorry for people, really sorry for people who you didn't think deserved it.

I thought about going away to college and leaving this place, striking out to see if things were different for a black nerd on the East Coast. But my grandmamma was getting older, and I didn't want to leave her. So I went to UC Berkeley.

I lost my virginity to a white guy in my dorm who want-ed help with an English paper. It felt…weird. He was really cute, and kind of sweet, but also kind of…dumb. In a hippie stoner way. I ended up writing his paper for him. He would come to my room late at night and have sex with me but not talk to me in the dining hall. I fell hard for him and then I realized he didn't want to date me or be my boyfriend. I cried outside his dorm room when he took this pretty skinny hippie chick back to his room, and the next day there were three words written on the notepad I kept on my door: Leave Me Alone. Not signed. But I knew. It was devastating.

The next jerk wasn't much better. That was a "real" relationship—another white guy, this one I met in one of my African American studies classes. He was a black wanna-be: he called all the black men in the class "brother" and didn't see when they rolled their eyes at him. To him, I was a trophy girlfriend—an actual black girl! He showed me off to his friends like a prize, and it was weird how that didn't feel much better than the hippie who was ashamed of me. After those experiences I started to hang out more with people I met at the Black Student Union—I had stopped trusting white men to see me as a fucking person. But the brothers on campus weren't exactly chasing me down either, and I was lonely. And horny. So I was laughing and complaining about this to this new black woman I met, Shandra, and she says, "Maybe you need to open your mind to other possibilities." She had this low, smoky voice, and I stopped and looked at her for a minute and the air just rippled with sex. I looked up into her eyes and for the first time I knew what it was like to have someone look at me, to just see me, for who I am, and look at me with desire. And it was thrilling.

Shandra was getting an MFA in some kind of sculpture, which meant she worked with metal and wood. She was tall and strong with broad shoulders and muscular arms, and she kept her hair cut close and natural. And I thought, no, no, I'm not gay, what am I doing? But I went back to her place, and I let her make love to me and it was a revelation. Shandra wanted my pleasure and knew how to get it: she had strong fingers and deft hands and gave soft loving kisses and whispered to me how beautiful I was, that I was a goddess. She tasted me and stroked me and brought me to a kind of rolling, shuddering orgasm I had only had by myself before. I was so grateful to her.

And so confused. I'm using female pronouns now for her and the name Shandra because that was how I thought of her that first night with her, but pretty soon he told me he was really a he and that he preferred to be called Abimbola, which meant "born wealthy" and was a name for both men and women in…Swahili? I forget now. When he told me it just made so much sense. He was very masculine to me—bigger than me and strong and he made me feel beautiful and feminine, like no cis male ever had. But it got even more complicated than that, because Abimbola kept evolving. His gender wasn't just one or the other; he didn't want to be pinned down like that. They prefer they pronouns now.

Anyway—he—I'm going to call him "he" because that was the pronoun he preferred when we were together—taught me so much. Taught me really to put aside labels and just pay attention to what I wanted and felt. Taught me that I deserved to have anything I wanted. He loved making presents for me, little sculptures out of wood and metal that sometimes made me laugh and sometimes took my breath away. He asked me about my secret fantasies. He wanted to *know* me. But he wanted to know other women too. He wanted to go out and please all the women. When I first learned that I was hurt and I cried, and he held me and said he was sorry. He said he didn't know I thought we were being exclusive, which seemed like a cop-out at the time.

But he was a good thing in my life because he taught me that I could have any fantasy I wanted, any experience I wanted. I told him about my fantasies about having multiple men, like a lot of men at once, and he laughed and said then I should have it. He wasn't even threatened or unhappy that I sometimes wanted a biological penis inside me. He had a BIG soul. He introduced me to all kinds of people, artists from off campus and pranksters and rebels. He helped set up my first gang bang, helped me vet and decide on each person who would be there. We had a mix of people with penises and people with strap-ons, and he checked in on me and made sure I was okay and held me afterward. I was high as a kite. I felt like I had conquered the world. Me! Star of my very own gang bang!

Abimbola and I were together for years while I was in college and grad school, but then he went off to make sculptures in New York: he has a partner now who's an MTF choreographer and they make these intricate pieces where dancers dance on sculptures that move, so that you can't be sure sometimes what is the dance and what is sculpture, and the dancers have all kinds of bodies, in shape and gender and disability. Abimbola dances in the space between genders, between motion and stillness, between freakish and beautiful. I owe him hugely for helping me find my own sexual…voice, and that led me to finding Leo and making this family of my own.

So when he moved away I cried but it was okay. It was time to move on. Sometimes when we get together we still make love, but mostly we laugh and share. He's one of the few people I have told about what we do, and he's happy for me that I found a partner who loves me—and such an unlikely one! Me with a porn king! Life is funny! And then Max came along and I finally had a child of my own. I live a blessed life. I don't believe in God, especially considering what fucked-up shit gets done in his name, but I believe in blessings. Abimbola once told me that nothing's sacred but everything is divine. Yeah. That's about right.

The Case of the Creepy Christian Camp

Chapter 9: They Took My Sister

Three weeks after Jess and Lindsay were safely launched on their new life, they got a call to follow up.

"They came in the middle of the night and took my sister," Paul's voice shook as he looked down at the table, one hand clenched and unclenched by his side. He was young, with messy red hair and red eyes—the first genetic, the second from long nights of crying.

When they had opened the door to their apartment and introduced themselves as Ginger and Mary Ann, he had almost run away on the spot. "This is serious!" he had yelled. "This isn't a stupid game."

They calmed him down. "We need anonymity. So we have code names," Isobel assured him. "You can't know our real names. That makes sense, right? Think about it a minute. Hey, at least we aren't Daphne and Velma."

"There's no way I'm going to be Velma," Mary Ann teased. "At least Mary Ann was a babe."

And strangely, their bantering calmed him down, and so did the smell of coffee and fresh-baked muffins, the decor of light blues and creams, the soft ambient music. They and Sequoia had designed everything in the room to radiate peace and calm. If he had walked down the hall and opened the door he would have seen an eye-popping array of weapons, a sling, a cage, everything black and white leather. But here, peace reigned supreme.

They settled him in and brought him coffee, cream, and a blueberry muffin. He sat a long time before he spoke. He picked up the muffin and started crumbling it between his fingers. Saw what he was doing, put down the muffin, and looked down, like he couldn't look at them directly.

"They came in the middle of the night and they took my sister." His voice was clotted with horror, forced out of a closing throat.

They waited and he took a gulp of coffee. Felicity walked to the sliding glass doors and opened them a crack, looking out at the gaudy strip, a rouged and raddled whore in the sunlight. She adored it. She sometimes looked out the window, thought of the quads and old brick of Ivy League academia she had been headed for and thanked every star in the sky she had escaped that life to this big weird sexy den of sin. But right now she needed to focus on Paul.

"I was staying home for the summer; I didn't want to but I was earning a few dollars before I went to college. And I wanted to protect my sister. Which I didn't." Self-loathing was in his voice now. Felicity wanted to comfort him, but that wasn't her strength.

"You couldn't have known about this. This is...unbelievable," Isobel patted his shoulder, but he didn't look up. She filled his coffee cup, and he looked around. She looked sweetly sympathetic, and Felicity's face expressed nothing but calm and compassion. But they were both thinking—*jackpot*!

"I know this is hard, but you have to tell me exactly what happened. Details matter. We might not be able to do anything...but we will try," Isobel patted his hand, urging him to continue.

"What exactly do you do? Who ARE you? What the hell do you *think* you can do?" He looked around. "They came in the middle of the night and *took* my sister, these guys dressed in pastel polo shirts, but big muscular guys. Terrifying. I heard her screaming. I ran in. She was screaming and screaming, and they took out handcuffs. They threatened to cuff her if she didn't stop. So she stopped, and I ran to try to get by her side and they threw me aside—like I was nothing. *Nothing.* They shoved me out of their way, almost out of the room, but I dodged aside and stayed right inside the door. I had to stay to see if I could help her."

His hands balled into fists. Then he looked down and realized they were full of muffin. He shook them over the plate. His hands kept shaking after they were empty, and he closed them again.

"They told her to get dressed. They *watched* her get dressed. The sick FUCKS! They told her to pack, and she told them to fuck the fuck OFF. But they threatened her with handcuffs again, so she packed. They made her pack—and they checked everything that went in. Felt in all her pockets. To make sure she didn't pack anything 'sinful.' My parents came to the door of the room and tried to get me to leave the room. They told me it was 'okay,' that these guys were going to help my sister. I started screaming. 'ARE you CRAZY? Are you NUTS? This is not the way to help anyone!'"

"My sister yelled at them too. She always said whatever she wanted. I loved her for that. She told my father he was a sick fuck too, and my dad ran in the room and slapped her and told her that *that* was why she needed to go, that she talked like a whore, and he finished packing her things, and they took her arm. I ran in and tried to push them away from her, but got shoved away again."

Tears streamed down his face. He kept talking.

"They checked everything she put in. Every piece of clothing got shaken out. They took her underwear and looked at it and threw it on the ground if it was too 'sinful.' They wouldn't let her take any books. Except a bible."

"The bible—when she packed it, did they check it?"

"Yes. Opened it, shook it, the whole works."

"Did they ask about her passport, make sure she had it?"

"YES! What does that mean? They're taking her to another country, oh, my God, I never even thought of that, oh God. Oh God, she could be anywhere. Anywhere."

Felicity grimaced to Isobel over his shoulder.

Isobel leaned forward and gave him a tissue, and he wiped it across his face and balled it up.

"Anyway, she wrenches away from them somehow, and she runs up to me, and we're both crying. She hugs me, grabs my hand. I feel something in it, so I palm it. They wrench her back and, oh my God." He leaned forward for a moment, put his head in his hands like he felt weak. "They pulled her back, and they put this thing, this *harness*, on her, like she was an animal, and they pulled her away and out of the house. I saw her face. I saw her face as she was leaving, and I ran to the bathroom and I threw up. Then I ran into my room and called 911, but when they came they said Kate was a minor; her parents signed her up for this, and it was legal. How can this be legal?! She's sixteen! She was abducted; she was TAKEN against her will. My mother was crying; my father did his stony-faced thing."

"What did you do then?"

"I packed, got in my car, and took off to a friend's house. His parents are never around so I knew it would be cool for me to stay a night or two—maybe more. And in the morning I called the number on the card. Your number."

79

The Case of the Creepy Christian Camp

The cards had been Felicity's idea, the backbone of the organization, just a white scrap of paper with a simple LGBT triangle, a phone number, and the words: "If you're in trouble." When you called, the voicemail message told you to call 911 if you were in immediate danger, to call a suicide prevention line—it gave the number—if you were suicidal, but if you were an LGBT minor who had issues with your parents or guardians, to leave a message, give as much info as possible, and wait. Young people got handed the card in bars if they looked underage, and they fell out of LGBT books in local libraries and bookstores and out of quite a few books spreading so-called Christian misinformation on LGBT issues. They got around, these cards, and connected the team with those who could benefit from their unique talents. The callers were discreetly investigated, contact was made, and, sometimes, rescues were arranged. It worked.

"Are *you* going to be okay?" Isobel asked, her voice like hot tea with honey, sweet and steadying.

"Sort of. I guess. My grandparents pay for college. They aren't as bad as my parents, and they're scared for Kate. They are freaked out because my parents won't tell them where she is. So I just need to find a place to stay until school opens. I can stay with my friend for a bit—he might not even mind if I just stay there or maybe I'll get a job, rent a room. I don't know. I'll be okay. But Kate—do you think you can find her, really? Can you help her?"

"Honey, all I can tell you is that we're going to try our best. We think she might be in the Dominican Republic, but we have to make sure."

"The Dominican Republic? Really? WHY?'

"We don't know…we have been getting information that there is a sick evangelical Christian camp that 'reforms' bad kids. Not just gays—all kinds of 'problem' children," Felicity spoke crisply, but her distaste was clear.

"We don't know much about it, but we've heard this is how they operate, this weird middle-of-the-night crap. We're trying to find out more. We need to find out a *lot* more—rescue is going to be hard."

"But we like a challenge, right?" Isobel smiled, and he winced. Felicity thought, he can't even stand to see someone smile. That's how miserable he is. That sister must be something special.

"I don't really understand. What do you do? What can you do?" He looked at them beseechingly.

Felicity took a breath, projected calm. She trusted him. His grief was abject and real. "We rescue kids. We go in and get them out of situations like this one—well, maybe not just like this one; this one is special. But we have done this many, many times."

Isobel patted his hand again and said, "Honey, we're good at what we do. We've saved a lot of teens. We promise, Paul, that we will do everything we can. A few weeks, maybe a month—you'll have your sister back."

"Hurry, okay? She's...she's special," he handed over a picture of a laughing girl giving the finger to the camera. "All these years, they've tried to break her, tame her—and she just laughed and did whatever the hell she wanted. Mouthed off to them, got smacked, and kept right on doing it. I tried to protect her but even though I was the big brother, she was the one who taught *me* about courage. I was always the good one, the good kid, trying hard to please them—to please *them*! FUCK them! But she was fearless. I don't know how she did that, in the face of what our fucking parents put us through. But when I think what those assholes might be doing—it's not *enough* to get her back. I want her unbroken. I want my badass sister back."

Felicity and Isobel looked at each other, eyes filling for a moment with tears, and then they saw him to the door with more promises that they would be in touch.

The moment he was out the door, Felicity flew to the phone, thankful that it was evening and she had a good shot of catching Sequoia at home.

"Hey, girl," Sequoia answered.

"We got it! What we've been waiting for. We have a clear SOS now from this camp in the DR—a girl passed our card to her brother. She wants to be rescued. Oh, Sequoia, this is some sick fucking shit. We have to get that poor girl out."

"Then we will," Sequoia said. "So tell me everything from the top, and let's get to work."

Chapter 10: How Mr. Howell Met Mary Ann and Ginger

In the words of Isobel Jensen

When we ran away, Felicity asked me where we should go. I had no idea. We were sixteen we had a few thousand dollars, and we knew that wouldn't last long. So I thought about it for a minute and I said, Vegas. Surely there would be some work for two cute girls, even underage ones, in the big sin capital. So we landed in Vegas, wandered into a sketchy, off-strip casino, and got hired as cocktail waitresses. They didn't look too hard at fake IDs when presented by knockout girls ready to work. We managed for a few crummy years, first in cheap motel rooms and then a cheap apartment, getting our asses pinched and living on crappy tips. When we turned eighteen we decided to try our hands—well, more like asses and legs and tits—at stripping. We found a club owned by a woman and pitched ourselves as a double act, stripping and dancing and, really, coming close to doing a live sex show night after night. Then we found that the club owner was pimping on the side, and he asked if we wanted to make serious money just by going to men's hotel rooms and lezzing out in front of them, and we said yes, hell yes! Why not make money doing what you love? And who you love?

Sequoia asked us later, were we scared? Did we feel degraded? No. We felt exhilarated; we felt like we had escaped.

The Case of the Creepy Christian Camp

We moved into a nice apartment—no ants! A dishwasher! We felt lucky and blessed and raring to go to work.

I felt terrible for dragging Felicity into this at first. She could have gone to any college, been anything she wanted, anything. If you love someone, you're not supposed to drag them into a life of dancing and whoring just to save your sorry ass. But I realized after a time, she made me realize, finally—I didn't have to feel guilty. *She* didn't feel regret, and not just because she loved me, because she really loved this life. She says she was on the road to being the biggest stick-in-the-ass closeted lesbian doctor in the world. Says she probably would have become a gynecologist while denying she ever wanted more from a pussy. Instead she was dancing for men for money, and the weird thing is, she loved it. I always had more problems with it than she did. She would go on stage and *dominate* through dancing. As soon as we started to strip, she made us take martial arts. I thought she was fucked in the head. Dancing in high heels every night and training in a dojo by day. But, she said, let's not be afraid of these bastards. And she was right, when we knew even the most basic things about taking a man down, it was more fun. We danced better; we flirted harder; we made more money. After a while we did more live shows than strip acts, and life was sweet.

Then Leo hired us one night. We knew about him, big porno magnate, and the girls said he was a pussycat, less sleazy than most, gave girls a good deal. Our little in-house sex show was getting some buzz, and we heard from our handler that Leo wanted to check us out. If he liked what he saw there might be opportunities. We could make porn, maybe. We had thought about it before but the offers hadn't been sweet enough to tempt us, and Felicity absolutely won't fuck guys, and I won't fuck them for money. I have to really like a man to find him attractive, and I mostly don't: who can blame me? But if we could do it *together*, just let people film the two of us, well hell, why not make bank? Our handler was all for it—thought our live act could triple in price if we were also porn stars. And let's face it, we were getting used to having money; we liked money. Who doesn't? And we also liked getting dressed up in hot little outfits and having sex with each other. So Leo set up a private appointment for midnight Saturday and paid enough that that was the only show we would do that night. He asked for some S&M action, which he had heard we would provide on special request; it was kind of an audition.

In Leo's words

That night I fronted the cash for a decadent suite of rooms: wet bar, hot tub, huge-screen TV, high-priced call girls, and drugs on speed dial. I think the concierge would have come up and personally given me a rim job for enough money. He might even have done it for free. But never mind. I relaxed with a flute of fine champagne in a silk robe, very Hef of me, and waited. These two had just started billing themselves as Mary Ann and Ginger, and with my love of tiki—well. I felt like a kid about to get the best Christmas present ever. Mary Ann and Ginger were going to do naughty, naughty things right in front of me? Oh yes, please!

At just before midnight there was a rap on the door, and when I open the door this bombshell redhead, in ripped white lingerie, throws herself into my arms, presses herself against me and murmurs, "Oh, God, *please*, hide me. She's a monster...." She pushes past me into the room, looks around in panic and runs for the bathroom, gesturing back over her shoulder to me, "Shhhhh." She put just that slight whispery, feather touch of Marilyn in her voice, that Hollywood damsel-in-distress look.

The Case of the Creepy Christian Camp

And just as she disappears into the bathroom, there's a hard knock the door, a stern voice calls, "Police! Open this door!"

I open the door and there's Mary Ann—Felicity—in the tightest, most flattering porn cop outfit imaginable, complete with night stick, handcuffs, and shades. Felicity has this highly trained, disciplined little body. People get so thunderstruck by Isobel's glamour they overlook Felicity, but she's just as beautiful, every bit as sexy. When I opened the door she stepped past me and before I could get out a word, she says, "Sir, I believe you might be harboring a dangerous criminal. I'm going to have to inspect the premises. If you stop me I can have you in for obstructing justice." Her voice was steel and if she wasn't wearing a miniskirt and platform boots, I might have believed she was a cop. Off she marches to the bathroom. And there's Isobel, huddling in the big open shower, which is a stupid place to hide—but this is not a cop show; this is a sex show. Felicity reaches in and turns on the shower. Isobel tries to leap out, but Felicity pushes her back, grabs the guard rail, and leaps in with her and they are wrestling, wet and gorgeous in the shower. I had the fleeting thought that this must have been dangerous as hell: stripper footwear in the shower? But they knew what they were doing, and the bars were securely installed. I didn't think about it long; I couldn't. I had an erection the size of her nightstick by that point. This was one of the best shows I had ever seen.

Then Isobel manages to leap out of the shower, her make-up miraculously in place (after all my time in porn, I notice these things), and her clothes almost completely off—just one small wet thong still covering her. She scrambles out, and Felicity hurls herself after her, and they fight again on dry land. It looks fantastic! It must have been so well rehearsed, if you can imagine a karate-dance-strip act. Isobel gets her hands on the cop suit and with one perfect tug that rips off too, then Felicity roars and pounces on her and gets her down on her knees with her arms behind her back, yelling: "You whore! You naughty piece-of-shit bitch!" She looks up at me and says, "Sir, she's a desperate criminal, and I have no backup. I'm going to have to subdue her completely before I can bring her in."

She hauls Isobel to her feet, and, twisting her arm behind her back, marches her over to the bed and handcuffs her to the headboard, face up, saying, "Sir, I'm sorry you're going to have to see this. If you could please stay out of way for a moment, sir," she waved him to the armchair near the bed. "I am going to have to teach this bitch some manners."

Isobel writhes and pulls against her restraints, and the kicker was, you can tell she loves it. Her eyes are wild and she is completely in this moment. She is not one bit phoning this in. And she yells, "Fuck you, slut pig! Don't you dare touch me with your dirty pig fingers!"

"Oh, you don't like my fingers, do you? Well that's too bad for you, because these fingers are going *everywhere*." She stands beside this writhing she-devil, reaches down, and pulls the last shreds of her outfit off and flings it aside. The she straddles her and starts playing with her breasts with one hand and reaches down with the other and slips two fingers in her pussy, and I could smell her arousal in the air, sweet and pungent. Isobel's thatch is just as fiery red as the hair on her head, and she has it trimmed that day into this little red heart. It is enchanting, titillating, delicious. I was in heaven.

I was sitting there, and, of course, doing what was expected of me to do—what straight man wouldn't have himself well in hand by then? But I was also just marveling at them. They were some amazing, gutsy dames! Before I started to concentrate on getting myself off, I had to take a moment to admire the consummate artistry here. This scene was well acted, well choreographed, imaginative, smart, not like anything I had ever seen before, and I have seen plenty. I was sitting back and thinking, yes, I want to make them stars. But I was also thinking that I *liked* them. Who are these women? What's their story? The love was palpable—this wasn't just a show. Felicity focuses more and more on that pussy, with a thumb on Isobel's clit and the other hand up to four fingers and then her whole small hand is in and she is fisting her! (Can I tell you I hate that word? Such a misnomer too!) Isobel tips over into a toe-curling orgasm and lets out this sound, like a cat and a goddess combined. She squirts, and there is no faking that, and I have to say that this all tipped me over into coming too, and it was magnificent, amazing—one of the top ten sexual experiences of my life, and I never even got to so much as cup a breast.

No one left that night. Felicity told me later that it was one of the best shows they had ever put on. She outdid herself, because she had heard about me and my money, heard I was good to my employees and could open a lot of doors. And Isobel was stupendous, all groans and whimpers and creamy skin. They kept going after that, with Felicity rocking and grinding her way to orgasm on top of Isobel, and I was right there with her too. But even after my time came to an end, and I was wrung out, they kept going, oblivious to me. I think for a while they forgot about me.

When they finally finished, they went to take a shower. I didn't even have the strength to go in the bathroom and watch them wash each other. I asked them to stay, talk to me about what they wanted and how we could—what we could do for each other. After about an hour, when we started to fade, I offered them some ecstasy. Isobel cut her eyes over to Felicity, who smiled. "Isobel doesn't have the best judgment in people," she said. "I protect her." I could see that was a job she took very, very seriously.

"I think he's okay," Felicity said, and she reached out and took two of the pills I extended out to her, and washed them down with a sip of sparkling water. "Here's to a special night." Her eyes were sparkling. They were starting to like me back. That felt almost as good as coming. Almost.

Amazingly it turned out they had never tried ecstasy before. True, Vegas was a booze and cocaine kind of town, and they had done a little of that, but Felicity said they only drank when they were home alone (other than the watered-down drinks they let customers buy for them at the strip joints) and never touched the coke they got offered.

When I asked her about it, Felicity shrugged. "What we do is fun, in its own way, but it's dangerous. If we don't keep our wits about is, know how to protect ourselves, we can go from sex workers to rape victims in a heartbeat. And who's going to believe it if two sex worker-strippers cry rape? No one."

But somehow, with me…they agreed. I'm sure it was partly because of my reputation as the nicest guy in porn—which I worked hard for. However, I think that we all knew they were something special, and I was something special, and what we could do together was very special indeed. They knew I loved women, in a real and genuine way. I would never take advantage of them.

We got high. I spent a half an hour dissecting every last bit of their act and telling them how much I loved it. "The shower scene? Oh my God. The wet karate fight? Fucking hell that was good. The part where she rolled her over and hit her with a crop until that scrumptious white bottom was as pink as strawberry ice cream? Just amazing." I babbled. They blushed.

"I LOVE sex!" I yelled from the balcony late that night, and somewhere in the Las Vegas night someone heard me and yelled back a loud, "FUCK YEAH!"

The women laughed, and I went back to the bed and

grabbed them up in a big bear hug. "Now you come here and cuddle up with Papa Bear and tell me the story of your lives," I said. "Because you girls—and this is not the e talking—you women are absofuckinglutely amazing. You can do *anything*. You are wasted as strippers—you could be the biggest porn stars in the world. You could be rich—as rich as I am. I'm serious."

"I don't know…do we want to be porn stars?" Isobel asked.

"Would we have to fuck men?" Felicity added. "We don't want to fuck men."

"Well…it would help." I said. "That is a difficult limit."

"Technically," Felicity said, "I've NEVER had sex with a man. And I don't want to."

"Never?" I said. In all her time as a stripper? That was impressive.

"No. Don't really want to. I mean, I have this." She grabbed Isobel and kissed her long and deep.

" Okay, we can work around it. I mean, there definitely is a big market for girl-on-girl action. Would you be willing to work with other women?"

"Hmm. Maybe…" said Felicity.

"Oh, really?" said Isobel. "You never have before…"

"Hey," she said. "I'm human. I just don't know about porn. I like live, performing for someone you know is turned on. But we did a photo shoot once, and …it gets clinical, you know. The lights. Taking direction. It's just not very sexy. We'd be faking it, I think."

"Well, I can see your point there…so what do you want to do? If not porn stars? I mean, I want you to work for me and make me tons and tons of money. I wonder…okay, I'm having this amazing idea…. You were so good as that cop…do either of you really know how to fight?"

They burst out laughing.

"What? What's so funny?"

"It's just that, well, fuck yeah, we know how to fight. We have been taking Krav Maga lessons for the past two years, and I've been taking karate lessons too. And Isobel here is a sharpshooter; she goes out and does weapons training every weekend at the shooting range. I don't like guns, myself, but I've been with her from time to time. Enough that I know how to handle a weapon."

"She has great aim. She would be really good if she worked at it," said Isobel.

"I don't like loud noises! Yuck! I like fighting! I rescue the people because I like to FIGHT!" She sang a snatch of the Shonen Knife "Buttercup" song and jumped up mock dancing and fighting.

Isobel laughed at her. "You're so high."

"You're high too, gigglepuss," she said, swatting her ass. Isobel caught her arm and brought her down onto the bed, pinning her underneath her and taking a long kiss.

I leaned back against the pillows, watching them frolic, smiling, turning something over in my mind. An idea taking shape.

"So why do you do it?" I asked. "Why the fighting and the guns?"

Felicity leaned back and thought a moment. "Well, you know, when we first got into stripping, my girl here was nervous. I mean the main dances were okay, but you know the real money is in the lap dances, right?"

I nodded.

"So I was giving the lap dances, I would wiggle all over them, let them feel me, and at first I hated it. But there was this girl at the club; she was smart. She told me, the reason you hate it isn't because you don't like men. You hate it because

91

you're scared. You feel powerless. So take some martial arts. I had always wanted to anyway, so I took her advice. And she was absolutely right. After that, I didn't love it, but it was a job. I kind of got into doing it right. I would dance and feel contempt for them, and get off a little on getting them worked up. Some guys even got off on my 'I don't give a *fuck* about you' attitude. And I wasn't scared when I knew I could kick most of their asses, or at least protect myself long enough for a bouncer to get there. Isobel wouldn't join me at first; she's such a tender thing."

"I had a crappy childhood," Isobel murmured. I nodded in sympathy. A lot of women I know have had crappy childhoods.

"But I insisted she take martial arts with me."

"That's about when you first started bossing me around." Isobel said.

"Well, you needed it...and we needed the money. And what's more, I know how sexy you are," she turned to me. "You've seen it. She's sex incarnate and if only she could tap into that, and feel safe and powerful, then I knew we could make serious cash. But not if she was scared. I don't want to see my beautiful girl scared." She held her, stroked her face. I was in the presence of love.

"So now we strip at night and train in the day. Pretty much our lives are stripping, training, and fucking, with occasional food and sleep thrown in."

"And what helps with that? Cocaine? Speed?" I threw it out there very innocently, no judgment, but I was thinking about Sequoia, about what she wanted to do. This was the start of our team, I was thinking. But not if they're heavy into drugs.

"No. I mean *occasionally*, we've tried it, sure, but we have to stay sharp."

"I've got something in mind for you girls," he said. "How

would you like to be my personal bodyguards?"

"Your *what*?"

"Bodyguards…and, okay, just a little extra."

"I thought so…okay, how *much* extra? We won't fuck you."

"No, that isn't part of the job. If you ever wanted to, I wouldn't kick you out of bed, but…no. There's two parts of the extra. One is that sometimes at my private parties you might do a little stripping or do a show like you did for me tonight—but not on a stage. It will boost my image to keep you two to myself. And you have to let people *think* we're having crazy sex. Image. You know. Man stuff."

They looked over at me and smiled. They knew man stuff.

"And the other thing?" Felicity asked.

"Okay, I should maybe hold back on this. My thoughts are still pretty loose on this but…"

But the E rolled through me and made me trusting. I held onto it for a second, willing myself to wait, but dammit they were *special*. I knew I should wait for Sequoia, but I also knew I could trust them.

"Okay, so I…I give money to lots of sex education programs, things like that…"

"Yeah? That's nice," they smiled at me.

"But I sometimes think, and my partner sometimes thinks, we could be doing…more."

They looked at each other, confused. "What do you mean, more?" Felicity asked.

"More looks like…well…we've been collecting horror stories, from lesbian and gay press, from the stories of people who got 'converted'…we got kind of obsessed with them."

"What kinds of horror stories?"

"Mostly about sexual abuse. Incest sometimes, especially from people who use the bible to rationalize abuse. It makes

93

Sequoia—my partner—furious…and I give money to charities that try to do something. So Sequoia got this idea that with enough money, and the right team, we could do…more. My partner is an amazing woman, astonishing. But we need people who can handle themselves. And we need people who had crappy childhoods themselves, who can understand what these kids go through." I took a deep breath and looked at them. They were high and smiling but listening so attentively, sharply.

"We want to rescue them."

"Rescue them. What do you mean…rescue them?"

"I mean just that. Find out who they are, go into their houses in the dark of night, and pull them out. Risk arrest, injury, and death. Take them far away from abuse and give them a shot at a better future. Rescue them."

Felicity looked uneasily at Isobel. It was just a long look, and a tear ran down Isobel's face. I held my breath. An invisible signal passed between them. I couldn't read it at all, but they turned their heads toward me at the same time, and it was Isobel who spoke.

"We're in," she whispered.

Chapter 11:
The Skipper Plans a Rescue

Keith Davis drummed his fingers and took another look at the papers spread out across his plain, utilitarian wooden desk. He pulled two maps of the Dominican Republic toward himself: a road map and a topographical map. He looked through property listings. He looked at a report compiling info from secondary agents, their moles in the Christian Right community. He shook his head. It wasn't enough.

He made a phone call.

Three days later, he settled into his seat on a plane to the Dominican Republic, first class, with Leo and Isobel across the aisle. He didn't look at them. He had argued hard against riding in first class; his income bracket meant he should be flying coach triple economy. Steerage. But while Leo had agreed to pretend they didn't know each other, he couldn't let one of his team fly anything but first class. That man was first class all the way, Keith thought. In every sense of the word.

The flight attendant came and took drink orders, presenting Leo and Isobel with elegant matching flutes of champagne. They leaned in toward each other, enjoying their roles to the hilt: rich mogul with his gorgeous young trophy bride, off for an exciting retreat in the Dominican Republic.

Nice, Keith thought. Very nice. And he thought it again many hours later when he bumped into them, ever so casually, at a little nightclub in Santo Domingo. They hailed him, slightly drunkenly, as their friend from the plane. He sat down to get a drink, thinking: my life takes me places I never dreamed it would.

"And what are we drinking tonight, Mr. Howell?" he asked. The man knew his liquors, he thought. It was good to know a man who knew the importance of a really fine drink.

"Tonight, my friend, we drink to possibilities and liberation with a fine local drink known as Mama Juana."

"Mama Juana! Is that shit legal here? And aren't you supposed to smoke it?"

"It isn't what you're thinking—it's made of rum, red wine, honey, and herbs and is said to be pure liquid Viagra," Leo said, smiling at his menu.

"Oh, no!" said Isobel. "Just what I need—to be out on the town with two men already horny as tomcats while they drink liquid Viagra! I'll have to preserve my maidenly innocence by beating you off with a stick." She fluttered her lashes at them like a born Southern belle.

"At your hands, pretty lady, I could even be into *that*," Keith said, using the opportunity to kiss her palm. The lady, after all, was seriously, ridiculously fine.

The drinks came quickly, deep and red and smelling like a forest, like licorice and cedar and cloves.

"To possibilities!" suggested Leo.

"To tonight," Keith said, winking at Isobel.

"No, my friends," she said. "To liberation!"

They clinked their glasses and all drank deep.

The next day began with an argument about who would drive the ATV they had rented to go out on the jungle roads. It went round and round; among his other expensive tastes,

Leo loved big trucks and vehicles of all kinds and wanted to blast through the pitted, pocked roads himself. Isobel let them fight it out. Isobel, bored, thought she might as well play her part; she filed her nails and checked her makeup while the boys fought over toys.

Keith argued, "We are going to be visiting white motherfucking evangelists! I have done my research. Have *you* done the research? No, you just want to drive your shiny toy in the jungle. Well, we can have some playtime tomorrow. But these particular assholes that we are doing recon on are part of the 'Christian identity' movement? There are no black kids in the camp that we know of. The info the moles have funneled back to us suggests that these particular wingnuts are very Christian AND very racist. They want to save white kids for Jesus because they think white kids need to have lots of white Christian babies. They think gay whites are committing race suicide. These are some fucked UP assholes, okay? So if they see a white man driving up with a black man in the back, there is going to be trouble from the get-go. And that is why I am going to drive. Can you get that through your cracker head?"

Leo laughed suddenly, loud and sharp: "Did you *seriously* just call me a cracker?"

"Well, I wasn't really serious. But would you prefer honky mofo?" Keith grinned back.

"I've really never been sure Greek counts as *white* exactly."

"When someone has as much money as you, it counts. And they won't know—you can pass, my friend. So put your crucifix on, and let's get into the jungle. I'm driving—and you guys, both of you, are riding in the backseat. Because you put me in charge, so I am in charge here and I *say* so. And then they will just see what they want to see, a happy darkie, just like Pat Robertson says, serving white people with a smile on his face."

"Jesus," Isobel muttered, with no irony whatsoever.

"Amen and hallelujah."

They loaded into the car and headed out. The process of figuring out where to drive today had been arduous; the kids who made reports just knew they drove on dark, scary roads. Daytime arrivals were confused by the streets—disoriented, hopeless. He had been sleuthing through the property records and bribing officials and hiring local private eyes to collect gossip and all that had given them was a place on a map that was simply a possibility, a likelihood.

The drive was long, hot, and sweaty. The lush foliage pushed up hard on the sides of the road—there was no place to pull over, even just to have a snack or a roadside piss, and only one or two turn-offs. The road was red, winding, pitted, and they bounced and jolted in the car. Keith put on some old-school rap to drive to, and when the car bounced extra hard Leo's hands twitched like he could feel the steering wheel.

Three hours later they found it. Keith could feel it—they had got it. The road stopped at an old guard house, and white military types with guns on their belts waved them to a stop. Keith stayed in the car while Leo and Isobel went to talk to the guards.

"Sir, ma'am, you can't go in there without being authorized." A blonde guy with a buzz cut stopped them.

"Oh look, darling. Perfect. A gated community—I was so worried," Leo said. "A lovely country—but so much hoi polloi. This should do nicely," he said as he strolled toward the gate.

Keith shook his head and angled it down to hide his smile. when Leo was angry, he played the rich man twice as hard. Isobel leaned on his arm and smiled her 1000-watt smile at the guard, who blinked at her. It took him a beat to regroup.

"Uh, sir, we really can't let you in there."

"My good man, I am considering buying property in your little community. I am sure it would be all right if I just took a little look-see, eh?" He produced a wad of twenties and fanned himself with them, while Isobel disengaged and went closer to the gate, squealing.

"It looks so darling and rustic! Just what we were looking for!"

While they distracted the guards, Keith checked out what he could without getting out of the car. It wasn't much. A few attractive, grass-hut-style buildings near the gate, then a sweep of road disappearing and hidden in foliage. A fence all around: tall, sturdy, and cutting into the foliage, which was deep and tall and thick enough to prevent most intrusions anyway. What this trip had bought them in information: almost jack shit. He couldn't even be sure this was the place—though the guard was promising. All it told him was just how hard this was going to be. No chance of getting in there through the jungle. No storming the gates without an army. He drummed his fingers against the steering wheel in frustration.

"Sir, ma'am, this is not a gated community; this is a children's camp. There are no properties for sale here." Keith heard the guard's word with internal satisfaction. He knew it. This was the place.

"It IS? Oh, how delightful," Isobel exclaimed. "It might be just the place for Alexis and Terence. Can we speak to the head counselor? What's the name of the camp? Do you have a website?" She spoke in her breathless bimbo voice, apparently oblivious to the strangeness of armed guards at a supposed children's camp.

"It's a private camp, ma'am. "

"Well, I should hope so," Leo swaggered. "We don't let our children go to a public *anything*. We're not savages, you know."

Behind his poker face, Keith enjoyed watching the guards squirm, trying to figure out how to repel these entitled and surprisingly tenacious intruders. The brighter of the two finally said, "The camp manager isn't here right now, but if you leave your names and contact info we can have them send you some info—we are of course too exclusive for a website."

"Oh, it sounds too perfect," cooed Isobel.

Leo handed over a fake card he carried for just such occasions. It had a phone number and email address for his alternate identity, a mover and shaker in evangelical circles. If there was research done, they should be able to vet him and get info—though he wouldn't bet on any being forthcoming.

They got back in the car, and Keith executed a difficult five=point turn on the narrow jungle road, while Leo complained that he could have done it twice as fact with half as much effort.

"Those white boys were looking at me like a cat looks at a songbird. I ain't leaving this car, and you certainly aren't driving me in front of them, so just shut up and hold on while I get out of here."

Though they were comfortably ensconced in a soundproof car, they waited until they were out of sight to break character, with Isobel waving at the guards from the back. As they turned around a bend in the jungle road, they breathed a collective sigh of relief.

Isobel growled, "GODDAMMIT! I hate playing dumb bimbo for apes with guns."

"You may hate it, pretty lady, but you do it like a pro."

"Okay, so Mr. Big Shot Planner: what the hell did we learn?"

"We learned this is almost definitely the place. And we learned this isn't going to be one bit easy, and it may be impossible."

"It can't be impossible. It CAN'T be. That girl is in there, and we have a job to do," Isobel's voice rang with determination.

"Well now, I can only think of one goddamn way to do it, and you aren't going to like it one bit."

"What is it?"

"Not now, babies. I have to think of it just a little more. I have to think whether there is any other way to do it. And I hope there is."

Isobel followed Keith back to his hotel room that night. His face registered surprise, but he invited her in, pulled out two beers from the minibar, and asked her what was on her mind.

She gave him a look he had dreamed about, sultry and speculative, then took a long swig of her bottle and turned away.

"I know what you have in mind, you know."

"You two aren't dummies," he said, sitting on the bed. "I imagine you both have figured it out."

"Sequoia won't allow it," she said.

"I love her, but she's not the one who has the right to make that call," he said. "So what we're saying now doesn't make a damn bit of difference. And since that's so, why are you here? You can have a beer in your own room."

Isobel walked over to him on the bed, put her hands on his shoulders. He stood up when he saw the look in her eyes. Everything about him stood up. But he ignored the voice that told him to grab and take and said: "Pretty lady, what's on your mind? I thought you didn't do anything without the spitfire's say-so."

"I don't," she said, and pulled his head down for a long, slow kiss that gathered heat and speed as it burned. He pulled himself away with an effort.

"Are you telling me you cleared this with the spitfire? Are you sure? Because she may be tiny, but she's mean as a snake and might be the only five-foot-two Chinese girl in the world

101

who could kick my ass."

His hands came up behind her back and he lightly rubbed his nose against hers. She smelled like jasmine and vanilla, like sweetness with backbone and passion. He kissed her again, feasting on her rosy lips, and then pulled back with a question in his eyes. She looked back with candor and a hint of a smile.

"Yes. I asked her. She said she never wanted to stop me from doing what I wanted, but she wanted me to wear this if we fucked." Her hand came up and rubbed her black leather collar lovingly. "So I would remember who I really belong to."

"Well, you know I'm not into *owning* anyone, so you're safe there with me."

"If I didn't know I could be safe with you, we wouldn't be about to do this," she said as she pushed him back onto the bed laughing, and he laughed with her as his hands came up and pulled her down on top of him.

He was surprised, after all the bangs and screams and wails he had heard over the years from their bedrooms, how sweet and tender and slow she was being, stroking his body, taking off his clothes, kissing every inch of skin laid bare by the buttons, so he let her set the pace, and he realized that she had had enough roughness from men to last a lifetime. What she was looking for here was friendship transmuted for a night into tenderness and passion, and knowing that, he rolled her onto her back and returned the favor of undressing her with slow, achingly slow, tender care. He still could get an erotic charge from the contrast between her pale skin and his dark hands. He took her nipple in his mouth and she responded with a soundless undulation that rolled through her and a soft hand stroking over his head, so he took it deep and pushed under with his tongue, and her hand pulled him into her breast. He took his sweet time with her beautiful pink-tipped breasts and then slid down to pay attention to her other pink and pouting lips, tasting and smelling nectar, lapping at it.

"Like rainwater with a twist of honey," he said, and she laughed again with sheer joy, and then his lips and tongue amplified that joy carefully to the point of fireworks and explosion, then lay beside her and gathered her to him and kissed her deeply so she could taste her own pleasure from his mouth.

"That was…spectacular, you know," she said.

"Well, really, pretty lady—it was my pleasure. And I mean that. You are pure delight."

"And what can we do for you?" she said, kissing him, rubbing her hands lightly against his erection from tip to bottom.

"You know, darlin', I will take whatever you're giving and don't need a damn thing. That was more than I ever dreamed of, right there."

"Well, Felicity did give me a limit: no penetration."

"I can live with that," he said, kissing her again.

"But! We did get some training once in this, and you look like you could use a massage. Hold on a minute," she said.

"As far as I'm concerned we have all night."

She scampered out of the room and came back wearing a sexy, silky robe, carrying massage oil and a small MP3 player. She got some music going that fit the mood: slow, relaxing, but with a sensual insistence in the beat. And she began to work on him.

She was stronger than he expected and started with medium-hard strokes, working into and relaxing his muscles better than he had really expected; he felt the tension of the day leave his body and she gave extra love and attention to his neck, so recently pushed to its limit in his own push to give sweet pleasure. His body sank into ease, when she whispered in his ear, "Turn over."

Her breath was hot and insistent, and the arousal that had banked down into warm embers flared up again, hot and ready. He turned over and now her hands were much more gentle, touching him everywhere, sweeping over him, and then she bent over and swept her hair across his belly and cock. When she touched him her hands were soft but also certain, and his massage closed with a very happy ending.

They held each other wordlessly for a long time afterward, and he felt himself drifting off, but as he did she whispered, "I have to go back."

He spooned her from the back, and hugged her to him. "Another limit?" he said.

"Afraid so…but it has been worth it."

"Oh yes. Worth every minute. Thank the spitfire for me, will you? She's been more generous than I ever dreamed."

Isobel touched her collar again, running a finger over it lovingly. "She knows where my heart is."

He reached up for her and kissed her one last time. "Good night then, sweet Isobel."

"Good night," she answered. He was asleep before she got to the door.

Chapter 12: The Skipper's Story

It seems like I was born horny. I masturbated early, and I broke into my dad's porn and used to just, mmm. My dad would hide stuff—under the mattress, under a seat cushion. I was *good* at finding it. Much better than my mother.

Anyway, when I got older I played sports, year round. My dad was proud; my mother was proud. I was okay at school, got into trouble just enough to show I was rambunctious, not enough to get labeled a serious problem kid. Had two sisters, one younger, one older, Marcy and Tanya. Nice. I like my sisters, they're good people.

Dad was in the Air Force, and we moved to Germany. I was around ten. I started hearing about "freaks." People on the street looking punk, people behind closed doors doing…what? My dad would talk about sex freaks, sex shows, like he was mad that they existed. I got curious. I knew Rick James was singing about a "super freak," but what did a super freak actually do? I wanted to know, and I wanted to know bad. And then my dad's porn started getting weirder. I guess he was curious too. People in black leather. Ball gags. Now, Germans fetishize black people. Which makes sense. When most people around you are blonde, black is really, really sexy: evolution at work! Diversify the gene pool. So there was this one photo shoot of two blonde German girls with a black guy and, oh, god—I wanted to be that guy. That porn was the first time I came, and it got on the picture, and I thought, oh, shit, my dad is going to kill me. Some guys think they're dying; some guys think they've seen God. I just thought, what will my dad do? I threw the magazine away. He never said anything. Well, what could he say? He wasn't supposed to have those magazines.

Then we moved back to Texas. No more German interracial threesome porn. Dad's porn got more boring and real girls got more interesting, and the best way to get girls in Texas is to play sports. So I played all the team sports. Baseball, basketball, football. I like the games—baseball is a little boring, but it was better than not playing. It's better than running track, that's for sure. Football is my favorite—I'm not fast enough to be great at basketball, and I like the strategy, the mind game, of football. Oh, yeah, and it was Texas; football gets you the real glory and the most pussy. Yeah, I liked the games okay, but I liked the girls better. And also I loved the grab-ass, the feeling of being on a team, of slamming into men and snapping towels in the locker room and the shower. And sometimes there would be a little friendly dick comparing and maybe that would lead, every once in a while, to two horny boys jerking each other off and then not talking about it. It happened. I bet it happens less now—people were less scared of being gay in some ways back then. Gays just didn't exist so if you jerked each other off it didn't mean anything. It was just something that happened. And it happened as much as I could make it happen because I loved *cock*! It took me a long time to realize that. We would make jokes about the girls being too damn tight and prissy, but you know at least as far as I was concerned that was a god-damned lie. I was in Texas, in high school, and varsity in football, basketball, *and* baseball. I was big, strong, fast, and good on my feet. I could get pussy. And I did! And I loved it! I was always getting in trouble with one girlfriend because I couldn't resist the next girl, and then she would be my next girlfriend, until she got mad at me and so on. I wasn't faithful. I didn't know how to be. I was greedy. And the other boys encouraged me to take what I could get; we were always egging each other on to act like shits to girls. It's fucked up, really. I didn't see that at the time.

Anyway, it didn't matter how much pussy I got; I would get in the showers and smell all that man smell and then I would tell lies like the rest of the guys about how I had this big erection because my girl was giving me blue balls and then we would "help a brother out." That's what we called it in the locker room when we talked about it at all, which we mostly didn't. Me, I was in the shower with a guy once helping a brother out and we got carried away and kissed. Almost got caught. That would have been bad shit, but we had some warning and we jumped back away from each other and said, oh shit, I forgot, I thought I was with my girlfriend. Oh boy, we never touched each other again. Too bad, too. He had a really nice cock.

I learned later there's even a word for what I was doing: I was on the down low. Yeah—when a black man has a little sex here, a little sex there with men, it ain't no thang. You don't date, it's just a little jerk-off here, maybe a blowjob there. And you don't tell your girl because she doesn't need to know and it doesn't mean a damn thing. On the down low. I was on the down low for quite a while.

High school came to an end, and I got a scholarship to play football, but not at a major football school. When it came right down to it, I was good, but I wasn't great. It was never the game I loved, it was everything that came with playing. But on my college team, no one "helped a brother out." Everyone knew the college girls were horny and good to go; if someone complained his girlfriend wasn't giving him any, we would just say, "Dump her ass." So my best friend Jack went to the same college, also on football scholarship, and sometimes we would hang out and just, you know, fool around a little. But no kissing and no fucking, because THAT would be gay. And we weren't gay; that was for faggots. Uh huh. I am not proud of myself when I look back, let me say that.

So I mostly concentrated on the girls then. I had this horny girlfriend for a while, Shirell, with a big heart and nice and smart too. I was actually faithful there (except for Jack and that didn't count, right?) for about six months, and we even did a threesome once with one of her girlfriends. That was the best day of my life up till that point. Me! And two pretty girls! One white and one black! I had an inkling then that, yeah, maybe I was a freak but I just said, nah, I'm twenty years old and horny; that's normal. What guy doesn't want a threesome, right?

College was a sweet situation for a while, but after two years it went all to hell. After the threesome I couldn't stop seeing the other girl too, and she told Shirell, who dropped me hard. And Jack worked up the nerve to tell me he had some real feeling for me and he was afraid he might be gay. I said some nasty shit and told him he was garbage and never to touch me again. That's maybe the thing I most regret of anything I have done in my life. Because I *loved* him, I did, but because I loved girls too I thought I could be "normal." That idea of *normal* has a lot of pain to answer for. Sometimes I wish I could just punch the word *normal* so hard it would die. And then while I was dealing with the stress of all that I got careless and injured myself so I couldn't play anymore. I was going to heal, but I hadn't been playing all that well anyway, and my grades were no great shakes either. My scholarship got pulled, so I joined the Navy when I healed up.

And that's when shit started getting really freaky. I kind

of knew *why* I was joining the Navy and not the Army or Air Force. My dad got mad at me. When you have a dad in one of the armed forces, it's almost an act of treason to join any other branch. The military has a lot of loyalty like that—like, if your dad's enlisted, it's treason to become an officer. That's another way to make sure the working class never gets ahead. At the time that was okay with me. I didn't want to be an officer. But I liked the idea of boats.

I wanted to have sex with sailors and lied to myself about why. That was when I started getting to do a lot more things than helping a brother out. Before, the most I did for another guy was mutual hand action, and okay, with Jack he would suck my cock and after a while I decided I should do the right thing and reciprocate. Told myself I didn't *like* it. I lied to myself a lot. But I had never fucked a man, not till the Navy. I think that's one thing people don't understand about why when women starting showing up on ships they got harassed. People think it's because you get too many men on a ship, horny and deprived, and they just will be too horny to control themselves. But that's not what happens when women get scarce, if you read your history. Actually when women are scarce they are more valued, like in the Wild West when a man might go years without seeing one. When he did, he might have to pay for her, sure, but those men were good to whores. They wanted a little feminine tenderness.

Men on ships don't want loving. Some of them sign up to get on ships because they *want* an all-male atmosphere and used to be they didn't want to admit that that's what they wanted. And here comes some girl, fucking up their fantasy that they are being forced to have sex with men because there are no girls, and they are ANGRY at her for that, but they can't actually ever even say that's what they are angry about, and that makes them even angrier. That's what I think anyway. That's

109

why the British actively recruit gays into the Navy now. That is smart. Very smart. Rum, sodomy, and the lash.

I got a lot of action on the damn ship. Cock on board and pussy off. Okay, I had to pay for the pussy sometimes. But sailors knew where to find it cheapish and clean enough with condoms. And I knew how to talk to a girl, find out whether she was someone who liked her job. People think none of them do, but that's not right. A lot don't but a few do, and if you pay attention you can find out which, and the ones who do are treasured

Then one day, one fateful day, we went to the Bay Area for Fleet Week. And my friend took me to this place. A real treat. He told me he was taking me to a sex party! Hot damn! I always wanted to go to a sex party! And that this sex party was chock-full of beautiful single girls who wanted to give blowjobs to sailors, he said, but he was winking at me when he said it. I wondered what the catch was, but when we get there, sure enough. I thought I had died and gone to heaven. Then I looked around and did a double-take and started laughing and laughing. Because there were a *lot* of beautiful girls there, and they sure did want to give blowjobs to sailors, and there was just one problem. Most of the beautiful girls had cocks.

Well, that wasn't a problem for me! I love beautiful women, but the one problem with beautiful women was that they usually *expect* to be treated like beautiful women, and you have to wine them and dine them, that kind of thing. I enjoy it, actually; all of that is fun too. But here! There was this blonde and I caught her eye, and I was young and cocky, so I just jerked my head for her to come over. She looked up at me laughing, and I took myself right out of my pants and showed her, without a word, and looked right in her blue eyes. She sank down to her knees and put me in her mouth and sucked me all the way to the back. I was just starting to get a chubby when I pulled myself out but I felt myself hitting her throat almost immediately. Now I'm not huge; that bullshit is racist. Leo, he's huge—but I'm a good length and thick and I could tell right away this girl had no gag reflex and loved her some cock. She was sighing and humming and I could feel the vibration all through me, and she worked her tongue with her lips, making her lips tight around me then letting her tongue push down against me as she slid me out and then slid back that hot ring of her mouth until I was pushed against the back of her throat and just pulsing her tongue right against the sweet spot, making it tighter and tighter. I grabbed her head and pushed my cock into her mouth and she moaned like she loved it so I pulled her hair back—she had grown her hair long, no wig—and I asked her if she liked cock. She nodded but kept her eyes down. I teased her with my cock, pushing it against her lips. She opened her mouth, pushed out her tongue to try to lick it but I kept it away from her and said to her, "If you want it, you're going to have to beg for it. You're going to have to beg me to fuck your mouth."

And she looked up and said, "Do it. Fuck me; fuck my mouth; use me like a whore! Do it! Please!"

It was so fucking hot I almost came right there. I said, "Yes, you're a good little cocksucking girl, and I bet you want a taste of cum, huh?"

She nodded, and I pushed my cock in and started fucking that sweet mouth with no restraint and I was saying things I had never said to a real woman, like, "Take it, you little tease, you whore, you cocksucking slut!" And I came rockets and she grabbed onto me and sucked me dry. And that was just the first half hour.

That party happened once a month, and we ended up staying behind and stationed there for about three months. Then we were supposed to sail out again. I went to the party

111

the month after that, and that night someone gave me some Ecstasy. I had never done that before. Because of sports I had never been big into drugs—jocks when I was young mostly just drank. But I wasn't playing sports anymore and someone handed me some of this stuff. I took it and started talking to this really cute black ladyboy, and an hour later I had one of those big moments, a real epiphany. I just realized...that there was nothing wrong with this, and I wanted to stay here with these beautiful women and fuck as many of them as I could because they gave me everything I wanted—they were beautiful as girls and as easy to be with as men and they even had cocks, and I realized that too, that night, that I LOVED cocks. I had always thought up until then that I was just sowing my wild oats and someday I would settle down with a girl and we'd get married and shit and I just realized, that, well, fuck that. I realized I was well and truly bisexual. I like beautiful girls with pussies and beautiful girls with cocks and big manly men with cocks and who knows who else I could love if I gave it a try? Tears were streaming down my face. I didn't want to lie about who I was or what I wanted anymore. So I marched down to my superior's officer and told him I wanted to leave the Navy so I could fuck as many "shemales" as possible. I don't think that's the most politically correct word these days. That was in the days of don't ask, don't tell, you know.

You should have seen that man's face. He got red as a brick, and he just kept blinking at me, and he said, "Come again?"

And I said, " Exactly."

He didn't even get it. So I just said, "Sir, get the paperwork all set, and whatever you need to do, because I have had it. I want out. Give me a dishonorable discharge or whatever, and let me out."

And he said, "Son, I don't really think you want to do

that!"

And I said, "I am NOT your son, and I know *exactly* what *I* want. Do you?"

So that was it. They didn't ask: I told. I stayed for a few weeks with someone I had met at the party, got a job bouncing at a gay bar, and had as much sex as I could with whoever would have me. And that was about it. Until trouble. In the form of Margarita Rimsalt.

I was working at a bar that had a regular drag show. I love drag queens. I love drag queens, and I love trans women; I love all flavors of genderfuck. But drag queens. You've got to be really uptight not to love drag queens, right? Anyway, Margarita performed with the show sometimes and we hooked up. She—he—she doesn't care about pronouns—anyway, it started just as sex but she fell on hard times, and I said she could stay at my place (I had a place by then), and I just got a kick out of her, as a guy or as a girl. Big sweet energy, huge. Funny and loud as a woman, kind of shy and sweet as a man. My cocksucking little buddy, Gilligan.

Anyway one night I come away from bouncing at the club, and I am walking back to our place. We didn't live far away, but it's this area of SoMa with lots of little alleys you don't notice at first, and I hear a cry from one of these alleys. I go and check it out, and it is my Margarita on the ground getting kicked by two college-looking white guys. I start toward them, and they look up and see me and start running. Well, I am a big black guy—the stuff of nightmares for dudes like them. But I am PISSED, and I take off after them and grab them by the collars and start yelling at them for hurting my girl. One of them has a bat. I didn't see it before because it was dark and they were running, but he comes up and swings it at me. He's drunk and slow, so I grab ahold of it and say, "What the FUCK, man? What are you trying to pull off?"

113

The Case of the Creepy Christian Camp

And that's how the cops catch us, me with a bat in my hand brandishing it at these white boys. I didn't hit them and wasn't going to. Didn't have to. I saw the cops coming at me, and my whole life flashed before my eyes. And of course, before you know it the dude-bro assholes were telling the cops lie after lie. I pointed back to Margarita and said, "Get her help, okay? She needs medical help."

So they go look and then they think I did that too. The white boys are telling them it was me, and Margarita's out cold, so there I am going to the pokey. And I am thinking, That's it. Goodnight, nurse. I wonder if jail is anything like the Navy.

Margarita eventually got her medical care and tried to set the record straight, but who are cops, even San Francisco cops, going to believe, a drag queen and a big gay bouncer? Or two "straight-as-an-arrow" white college kids? The cops thought I was her pimp and I was beating her. The two boys were trying to stop me, and she was too scared to tell them the truth because I was such a violent beast. And to make it worse, Margarita had been drinking herself that evening so she was sloshed before the beating. That's what started it, I found out later. They yelled some shit at her and she was too drunk to be careful. She yelled all sassy back, so they dragged her back into the alley. They tried to get her to suck their cocks but they were too drunk to get hard and she laughed like hell at them for that. So they decided to teach her smart mouth a lesson. Fuck! The funny thing is, when he's Beto he's kind of shy, won't stand up for himself. But Margarita will not back down.

So they assign me some attorney who you could tell had about a thousand cases and didn't believe me anyway. The girls at the club threw a benefit to try to get a better lawyer and meet my bail, called some gay groups to see if they could get someone for me, but while I was waiting for them to get enough dough together I spent some time in lockup. The food was crap

114

and the company was worse, but at least I was big enough and strong enough that no one really tried to fuck with me.

After about a week they tell me someone wants to see me. And this guy walks in. Slick. Classy. Nothing flashy but everything expensive and top of the line, and he says he's heard about my case, heard about what happened, and he wants to pay my legal fees.

So I ask him the obvious: "Why?"

And he says, "I think you might have talents we could use, Mr. Davis. But let's discuss that after we get you out of here."

I was not comfortable with that and I said so. He cocked his head and said, "The girls at the bar are trying to raise money for you. If you don't like what I have to say, they can pay me back. But I have high hopes...."

So he makes my bail and we go get a drink. He takes me to the Tonga Room, which I had not been to before. It was surreal. One minute I'm in an orange jumpsuit and the next I'm drinking something fruity with an umbrella in it. The room is misty, tropical. Sounds are playing through the speakers, and this damn boat is moving back and forth in this pool. I am sitting there under one of those grass-thatched hut things, listening to this weird guy tell me he wants to hire me. Sort of.

And then Sequoia walks over and joins us, and did you ever just know you loved someone when you first met them, right away? I'm not talking about hearts and flowers, love at first sight, romantic kind of shit. But like someone was a part of you for a long time, and that part's been missing, and now here this person was—familiar, like family, right away. It's what she has going for her: you see her and you trust her. Just like that.

So I heard them out. To rescue gay teens from abusive parents: well, okay. But, "Well, I have a question. I just want to know: why me? I mean I have heard the story of how you guys

115

met. I get what you are bringing to the team. *You* have money (I gestured at Leo); *you* have all your super brains about people who are hurt and need rescue and it's your idea (I gestured at Sequoia). And you're telling me you already have some muscle. So what do you think I can do for you?"

Sequoia spoke slowly, feeling her way, "I think you underestimate yourself, Keith. It was like this...one of the girls at the club is a friend of my uncle. Charlamaine?"

"Oh yeah, I love her...total sweetheart."

"Yeah, she is. Anyway, she saw how long it was going to take to raise enough money to get you out—they set the bail high. Well, black man with a dishonorable discharge beats two white boys and a drag queen. Even in San Francisco that's a high bail. So she called me; she knows about my honey pot," she gestured over at Leo. "And we go back to when I was in high school; she even knows about this...thing...we're doing. We kind of dreamed it up together. And she says she thinks you're what we're looking for. So we researched you: football, doing well in the Navy before you walked out, threw yourself into the fray to protect an innocent and didn't *actually* touch a hair on those white boys' heads. You're smart; you're brave. You have some military background so you have some discipline, and you keep your head under pressure. Isobel and Felicity, they are great; they fight like champs, but we need someone who can think strategically, plan things out. That's you, we think."

Well, that felt good to hear. And a hard job being offered, just accepting what they were telling me. But I knew in my gut that I need someone by my side in this, someone I could trust utterly: I didn't even know these people. So I insisted Margarita be included. He's my buddy. You don't desert your buddies.

So Leo laughed and said, "Okay, well, what can he do? We don't need dead weight."

"Cars. Vehicles. He's a mechanic at his day job—a mechanic drag queen, you should hear her complain about her freaking nails. And he can drive like no one's business, a born getaway driver."

They looked at each other; Leo grimaced, and Sequoia smiled this funny smile and said, "Well, the Lord provides."

Leo threw his hands up in the air: "I give!"

I learned later they had been having an argument about that exact thing. Leo loves cars and wanted to do the rescue driving but Sequoia said, no, he was our deep pockets and too valuable to risk; if he got caught everything would explode in our faces. So they *needed* a driver.

And then Leo waves his hand and two smoking-hot girls came over from another table and sat down with us. A tall redhead who moved in a pool of her own light like a movie star and this little Asian girl with fight in her eyes. The pretty lady and the spitfire.

And Leo laughed and said, "Okay. Looks like we've got ourselves a team. I think another round of Mai Tais are definitely called for."

I smiled. "Let me go call Margarita. She should be here for this."

Chapter 13: Gilligan's Story

My mother had a great closet. Even when she didn't have much else but mouths to feed, she had a great closet. I was the youngest of seven; my mother popped us out in sets like collectibles. First three boys, then three girls. Everyone held their breath when I was born. it was a big epic power struggle. Would there be more manly men in the house or more girls? My dad told me when I was little that when I was born he smoked a big cigar and bragged and my brothers were allowed one beer each to celebrate: men were better! We won! Oh, he was wrong about that, honey!

They were so happy I wasn't a "stupid girl" like all my sisters, who loved Disney princesses and ruffles and flowers and Barbie—all the *good* stuff. But my sisters were closer to me in age, so I grew up playing their games, playing with their toys. My brothers' boy toys were old and broken; Mama didn't want to buy new. And why buy new boy toys when money was tight and I was perfectly happy with my sisters' toys? I loved my childhood. I was the baby when they played house and a model when they played dress-up. I had a drag queen's dream childhood.

When I was two, someone showed me *The Wizard of Oz*.

I remember my mother saying, 'No no, those winged *monos de diablo* will give him nightmares!' My mother never really got that Spanish and English were two different languages. Anyway, I watched it, but the monkeys?! They wore ugly jackets and bellboy caps: this girl is not afraid of bellboys. At first I wanted to be Glinda, with pretty red hair and a giggly bubbly voice. And who wouldn't want a big floating bubble as your ride?! But then I decided Dorothy was a better choice: she had big brown eyes like me—and ruby slippers. I was just an itty bitty thing, but I remember *wanting* those slippers, dreaming about them. My parents found some used costume ruby slippers one day at a thrift store. I cried until they got them for me, and after that every day first thing I would put on my slippers and prance up and down. "I've got ruby slippers! I've got ruby slippers!" I would put a sweatshirt over my head to be my long pretty hair—yellow one day, red the next. But always ruby slippers. That sounds like a cliché now—I was such a friend of Dorothy—but it is the honest truth; I swear on my knock-off Prada bag. I don't remember all of it, but my sister Lola told me.

I remember when I was four, Carlos, the younger of my two brothers—he was about eleven—tried to pull me away from my sisters to go play ball with him in the yard "like a man." I cried and cried and said, "I don't wanna be a man! I wanna play Barbie!"

Carlos slapped me. Gay bashed at age four. Okay, not gay bashed…gender bashed? Queer bashed? Anyway. Life was not all Disney princesses and ruby slippers.

That's when my brothers started yelling at my sisters that they were ruining me with all this "girly shit." I started to wake up to the fact that being me was not going to be an easy road. But I still would not play ball. I hated it. Balls flying around all the time, smacking me in the face, me squealing and running like my sisters, legs flopping and arms flailing, my brothers screaming at me not to run like a girl. But girls will be girls.

By the time school was about to start I knew I was doomed. Then on my fifth birthday, my oldest brother, sixteen years old, gave me a set of matchbox cars from the money he made working at my uncle's garage. And I did kind of like those cars. They got me some hot wheels tracks and my brothers set it up for me and we started playing with the little cars. Magic! My brothers stopped giving me shit. Maybe they didn't know that in my head the little red convertible was being driven by a beautiful girl spy on the run with her long hair streaming in the wind while she hugs the curves driving in the French Riviera; all they cared about was I had my head down and was going "vroom vroom."

So after that at school, whenever I was out in public, I was the little car dude. I had a racecar lunch box. I wanted Barbie, but when do you get what you want when you're a little drag queen? For years, I had car-themed birthdays and played cars with other boys at school. I learned to run just "boy" enough that they didn't know that inside I wished I was wearing a pink dress with ruffles with rosebuds and little pearls, like the kind my sisters got to wear to church. But when my brothers weren't around, my sisters would still dress me up in their clothes. We would play fashion show, girl rock band, and my very favorite—*telenovela*. *Telenovelas!* We watched them on daytime TV whenever we could and acted them out. I usually got to play the bitchy villainess who steals the good girl's man—I know, *typecast*—right from the start! But then at the end, the good girl would overcome, and I would design the bride's dresses with toilet paper ruffles and bed sheets, and we would all giggle and laugh and start all over again. I loved my sisters.

Anyway, my mama, she always thought it was funny when I would dress up, and sometimes we would get her to judge our fashion shows, and I won a lot of the time. My sisters said it wasn't fair and she let me win because I was the baby, but *I* think they just didn't have my eye for color. I got it from my mama! When my brothers would bitch and whine about me not being manly, she would say there was time enough for that later. I would grow out of it. Like a girl ever grows out of loving a good fashion show.

So it really freaked me out when one day she came home early and she caught me putting on my sister's makeup when I was nine. At that time my sisters were eleven, twelve, and fifteen, so only my sister Lola was allowed to wear makeup, but Mama came home, and all four of us were sitting around done up like little tramps. Little girls don't know how to go easy on the eyeshadow. And she shrieked, *"AY AY AY!"* just like she was a cartoon character. She almost never hit us, but she just started *slapping* my sisters—but not me. Asking them what they were *thinking*; they all looked like *putas* (and my mother never even swore) and look what they were doing to their brother: was this what they wanted—was it? —to turn him into a…*maricon*?! And she spat out the word, just spat out the word like it was dirty, like she had gotten caca in her mouth and needed to spit it out as hard as she could.

My younger sisters Marisol and Ana froze and then started to cry, sobbing and wailing and saying they were sorry. But Lola! Lola is my oldest sister. She does not back down. She is a firecracker. She was already starting to fight with Mama all the time, so she just started yelling: "*No me hace culpa de mi!*" Don't you blame me! She got *politico* and she yelled at Mama, "He is what he is! You better get used to it!"

I was nine. I just stood there in shock with bad makeup running down my face with my tears. I couldn't understand why my beautiful mama was freaking out when she never had before. Why did it suddenly get all real for her? It made it more

121

real for me too.

I started trying to piece this all together in my little co-conut. Okay...I knew that boys at school would call me names and beat me up if they knew. I knew *that*. Because they hated girls. When a boy dropped a ball or ran too slow, they would call him "woman!" and say it like it was the worst thing they could think of. So I was different because I *didn't* hate girls or think the things they did were stupid, and I had to hide that.

But sometimes the girls at school would run after the boys and chase us and try to kiss us and we would all yell and run away. I saw sometimes, just a few boys who I *knew* could run much faster than me wouldn't run so hard. They would get a kiss and then they would say it was *gross,* but you could tell they really liked it, and that was very confusing to me because I *really* didn't want the girls to kiss me. This was hard for me because the girls *really* liked to kiss me. I was a good looker, and I was *nice* to them. AND I wasn't fast enough. The fastest girl in the class liked me, so I always got caught. The boys teased me for being a ladies' man. But I did not like it!

So now according to Mama there is this thing called a *maricon*, and that was what I was according to my sister and my mother, and it was really bad bad bad if you listened to my mother, but according to my sister it wasn't so bad. I didn't even know what it was.

So I snapped! I yelled at them that I wasn't a *maricon*, I wasn't, and they were stupid stupids! I did not have the clever verbal wit that I have today, you understand. I ran to my room that I still shared with Ana and Marisol and I cried and cried. Then Marisol came in and we both cried together, and then we played Barbies and reenacted the whole scene.

My father? You're wondering where he was in all of this? Me too, honey. He was away for work, always on the road. He drove trucks, semis, really big trucks. When he would finally get home all the girls would run and hang on him and get picked up and swung around and hugged and I wanted to too. I would yell, "Me! Me! Me!" So he would pick me up too and swing me around and hug me and put me down. I loved the way he smelled, that big man smell and soap and aftershave. There was nothing in the whole world that smelled as good as Papa, and even now it's a turn-on: that *man* smell. It smells so good you just want to swoon into strong arms and be held. But mostly he wasn't home.

I was trying to figure out how I could find out what it meant, this word that I was, maybe. I couldn't figure out who to ask. I just wanted it to not be true, whatever it was. So I listened and pretty soon I knew it was these terrible men who liked to dress up like ladies and men put their things in them. Having a man put his thing in me seemed terrifying to me, and that made me relieved a little. I didn't want *that*, so I must be okay. But sex just seems horrible to a nine-year-old boy. I remember at ten some boy brought to school a porno picture of a girl giving a blow job that he stole from one of his dad's magazines and we were all, "Oh gross! NO!" The picture showed a girl with enormous breasts and a guy's cock sticking out big and hard. And the picture was cut off so you couldn't see his face. The girl didn't have it in her mouth all the way; she was kind of holding it and smiling in the camera with her eyes and licking it like a naughty girl about to eat a big ice cream.

The boys were saying, "Ooh, ooh, I am never *never* going to put my *pepe* in some *puta's* mouth. No way!" I said it too, but inside this voice spoke up for the first time and said, " Oh, little children, you are fooling yourselves!" But what I noticed is she seemed pretty damn happy about that big, hard thing she was licking. And that voice inside me said…"Yummy." I looked at the rest of the boys, and for the first time I thought, Whew, they are *cute*! How did I not see before that they are cute?

123

The Case of the Creepy Christian Camp

So then I knew something was really, really wrong with me. You would think maybe I would get closer to Lola, who was trying to stick up for me but *no*. I was not that evolved. I wanted to kill her because she knew what I was and she would blab. Everyone else wanted to *believe* I was "normal" so they did. I stopped dressing up—never again after that time when my mother shrieked. No more…except when no one was home. With seven kids that is pretty much never. But there was Lola, and she would smile at me in this way that let me know she was sorry for me. She still saw it, and I hated her. I love her now, of course. I do. My sister Lola and my oldest brother, Oscar, are the only two in my family I am still in touch with. Lola and her girlfriend, Janet. I just wish they would wear less sensible shoes. What is it with lesbians and ugly footwear? I say they're clichés, and they say I am too, but at least they get to be comfortable. Like comfort matters!

I retreated into the cars. It was the only boy thing I really did like so I played it to the hilt. I came home every day and played Grand Theft Auto. I hung out with my brothers. We would fight sometimes over whether to watch sports or play more Grand Theft. We worked on cars. My middle brother, Carlos, started working at my uncle's garage when Oscar went to college, so then I would go over and hang out there. I knew inside and out how to take apart a car before I was anywhere near old enough to drive one. I love the smell of cars and gasoline…and the smell of guys who work on cars.

From age ten on, I was mean to my sisters and made fun of them when they dressed up or played with makeup. I sneered at them and called them names because I had my invisible silk panties in a bunch that they could still do that and I had to wear ugly-ass ghetto jeans. And then they started to get boyfriends, and their boyfriends were so cute! I hated myself because I was never, never going to have a cute boyfriend, not

124

ever. They had boyfriends and *quinceañeras* and pretty dresses and lip gloss and giggling and sleepovers, and I envied and hated them for all of it. I had cars.

Lola left for college, full scholarship. Lola was a smart girl. All Marisol and Ana heard for a few years was, "Why can't you be like Lola? She never had boyfriends! She never did anything but study and make herself better!"

Lola bought me my first *Love and Rockets*, when she was first in college, with the early stories about Maggie the Mechanic. I wanted to be her so bad, a cute girl mechanic who flew around the world and had adventures. Everyone just thought she was so adorable, and then she had a...girlfriend. Hopey the badass. That was a shocker. I was fifteen by then. I was starting to get the idea in my head that I wasn't going to be able to keep my secret forever, and Maggie and Hopey gave me hope I wouldn't have to hide forever. I started to realize I was waiting. I was biding my time.

Six months later, Lola brought her girlfriend home for Christmas. Mom opens the door and there's Lola with a new butchy early nineties lesbian haircut. This was when they used to shave off weird parts of their hair, do you remember? There have *never* been uglier haircuts in the history of the world. But Mama didn't get it. She was not what you would call *up* on lesbian fashion. I wasn't either but that voice in my head said, "Child, that is one *hideous* do." I was sitting there fantasizing about giving her a makeover, so I sort of missed the clues. Lola had this girl next to her, Sandy, a cute blonde girl who just had regular short hair and big blue eyes and freckles. Mama had been cooking for Christmas, and the house smelled like rompope and tamales. She wipes her hands on her apron and reaches out to welcome the girl, the perfect Mexican lady hostess, and Lola decided to just do it right that moment. She just blurt out, "Mama, she is my *novia*. My girlfriend."

125

Mama just stands there puzzled, like someone had hit her over the head.

Lola says, "I'm a lesbian. Mama, *soy lesbiana*." She said it twice like she had to make it true in two languages, like she had been a lesbian in English up till then but now she was one in Spanish too, here at home.

Shit hit the fan with a bang and a splatter. Oh my god. There was *crying* and *wailing* and *screaming* from my mother. Telenovelas, watch out. My papa, home for Christmas, rolled his eyes and tried to get Mama to calm down.

Lola was yelling, "Mama, I'm your daughter. *Su hija*! I'm still your daughter! I love you, Mama, please."

Mama was saying, "No daughter of mine! Filthy! *Puta!* No, no! How can you do this to me? To God?" And then she just starts in again on the screaming and crying. Well, my mama was a drama queen, so I guess I get it from her.

Papa just looked on while this was happening, just like a man, all awkward and closed up. But, see, Lola was his pet, the first girl, his baby darling who got anything she wanted. She was always kind of his favorite of all his kids; she came along before he was on the road so much, so he knew her, changed her diaper. She was his little girl. So he tried to put the brakes on Mama's big production.

He said, "Hey hey, *calma! Callate.* It's not the end of the world, stop screaming, let's talk. It's probably just a college phase, okay?"

So mama turned on him too and yelled, "You want our daughter to be a freak, a *camionera!* She's filth!"

Sandy, who had been looking on, started to tug Lola's sleeve and say, "C'mon, let's go, let's just go. This was a mistake."

Marisol and Ana cried just like they did when Mama slapped me six years before. The voice in my head said, *Oh boo hoo hoo, you lucky straight bitches.* Carlos and Romero said, "Fuck this shit!" and went off to their girlfriends' houses. I sat there numb. It was my future on the line too, I knew that now, but I wasn't ready to let anyone else know that. After about three hours of everyone trying to calm my mom down, Oscar got home from grad school. He clearly knew about the whole deal and had hoped to get there after the fireworks. But he gets in and asks Mama why it's such a big deal, and she goes from crying mode back into shrieking like a harpy. Mama yells at Lola to go, to get out, to never come back. She storms up and down and makes hand gestures and cries and plays it to the hilt like a diva.

So Lola just looked at my dad, and he walked her to the door and said it was best she go right now; he would try to calm her down. Lola and Sandy walked out, and Oscar said, "This is wrong; this is wrong," and he went out after them. And I went to my room and sat there for ten minutes and then beat off to George Clooney. I know that sounds weird but it is exactly what I did. I just wanted to be in a different place for a while, one where I had beautiful blue silk lounging pajamas and a *chaise longue* and a movie star boyfriend.

Sometimes people ask me why—if I love all that girly stuff, love dressing up like a girl and whatnot—I don't want to BE a girl. I puzzle about that sometimes, but what can I say? One's not the same as the other. I want to wear dresses, but I still love my cock. I love the stuff that women get to do. I don't want to be one. I want to be what I am, a gay swishy boy.

I was growing up. Getting bigger. At sixteen, one of my older brothers gave me his old car that I had helped fix up when he got himself a new one, and I just started to drive. Out of Highland Park and over to Silver Lake, which was becoming the new hip gay neighborhood. Then out to West Hollywood. Watching gay boys. Wishing I were old enough and brave

127

enough to just walk into a bar. One day a guy walked up to me in the Tower Records and made some conversation about a CD I was buying. He was a big bear, but I didn't know the word then. He smelled a little like papa. He asked me if I wanted to get a drink somewhere. And I *did* kind of want to but I said no and ran back out to my car. I sat there and breathed hard.

But after that it got easier. I went over to West Hollywood and walked around and saw people sitting in bars and laughing and holding hands with their boyfriends and thought, *oh, honey, someday*. Someday that was going to be me, sitting and drinking cocktails and not being afraid anymore.

One day I met a boy closer to my own age at a coffee shop. He assumed I was gay. I didn't have to tell him. I don't know how he knew when I was dressed up like a *cholo*. He must have had excellent gaydar. He came up to me and told me his name was Kevin; did I want to go get a coffee? I felt so relieved! He introduced me to other people and boom! I had friends. I got a fake ID; I had just turned seventeen. One week I was lonely, driving by and wishing I knew people; the next week I was hanging out at gay bars getting my first kiss, and then my first almost everything else. After years of wanting and being scared it all happened so fast. First time I felt a cock in my mouth it was like the heavens opened up and angels sang. I was like, this is it. Now there are *two* things I know how to do in this world: fix cars and suck cock. My new friends fed me club drugs—a little e, a little speed. I stayed out late, then later, then all night, and my mother scolded me. But she didn't scream. She gave my brothers hell for joyriding, getting drunk, and hanging out with their girlfriends: she knew exactly what they were doing and she didn't like it. But with me, she was baffled. What was I up to? She was a little nervous, but she wasn't angry.

One day my new friends took me to see a drag show.

There I was, a little drunk, sitting there waiting and out comes this gorgeous creature, very fishy, and starts lip-synching. A black girl, tall and beautiful, lip-synching to the classic, "I Will Survive." She was good. It was camp and funny and touching and strong. I was watching her and I was thinking, *me me me*. I wanted to do that. My friend Peter nudged me and said, "You would look goooood doing that." My heart beat like a drum. I had been shy all my life, little Beto hiding in his mother's closet, letting his sisters practice makeup, trailing after his brothers and fixing cars, sitting there numb while Lola did her big dramatic scene. But if I did this, for the first time I would be the star.

I entered a contest. I came in third, and I was lucky to do that: I was wearing my sister's *quinceañera* dress, all ruffles, a pink nightmare, big fake freckles like I was playing a kid on Sabado Gigante, and lip-synching to Shirley Temple's "Good Ship Lollipop." My act would have tanked except I got one of those long twisty lollipops and mama I worked it!

So then I got to meet the regular girls around the club. Started hanging out there. Got my own drag mama, Madame Pomp Adore—she sat me down and taught me what I needed to know. Lipstick that won't budge when you suck cock. How to walk and how to tuck. How to glue on eyelashes when you're high, how to pin on a wig and balance in heels. One day I went home a little drunk with some of my makeup still on, and my mother did her diva thing. Screaming, crying, pointing at me, calling names. Jesus, Mama. As soon as I saw her launching into her act, something came over me. I started doing what she did, mocking her. She was throwing me out of her life and I was pretending to cry and pacing and wringing my hands and wailing. "OH NO, my baby boy, he's GAY, let the earth open up and swallow me WHOLE, how can I live with the SHAME?" Ana and Marisol didn't cry. They stood and watched pop-eyed with shock. Then I ran to my room, packed a few things, and left. I had another mama now, and she had an even better closet. So I drove to my drag mama's house.

She was just about to move to San Francisco so she said to me, "Girl, just move with me. Get a new start." So three months before my eighteenth birthday I moved from LA to SF and never looked back. Okay, I called my sister Lola. She came up to see me and caught my show: I was calling myself Anita Tequila back then and doing a lot of Gloria Estefan lip-synching. "Conga." "Turn the Beat Around." So much fun. I knew the name wasn't great, but it takes a while to find the right one.

One day this big bouncer comes in and my heart stops and I think: *I want that chocolate bear.* He was just so damn big, and he smelled like the hottest kind of danger and the sweetest kind of safety. Keith knew how to treat a lady, and when he saved me from those asshole gay bashers, oh, honey! What's not to love?! Okay, I know he's bisexual and not a one-woman man, but I can live with that. When you love a tiger you have to let it walk the jungle. That's not to say if I catch him with someone I won't scream like I madwoman and cause a scene. Honey, I am my mama's child.

So when he came back to our apartment one day and told me about the group, I said absolutely yes! They saved my Brown Bear. They save little boys like me. I got out by myself and that was okay for me, but there are kids out there playing in their mama's closets right this minute and they need *help.*

But I swear if you call me Gilligan I will tear your face off. I hate these fucking code names. If I have to be some ancient TV character, I want to be Endora. Now *there's* a role model for a drag queen!

130

Chapter 14: Forming the Team

Leo called Sequoia and crowed about the success when Keith Davis was exonerated in court. The best lawyers had done their jobs, and Keith was a free man. They all met up in Vegas: the perfect place to celebrate. Leo gathered them in his home tiki bar, lovingly built from his years as a collector, inspired by visiting the finest tiki bars in all the world. He looked proudly around the room. This felt right. As soon as he had met Felicity and Isobel, and then Keith and Beto, there had been a sense of family.

He looked around at their faces and began: "I've gathered you together here, and you know why. We need to become a team, and if we're going to do this, a lot of details need to be sorted. Sequoia dreamed this up and has been planning it for years, so I'll let her start."

Sequoia beamed, and her smile was as warm and comforting as a fire blazing cheerfully away in a fireplace. "Well, we need a lot of things to get up and running but first and foremost we have to find a safe way to let people know about us. I can very carefully start putting it out there among counselors and sex ed teachers that I trust, but word of mouth is dangerous. Sooner or later it will get back to us and let's not kid ourselves: we are going to be breaking the law. Since we are, we need to know in our bones that what we do is ethical. Whoever we rescue has to ask for it and has to, in our best judgment, be old enough to make that call. Younger than a certain limit and we call child protective services and we back away."

Isobel grimaced. "Child protective services is a farce in these kinds of cases and you know it."

"No I don't. What I know is sometimes it is and sometimes it isn't. It's saved some lives and wrecked others. I am sorry it never helped you—but we can't steal children from their parents, and you know it. But there are teens out there who know their own mind, and they have the right to decide not to live with abuse. The only choice for most of them is to run away. But how young is too young: fifteen? Fourteen? Twelve? I don't know, and the thing is, I think it depends on the kid, and how do we get to know them well enough to decide? But it's important, right?"

They nodded. Felicity and Isobel had run away and had bad memories of cheap hotels and minimum-wage jobs before they were old enough to start stripping—and that was a big step up for them. Not every kid had a drag mama to run away to, or a lover to stand by them. The streets, prostitution, drug use, suicide—all threats for gay teens and even worse for trans kids.

"Okay, so how do we get the word out there? Word of mouth is tricky and dangerous. Miscommunications aplenty. And it only goes so far. And how do we get this thing started?" Sequoia drummed her fingers on the table in frustration.

Leo said, "We need spies. People with ties to churches. That's going to be tricky. I think I might have to convert, start spreading some money around." He made a face and took a big swig of his Mai Tai.

"You think they're going to want a known porn king associated with them? Think again."

"Shit. Yeah. You're going to have to do it," he said. "Or maybe I'll need a second identity."

"Not every abuse case is Christian, you know. People abuse gay teens with all kinds of belief systems," Isobel chimed in.

Sequoia smiled. "There's nothing you can tell me about the abuse of gay teens that I don't know. All the statistics. Here's the thing, though—there's a lot of prejudice out there, but only the right-wing extremist Christians claim that floods and hurricanes are getting more common, not because of global warming, but because God hates gays. Statistically, they are the most likely and the most extreme of abuse cases. I'm not saying we ever refuse to help others—just that this is the best way to reach the most kids."

Beto spoke up: "About that second identity—I can probably get you a fake passport, papers. Some of the queens that have passed through the club have had problems with *La Migra*."

Sequoia spoke, thoughtfully, groping for her words: "I know some people in the progressive Christian movement. Maybe…maybe they would be willing to 'convert' to evangelism, get us an in, some info. But what can they do? They can't exactly walk up to kids and say, 'Hey, are you gay? Do you need an escape route?'"

Felicity, who had been staring off dreamily for a long moment, snapped to: "You're thinking about this the wrong way, all wrong. You keep thinking we find them, how do we find them. We don't. We let them find us. We take cards, with nothing but an upside-down purple triangle and the words, "Need help?" And it goes to voice mail. They give us their name and whatever additional information they can, then we follow it up and see if they need what we can offer. If they need other services, fine, we refer. Suicide hotlines, whatever. The voice mail is set up so if it falls into the wrong hands, they can't trace it. It's just a number set up by a fake nonprofit that routes people to the right services. It offers services, asks them to leave the nature of their emergency on the voice mail. Then we do research to make sure it's legit, not a trap, and make contact."

"And what do we do with these cards? How do we get them into their hands?"

"Oh now that's the good part. We walk into Christian bookstores and leave them in their foul literature about gays. We put them in sex ed books and books about homosexuality and transgenderism in libraries and bookstores. We give them out to sex ed teachers and just tell them it's a clearing house for referring people to services. We can do this. No problem. The best part is, we don't even have to answer the phones…"

"Okay," said Sequoia. "Let's do it. And another thing, when we write emails, we're going to need some code names. Google is big brother, and nothing should be done electronically that links us to each other."

"I have an idea there," Keith said. "I mean just look at us…Ginger and Mary Ann," he nodded at Felicity and Isobel. "Mr. Howell, drinking his Mai Tai from a coconut. And me, the Skipper. Fits like a glove."

"No way," said Beto. "That's stupid! We're going out to rescue people, and we name ourselves after a band of idiots too dumb to even rescue their own damn selves?!"

"No, no, now, wait a minute," said Sequoia. "I loved *Gilligan's Island* when I was a kid."

"Me too," said Leo. "It started my lifelong love of tiki, actually."

"And you know, at the beginning," Sequoia said, warming to the theme, "it was all about—having to pull together. Being more together than you were separately. Like the time they built a raft but it sank because each one tried to take too much gold. And I always thought the point was, they only thought they needed rescuing. When actually what they had found there was already paradise, right? There was this episode I saw as a kid, and someone had come to the island and put them in cages—that was always happening. But this one time you could see that the cages didn't go all the way around. And now I know that's because it was a cheap show and the cameraman screwed up, but back then I thought, *oh yeah*. They could each be free if they really wanted to—being trapped was just a state of mind. So we're going to help kids walk right past the cages, help them see that they don't go all around. I like it."

Felicity grinned. "Well, you know this makes you Lovey, right?"

Sequoia grinned back, ear to ear. "Back in my neighborhood growing up there was this blind man on the corner I always used to give money to. And all day long he would smile and say, 'All I can see, all I can SEE, ALL I can see is love.' Lovey? Yeah, I can live with that."

"Well, I am no professor and if you even *think* about calling me Gilligan I am going to scream till my weave falls off," Beto said, making a grand dramatic gesture. Which knocked over his drink and sent it flying into Keith's lap. Everyone sat for a beat staring at the spreading stain, and Keith just smiled.

"Aw, come on now," said the now-Skipper, putting his arm around his shoulder. "You know you're my little buddy, right?"

"Guys?" said Isobel. "I'm in. I'll be Ginger, I kind of always have been anyway, with this hair. But we're missing someone, aren't we? Don't we need a professor?"

And Sequoia leaned back and said, "There's a space here just waiting for him. So I think he'll come along. And we wait. Yeah, we wait."

Chapter 15: The Professor

I don't blame my mother, because I hate it when people blame their fucking mothers. I have three of them, and I don't blame any of them. Okay, the second. A little.

This is how I like to think it happened. My mother was a bad-ass punk teenager who snuck out to have wild, stupid adventures with a fake ID and a fearless heart. She met a man and fucked him in the back of his Volvo. He was a professor, a brilliant scientist. (Hey, it's *my* fantasy, okay?) He also was married, and didn't know why the fuck he was doing this, but my mother was a blue-eyed, blue-haired vixen and she seduced him. She got pregnant. Her parents promised support, and they begged her not to get an abortion. She was young; she was stupid; she gave in. Two years later she's realizing that if she doesn't get the fuck out now, everything she likes about herself is going to disappear, so she goes out, gets in trouble, ends up in jail. Her parents kick us both out. She takes me to the safe surrender hospital, pins the word "Max" on me, and takes off. And more power to her. I'd have done the same.

My second set of parents had been trying to get pregnant, and then to adopt, for years. They wanted a *white* baby; they're that kind of racist. "Oh, we're not prejudiced; we just think people are more…comfortable…with their own color. The caseworker called one day and asked if they would consider a toddler. I was about eighteen months old, they think. My mom says they just fell in *love* at first sight, which just goes to show. The social workers managed to wrestle me into a dress and I *was* adorable—I know, they took enough pictures. You know, black hair, pale skin, big blue eyes. My second mother has similar coloring, which was a real selling point. I looked like I *could* be theirs. But no way could I ever be theirs.

My parents tried to call me Maxine at first, but according to my father, I wasn't having that for a minute. I was never Maxine: I was Max. That's the first thing I remember, just fiercely telling people that I'm Max. I don't remember a thing before the hospital, and I don't remember the hospital. I do remember, vaguely, being given to these new people and told they were my parents now and that was very confusing. I knew they weren't. Where was my mother? I knew I wanted her. Anyway, they got the idea. The one thing I knew in the whole world was my name and that wasn't changing. I am MAX. Then, now, always.

Sometimes I wonder what it was about me already that made my mother pick that name for me. It's there on my birth certificate: Max. That's why I think I would like her. But I'll never know. She chose to give me up and I'm not mad about that. I respect her right to do it. Her choice, you know? And more power to her.

They brought me home and put me in a room decorated in pure subjection to the Barbie princess hegemony. I do remember thinking, *But this is a girl's room!* They gave me dolls, and I tore their heads off. Once, I took something like six Barbies, tore all their heads off, tiger-striped them with paint, and dumped them in the sink. That freaked my mother out, but Dad said to give it time. The thing about Dad was, he had no

137

real investment in girliness. He had a sly sense of humor that my mother didn't get. He got a kick out of me.

I don't remember my bio-mom reading to me but she must have, because I started demanding to be read to after a few days. They hadn't thought of that. Fuck! How could I have ended up with people who wouldn't even think to read to a child? And when my mother would read, I remember, she read with this singsong sugary dumpling voice. Dad was better—gruff, not a lot of expression, but at least he didn't call me things like "Mommy's special pretty pretty girl" and "sugar pumpkin pie." She used to call me that. OH MY GOD. So pretty soon I would try to tune out her tone, and just focus on matching the words to the marks in the books. I started learning, but not fast enough. And I wanted to read *when* I wanted to, *what* I wanted to. Mom would take me to the library, and I would pick out books with bulldozers and tigers and motorcycles; she'd say "No," and we would come home with more freaking fairy tales. I hated fairy tales! And Disney movies! I did not want to watch *Cinderella* or *The Little Mermaid*, not ever. We compromised on *The Jungle Book*. Having a big bear friend and singing with orangutans, that I could get behind.

Anyway, so after a bit I asked my mother to teach me to read because I couldn't pick it up fast enough. And she said no. The damn social workers who visited every once in a while for the first few years advised her not to: don't let Max get ahead of other kids. I was already weird enough, was going to have trouble fitting in. Well, according to my dad, I freaked out. I usually was pretty good tempered—I mostly had the attitude even as a kid that I had to pick my battles and it wasn't worth arguing about everything. I ate everything they told me and never angled for an extra cookie. I would wear pink as long as they didn't try to put me in a skirt. I played with dolls; I just chopped their hair off and pretended they were action figures.

They didn't know that *my* Barbie was actually a superhero or a ninja. But when they would seriously challenge me about something important, no. I would scream until I got my way. So I won that round. I would grab my copy of the *Where the Wild Things Are*—my favorite book—and read it until I knew every word. The best thing my mom ever did for me was sewing me my own "Max" costume for my fourth birthday.

So sometimes when a couple adopts a kid, it kind of flips a biological switch inside them, and sure enough when I was two my mother got pregnant. And had twin boys. And then she got pregnant AGAIN, and had twin boys AGAIN. Then my dad had a vasectomy. I remember him lying on the couch with an ice pack on his crotch and groaning. So by the time I was eight, Alex and Brian and Nate and Steven were running pell-mell through the house breaking *everything*. I loved it. I came up with all the best games, I taught them how to build forts, I sat on them until they treated me with respect, I arbitrated their fights, I taught them how to misbehave without getting caught, and I stood up for them in the neighborhood. They were my wild things, and I was their *king*.

Mom tried for a while, but by the time everyone was walking and talking, she was 45 years old. And she was worn out. She just got too damn tired to try to assert any kind of control on me. At home, I was just one of the boys. I remember once standing next to her, waiting for my turn in some game, and she actually looked out at us all and sighed and said, "I wish I had a girl." And then she saw me and she caught herself and said, "Well, I do, now, don't I? And one day when you grow up you'll put all this silly boy stuff side and be a proper young lady."

And I said, "Oh GROSS!" and ran off to play. Some of the times that stuff worried me: Was that true? Would I just wake up one day and be a girl? Because I really didn't think I was a girl, see. I knew my mother thought I was one, but she was STUPID.

When I went to school it got worse. After about second grade there was this big division: girls against boys. And the boys wouldn't let me play with them at first; in order to join them, I had to scare the girls by throwing frogs and bugs at them. Well, okay, I did it but I didn't like it. I kind of liked girls. They were pretty and I wanted to shyly go up and kiss them and stroke their soft clothes. I just didn't want to BE one. So I was kind of a loner, sometimes joining the girls and sometimes the boys, depending on who needed an extra person or what was going on. I was fast and coordinated and good at sports, and the boys would let me play on teams, but they didn't want me to race them or do anything one on one—because they didn't want to get beat…by a *girl*.

When I was eight, I got into a fight at school with another boy about who was the leader of their "gang." The boy told me I couldn't be the leader because I was a girl, and I said I could so. He said the leader of the gang had to have a "chick"—and some pretty little blonde girl backed him up on that. I think he promised her stickers. So I got a "chick" as well—my friend Harriet. We stood toe to toe, seething at each other, and then I said, "Well, I can KISS my chick," and bent her backwards and kissed her. The other guy grabbed for the girl, but she ran off screaming. I won that one!

I don't know when I "knew" I liked girls and not boys. It got confusing: I felt like a boy and I liked girls, but I didn't want to be a girl, but I could see that most of the boys were assholes and they weren't nice to girls, including me. So why would I want to be one of them, except that the alternative was to be a girl, and I wasn't that. My room just gradually changed from age five to age eight from Disney princess schlock to dinosaurs and trains and insects. I liked transportation of all kinds, nature and robots and astronomy. I've always had this sharp memory and no real problem learning anything. So when I was little I thought my parents were just dumb because they didn't know anything about trains or cars or science or dinosaurs and also they didn't know I was a boy. Just one of the tons of things they didn't know. I liked them okay. I kissed my mom a lot when I was really little, and part of that was because she was super pretty. I would tell her, "Mommy, you're so pretty!" and she would say, "You will be pretty too if you wear the pretty dress I got you." And I would say, "Yuck!" Pretty wasn't what I wanted to be. Pretty was what I wanted to kiss.

I got a little older, and I was always a talker. I would go to school and talk and tell stories and if there was a grownup who seemed cool I would talk to them. I got into gifted programs and through that I met some cooler adults and that's how I met Ms. Devine. She came and did some human sexuality class at my school when we were ten. My parents were very Catholic and wouldn't have let me go, so I forged their signature on the permission slip; I learned you had to hide some shit from them because fighting them—I could do it and win, but it always made my mom sad and I didn't actively want to make her sad. If I could have made her happy and not have made myself miserable, I would have done that, but I couldn't be what I wasn't just to please her. Pleasing other people has just never been *that* important to me.

So we had this class, and Ms. Devine read our questions. I put in the question I wanted to ask. I knew it was a risk—people were already guessing I was different, and they might guess I wrote it but I put in anyway, "Do people always have to grow up to be women if they're girls and men if they're boys?" Ms. Devine said, "Nope!" And she talked to us about it. So that's how I found out. I stayed and talked to her after class, and I told her it was my question. My heart was pounding.

141

And she looked at me and she knew and she smiled at me. The first time anybody ever sees who you really are and smiles at you is a special fucking moment.

But that was also the beginning of things getting really hellish. Boys and girls were starting to "go out" and I wasn't just a tomboy anymore. Ms. Devine gave me some numbers to call if things got bad, and for a while I stopped playing sports and just—well, my parents got me a computer. I had to beg them for three Christmases straight, and then finally there it was and after that, there were a couple of lost years while I taught myself to program. My little brothers were getting obnoxious; my mother was worn down by all their shenanigans and was getting older. She became more of a Catholic martyr every year. She made my brothers do altar boy shit. My father checked out more and more, beer and TV, TV and beer. Worked longer hours, he said because he had to support us. Money got tight—they hadn't really planned on having five kids. He took a second job on weekends. We never saw him.

And sometimes I would go to the library and just hide there if my brothers wouldn't let me be. I was about twelve or thirteen then, and that's how I found one of the cards. I was getting desperate—middle school was sucking sweaty donkey taint. Believe me, it is NOT fun to be trans and know it in middle school. I started getting in fights with boys, which I won about half the time because I'm fast and as a fighter I am mean and sneaky—four younger brothers, right? But sometimes they were just bigger and *stronger* and pinned me down and wham! Wham! Wham! And then they would say, "Ooooh, we're not supposed to hit girls." Like they just remembered that. And they would stop. Like they were punishing me for not being a girl, and then insulting me for being one. Fucktards.

My mom got mad at me for fighting, and my dad would just shrug and wander away. Once my brothers jumped someone who had gotten me, but it was weird—"Stop calling our sister a boy!" they yelled. That's not what I wanted them to say. I *was* a boy; I just didn't want to be beat up for it.

So one day I called the number on the card. They managed to get in touch with me: Lovey pulled some strings to get me referred to her as a psychiatrist to help with my fighting problem. My parents didn't know what to do, so they went along with it. That's how we met.

Chapter 16: Lovey on the Professor

We got the call from Max, and I pulled some strings and got myself called in as a specialist to check out what was going on. They agreed to come to my office.

First, I met the parents. I had the file on Max. Strongly gender identified as male, refuses to wear dresses, parents in despair, drearily religious but not abusive. At least in any legal sense. I had them in my office and they were nice enough people, wanted what was best for their girl but Max—they called him Max—had never played along with that fantasy. So fine, their girl was a bit of a tomboy, they could accept that, but that didn't mean that she was a boy! No matter how many times he told them.

"If the Lord meant her to be a boy, why make her a girl? We are what we are—there's no changing it," is what his father said. The mother nodded along as if he were speaking wise and profound truths. They dressed like a modern-day Ozzie and Harriet: fifty shades of beige. He was wearing slacks and a bland sweater; she had on a beige skirt and a white blouse. They weren't just white bread; they were *stale* white bread. They looked at me just a little like they weren't quite sure what a black woman was doing with a fancy degree like mine. But I

144

know how to get through that. I just work the big black woman with a heart of gold angle. Thank God for Oprah; she made my life so much easier. Pretty soon it all came tumbling out: how worried they were about Max, how they thought "she" would outgrow this tomboy phase, blah blah blah.

But abusive? No. I asked them what they did to punish Max and there was no defensiveness, no guilt or evasion or bluster. they didn't punish him for refusing to wear a dress; they sent him to his room when he came back from a fight. Hell, even *their* pronouns kept slipping—I had to force back a snicker when his mother asked, "Why can't he just be a girl?"

Then I met Max. I'd felt sorry for the kid before he came into my office, thinking, damn, this kid has had to put up with old Stan and Carol here for his whole life. I was bored to pieces with them after ten minutes. And all the standardized tests on this kid showed he was off-the-scale smart.

I was expecting an anxious, confused, smart kid. But in walks this cocky little number, almost swashbuckling with swagger and mischief, who swings into the chair and puts his feet right up on my coffee table, and he winked at me. He *winked* at me.

I cracked up. I couldn't even maintain basic professional decorum. I said, "Young man, you are a piece of work! Shame on you for giving your poor parents hell."

And Max grinned this heartbreaking grin of his, and that was it—I fell in love with this kid. I didn't know what to do about it, but I just loved him. He said, "C'mon, dude, they tried to get me to wear a dress. ME! A DRESS! Are you kidding me?"

"You got a problem with dresses?" I looked down at the African print I was wearing that day, cut to show off my fine womanly curves.

He grinned again, "No, I have no problem at all with

dresses. I love them. On girls. Beautiful girls that I want to date and bring flowers to and kiss and all the stuff that boys like to do with girls. But I'm not a girl, and my 'parents' just don't get that." He made air quotes as he said parents. I rolled my eyes.

"Yeah, boy, you are in a pickle. Because I talked myself blue in the face about how biology and gender identity don't always match up and that it was unlikely you were going to 'grow out of it' if you have been identifying as a boy since… since you were how old?"

"Always. As far as I can remember."

"I told them all that, and it didn't even seem to register. But despite all that, you're lucky. You have a gift, Max. A couple of gifts. You're a super-sassy, super-smart boy who knows who he is. Some people go their whole lives not knowing. So you have to take pity on your parents. Give them a break. I'm not saying give in and wear a dress, but wear a pink shirt every once in a while. Give 'em a thrill."

Max frowned. He leaned forward, and I could see the pain that swagger was covering up.

"Look, I'll level with you. I'm just *tired* of this. I was adopted, and these people—we just aren't a good match. I like my brothers okay. But are these people my parents just because they adopted me?"

"Yeah, Max. They are. That's what adoption is. And just because you feel like they don't understand you—and you're right, they don't—that doesn't make them any less your parents. Believe me, there are tons of people in the world whose biological parents don't understand them either." I thought of my brother then, like I do every day.

"Okay, okay. But I am fifteen now! And I am wasting away in podunk nowhereland, going to high school with morons, getting the shit kicked out of me every Tuesday, Thursday, and alternate Fridays. Fuck this! Can't I get the hell out of here somehow? Get myself emancipated or something?"

"Well, you would need to get a lawyer for that, and you would need to pay a lawyer for that. You have any money?"

"No," he said, looking a little deflated.

"If they were abusive, you could get one pro bono, but you don't have much of a case: they ever hit you?"

"No. Dammit."

"No—believe me, you're better off without your parents hitting you. Here, look, let me get you a lawyer's card"—and that's when I made my big mistake. I turned my back on him, bent down to reach into my purse to get the card of a lawyer who specializes in gay family issues. I had just met him the other day and thought, *well, I don't think there's anything that can be done here, and if the kid isn't being abused I really can't stage a rescue for him—but he deserves to at least take his case to a lawyer if he wants and see what happens.* It's a bad thing when a parent can't acknowledge what their kid really is. Is it abuse? Maybe. A subtle one. But it happens all the time on a less dramatic scale with most parents and kids.

Max left the office, but he didn't leave my mind. I kept thinking about him, about what I was sending him back to. Beatings from kids at school, no understanding at home: that's not abuse? I don't know, but it's tragic. But what the fuck to do about it when the parents aren't monsters? There are lines we can't cross.

Then we started getting the emails. To our private email addresses, the ones we only gave to each other—encrypted and code-named, where we planned our rescues. Cocky little emails. The first one: "I know what you're doing." Scared us half to death. I didn't make the connection. And the next one, "Your current security is as safe as a straw hut in a hurricane, by the way. I can help. Signed…The Professor." That's when I knew. When I read the third one, "I can make a radio out of coconuts," I did a spit take and spewed green tea all over my keyboard. I'm lucky it didn't break. Oh, I knew who it was then.

The team had a meeting. Arranged by phone, flying everyone to Vegas because we couldn't organize by email. Leo and Keith were pissed; Beto thought it was hilarious; Felicity and Isobel were worried but amused. I told them what I thought was happening.

Leo went into defense mode: "If this snot-nosed little kid is trying to scare us, he can go fuck himself. We can change passwords, upgrade our security, lock him out."

"Well, yeah, we can," I said. "But I have met him. He's scary-smart, and we don't know what we're doing. To protect ourselves we have to let someone into our secret. I say, why not let him do it? Give him what he wants."

"You want to negotiate with a terrorist?" Keith said, but his eyes were smiling.

"Terrorist, ha!" I snorted. "This is a kid in a tough situation. One we can't help by our normal methods; he doesn't meet our criteria. But he's got us beat, and I think he's right—let's turn crisis into opportunity. Anyway, we said the Professor would come, right? Well…here he is."

"You like this kid, don't you?" asked Felicity. She was half-smiling.

"No," I said. "I fucking *love* this kid. Let's go get him."

We didn't sneak into his room at night and make off with him. No. I contacted the parents and sat down and had a meeting. Told them I thought they should let him move to Berkeley and further his education through one of the programs and schools for unusual kids, take classes at the community college. He wouldn't have to get beaten anymore. And he wanted to go.

They frowned and said, "But where would he live? He's too young for college. He's too young to live on his own. We can't afford to rent him a place or pay private school fees."

And I said it. "He can live with me." Their eyes popped. Send their fifteen-year-old kid to live with this black woman in the wilds of Berkeley? Could they do that? But they liked me. And they were tired.

I started making the case. I leaned hard on the problems he was having at school. Berkeley has independent study programs and support groups for "people like Max." I didn't say transgender teens. Let them think Max was getting help in learning to be a girl. Whatever they needed to think. I saw shock gradually fade into doubt.

"Why would you do that? You can't take in every kid who has problems. why Max?"

And I smiled a big, nonthreatening, nurturing smile. I channeled Oprah full force and said, "Well, now, you *know* why. Because Max is special."

The mother stood. She looked bewildered. "We will think about it. And talk it over with Max."

I stood as well, nodded, and gave them my contact info. I stayed in Long Beach overnight and got the call in the morning. That afternoon I picked up Max and at 42 years old, just when I was sure it wasn't going to happen, I became a mother. Because I had told the exact truth: Max was as special as it gets.

Chapter 17: The Professor's Birthday and the Plan

"Everyone gets lei'd," the banner in the entry way shouted in giant puffy glitter paint. kids careened around with bags of leis, hurtling up to newcomers, throwing flowers around their necks, then racing away, out to the trampoline, tearing around to check that everyone sported a lei, and back to the door to catch the newcomers. In the backyard a flag flew from an improvised pole, a transgender pride flag with the words, "Happy 18th Birthday, Max." Sequoia smiled at the culmination of all her hard work.

She looked over at Max and saw him standing there scowling at it all. She smiled; she knew that scowl. It was the fiercely proud scowl of a boy who's trying not to cry with joy. Her yard overflowed. A tiki bar dispensed fruity drinks in one corner of the yard. An inflatable palm tree waved over a cooler full of soft drinks. A birthday cake in the shape of a red Mustang sat waiting for paper plates and plastic forks. And the whole team was there. Margarita, dressed like Marilyn Monroe, sang "*Feliz Cumpleaños, Señor Presidente.*" Keith macked on one of Sequoia's colleagues. Leo whistled behind the bar in the loudest Hawaiian shirt on earth and mixed fruity drinks with crazy straws, from virgin for the children all the way to very slutty indeed; Isobel and Felicity jumped on the trampoline and led the kids in games. Sequoia mingled and beamed with pride. Drag queens, sex educators, Sequoia's colleagues, transgender teenagers, even some of their first rescued children, and all of their children, were rubbing elbows and getting loose. Even Max's parents and brothers were there, looking a little flustered and out of place, trying not to gawk at the drag queens, doing their best. Max went up to them and hugged them for a long moment.

Despite his advanced age, Max was getting the birthday from Sequoia that he had never gotten from his parents. Oh, he got birthday parties all right: pink and rainbow unicorn-fairy-Care-Bear-princess parties, going back as long as he could remember. Sequoia was giving him a boy party: sports car cake, Spider-Man cups and plates, and, since the party was in June: water guns. Everyone left a little tired, a little wet, a little sticky: the way you were supposed to leave a good party. Sequoia was a firm believer in the healing powers of the party.

But the next day the guests had gone, and the team gathered back at the house for cleanup and a meeting. They walked through, gathering cups and trash and tidying up, singing along to Tracy Chapman. The sun came in through the window and lit up Sequoia's cheerful, cluttered house. Books were everywhere. Her cats, Zora and Octavia, dozed in a pool of sunlight on the floor. A draft of a paper she was writing sprawled out in the coffee table. And when the place was restored to semi-respectability, they sat down around the big oak dining table with cups of hot coffee. They had all given Max presents the day before: silly presents, boy presents, man presents. Hot wheels and a train set, ties, and cool sunglasses. But in front of him now was the real present.

The box was wrapped in shiny navy blue paper, and he opened it slowly, knowing it would be special. But he wasn't expecting what was staring back at him. A penis. A packie: a non-erect cock and balls that he could wear under his pants: a package to say to the world, "Yes, I am a man." He had been researching them, and he knew from the label that this one was top of the line, expensive, and could be affixed with surgical adhesive so that it could fool anyone. It was matched to his skin tone. It was…perfect.

"*Mazel tov!* Today you are a man," Sequoia said. "We all chipped in. We wanted this to come from all of us…"

"And because you're a man…" said Keith.

"No!" said Sequoia. "Not now. Not today, okay? Please." She felt rage and fear well up in her and cast Keith a pleading look.

"Yeah, sweetheart, I know. But it has to be now. No time better. We're all here, and those three need to get back to Vegas tomorrow. This needs to get started. And if he says no, I need to know as soon as possible so I can try my best to think of something else." Keith drummed his fingers on the table. Sequoia knew that meant he was nervous. He wasn't taking this lightly, then. Max looked back and forth between one and the other.

"You better just tell me what this is about."

"Well, you see," Keith started.

"And the answer is going to be NO!" said Sequoia.

"Now, the boy has a right to make his own choice, you understand? Eighteen. That's what that means. And he has been making choices for himself for a long time," Keith turned in his chair to face Max, steepled his hands together, groped for words. Then he opened a folder lying in front of him and slid a picture over to Max. The picture of Kate, laughing and giving the camera the finger. Max looked at it and smiled.

"Okay, and? Who is this ball of fire?"

"That's Kate, and you remember that Christian camp in the Dominican Republic? She's there. She's being held there against her will."

"Oh," he looked back down at the snapshot. "Sure, okay. I did some of the online research on that place. They have good security."

"Yeah they do. Exactly. When we went to scout that place, we couldn't get too close. Got stopped at the gate. The jungle's pressed against all the walls. And I wracked my brain to think of another way to do it, but...we need someone on the inside. One of us, not just our moles. Someone who can pass as a teenager," he said, and looked at Max meaningfully.

Understanding flashed in Max's blue eyes. "Absofuckin-glutely," he said. No hesitation. It was what he had wanted for years—to be in on the danger, the 'real work.'

"Now, no!" said Sequoia, and her eyes filled with tears. "Max, don't you dare say yes before you even think about this. It's dangerous. Really, really dangerous. They do not play. They are gun nuts for Jesus."

"The thing is," Keith continued, "it's not like I'm happy about sending you into a risky situation. And I don't want to break your mother's heart," he nodded at the fuming Sequoia. "Maybe, just maybe, we can get one of our evangelical moles to go in there and get us a little intel. But we can't risk blowing their cover, and we can't ask them to do anything dangerous."

"And you can't ask *Max* to do anything dangerous either!" Sequoia cut in.

"Well, yeah, honey, we can. He's eighteen now, and we've been rescuing people on the assumption that even someone sixteen or seventeen has a right to make their own choices. Max is an adult now—a lot more adult than most eighteen-year-olds. And we need him bad—we've got no one else who looks enough like a kid. Felicity here comes close, but...no. She's 28. And, okay just maybe she could pass, but you know how many Asian evangelicals there are? Not a hell of a lot. And these folks,

153

from what we can tell, are particularly *racist* evangelicals. So it can't be her. So who do we have? Max. We got Max. He knows the ins and outs of what we do, He's the right age; he's trained in self-defense; he's ready to go. Sequoia, I wouldn't ask him to do this if there were any other way. "

Max looked down at Kate's picture again. He was itching to go, would be raring to go for anyone, but the badass laughing girl in the picture was someone he really wanted to meet. Wasn't it every teenage boy's dream to rescue a damsel in distress? So he took a long moment and turned to face Sequoia, looking her square in the face. "I am ready to do this. I'll be careful, Mom." He leaned over and kissed Sequoia on the cheek. "When can I go? Tomorrow? Next week?"

"I wish we could, baby," Keith said. "But we have a lot of preparing to do. You need more self-defense and physical work. They run the place like a boot camp. And we need to get our mole hired somehow. There are strings to pull and plans to make. All right, well, there's one more thing. This is a dangerous assignment, and I want you physically stronger and I think…I think you'd better go in packing."

"Packing? You mean…with a gun? I haven't trained with a…"

"No, no" Keith said, and nodded toward Max's birthday present. "I mean…*packing*."

Max looked down at his present and grinned ear to ear.

Chapter 18: Camp

The camp sent a list of things allowed and not allowed, and the list, Max said, sucked ass. He sat making faces as he read, seeing his life constrict. No books—except the bible and books from one particular Christian publisher. No fiction. No games. No personal adornments: no jewelry except for one small plain cross necklace—for girls only. No hair products but shampoo. The worst: no computers, no tablets, no MP3 players, no cell phones. The thought of spending a week, maybe weeks—who knows how long it would take to get the job done?—with no Internet access in 00-degree heat, worrying about *literally* sweating his goddamn nuts off (though the surgical adhesive was supposed to withstand sweat) made him want to give up, right then and there. At least he didn't have to go through the horrific "kidnapped" scenario. Maybe fieldwork wasn't his thing. Maybe his style would always be a nice, cool room with access to video games, monitoring things on the computer and just watching *Archer*. Leave the rough stuff to Felicity and Isobel.

But they couldn't do this, and he could. And there was a damsel in motherfucking *distress*. His eyes strayed to the picture of Kate. Paul had given them several snaps, but the first one he had seen was still his favorite: Kate giving the bird to the

155

photographer, eyes crossed and tongue out. Paul had taken the picture on her sixteenth birthday, three months ago, and Kate's parents had stuffed her into a ruffly pink monstrosity of a dress for the occasion. Her blonde hair caught the light, and she might have looked like a Sunday school teacher's dream except that the real Kate wasn't a lifeless doll in pink lace and ruffles. She was the face alight with rebellion—and the middle finger raised in protest to all of it. He looked at the other pictures. Kate caught in the middle of a laugh, Kate bent over a guitar in ripped jeans.

Max tucked his favorite picture and a few of their cards behind the thick cover of the bible, glued it down neatly around the edges so no sign of his handiwork was apparent, threw it in the suitcase, and steadied himself. Yeah. He was doing this.

The flight to the Dominican Republic was long and grueling. No first-class service and flutes of champagne for him—there might be spies. He was shoved into the middle seat on an aisle between the same fat man and the same crying baby that are always, in every single airplane, sitting in the window and aisle seats in a three-seat row. He couldn't even nod off to tunes on his iPod—not unless he wanted to leave it behind on the plane. He read a cheap used copy of a James Bond novel, which he would leave behind in the seat pocket. He popped in some earplugs and absorbed himself in the sexploits of Bond, Pussy Galore, and her lesbian crime gang.

On landing, he was greeted by a small man in white shirt and conservative tie with a sign reading "Mike Hunter"—his name for the duration. He smiled at his little rebellion. The jagoff—as he already thought of the guy with the small wispy mustache and the sweat stains—ordered him out to a shuttle, telling him it would be a three-hour drive to the camp. Max whistled the "three-hour tour" bar from the *Gilligan's Island* theme and was told not to get cute. Whistling was, apparently, disrespectful to the Lord. His eyes got wide; he'd known he was heading into Crazytown, but shit just got real. He and his keeper waited for another kid, who came shuffling off his flight looking fat and sullen. The jagoff held up a sign with the name flanked by crosses. *Shit, John Joseph Christianson. That's a hell of a lot of Christianity in one name.* The kid walked up to them looking as miserable as—well, as a normal fourteen-year-old kid going to Christian camp. On the whole, Max approved of his gloom, but the jagoff, a Mr. Davis, told the kid that they would both be learning some lessons in respect soon enough. Mr. Davis was a chinless blond man, doughy and shapeless; his nose was peeling from sunburn. When he said they would learn respect, a sadistic smile played around his thin lips. Max bit back a wave of anger. How long could he go before he ended up yelling at these assholes to go fuck themselves? He felt profoundly grateful to be there as a boy; a boy could be deferential and polite with a little reserve, a girl would have to be sweet. And he had *always sucked* at being sweet. He thought about Kate again and wondered how she was doing: how badly had she failed to be sweet?

They bumped and sweated and jostled and suffered through the long ride to camp, listening all the way to Mr. Davis drone about how much their parents loved them to be sending them there, about how, without this intervention, they would probably die of the sins and bad choices they had been making. The shuttle had air conditioning, but neither Max nor John asked to have it turned on. It would have been pointless. Mr. Davis had already said that suffering was purifying. They glared at each other like two dogs on leashes. The camp appeared around a bend, and they slowed to go through the entrance. Max's eyes widened when he saw the gun in the hands of the paramilitary strongmen at the gate. As they rolled through the gate he stared, absorbing it all. John Joseph kept

157

his gaze firmly down, as if refusing to accept that he was really here. The camp looked tidy and well kept but bleak. Two large cinderblock buildings squatted in the middle of the camp, bearing signs that read CHAPEL and CAFETERIA. Ugly little cabins cowered off to the side—nothing like the cheerful, thatched huts with bright painted doors Max had seen going past on the outskirts of the city. Across from the cabins on the other side of the camp stood some farm buildings, and Mr. Davis bragged that the camp had its own chickens and pigs. Max wondered why that was worth boasting about. Mr. Davis led them to their cabin and told them to pick a bunk. Only two were available, the top and bottom of the same bunk bed, and Max strode forward and claimed the lower bed quickly. Easier for nocturnal comings and goings not to be noticed if he didn't have to climb down past a roommate in the dark. John Joseph glowered at him, but hefted his bag up to the top; then Mr. Davis led the way to a room where they were given what Max privately termed a "Christian asshole makeover."

It was military in flavor: he sat down and got a crew cut, then he was issued pants and a shirt and given a plastic bracelet, like the kind given in hospitals. The pants were dark, and the shirts were white, heavy, and long-sleeved, with crosses stitched onto the cuffs. *Excellent clothes for the tropics*, he thought. *If you want to torture kids.* And he suspected that that was exactly what they did want. His bracelet was yellow. He suspected this bracelet told his "crime." He knew he had been reported to be blasphemous and rebellious, refusing to be reborn into the Lord—the most general category. The kid he had come in with, John Joseph, was given a lavender bracelet, which he stared at miserably, turning it around and pulling at it. The military-looking "quartermaster" barked an order at him to stop it. *Jesus, the poor bastard*, Max thought. He was pretty sure he knew *exactly* what lavender meant.

158

Next came the chapel, where they were led to a bench in front. Entering the chapel answered a few of the questions that had been forming in Max's mind. First: *Where the hell was all the money the parents poured into this place?* He knew from Sequoia that they had shelled out big bucks to get him into this third-world chicken farm. But the chapel? The chapel was deluxe: air conditioned, state of the art, padded seats, a huge screen behind the podium. The walls sported huge tacky paintings of bible stories: Jesus and the talents, the loaves and fishes. This Jesus, Max noted, had golden-brown hair and sky-blue eyes. This was white boy Jesus. That had always driven him nuts. What were they thinking? How could they possibly believe that Jesus would look white? But that wasn't the most important question he had. The most important question was: how would he find Kate?

That question turned out to be instantly answerable. There she was. Three campers stood on a table at the side of the chapel, each holding up one pole of a large banner that read "SINNERS!" in red dripping paint. And in the middle, right under the Ns, stood Kate.

His seat was right in front of her, and the sermon—did they call them sermons?—was just beginning. The subject was the sin of vanity. He learned that the three girls had been accused of venal loathsome vanity because they had been wearing nail polish when they arrived. Two weeks ago. Apparently the sin had not been adequately expiated, because the preacher's face was still livid with outrage as he began the sermon with a discussion of the sin of vanity. He foamed and frothed about the worldliness of their corrupt, wicked hearts. He went on a rant about how their "pretty little bodies" hid the suppurating, festering condition of their souls. The phrase "pretty little bodies" was repeated, and he spat the word so hard Max thought he could feel the spray. Max thought he would not be

159

surprised if the guy had a hard-on and was glad the podium hid it from view. Max glanced over at Kate; her face looked carefully schooled, blank even, but he read into it deep fury. He hoped he wasn't just seeing what he wanted to see. He hoped she was keeping the bullshit at bay inside, and when the preacher launched into a more full discussion of the sins of the flesh, Max took a second, when eyes were distracted elsewhere (the sins of the flesh came with visual aids—huge, graphic, disgusting pictures of untreated STDs) to look up at Kate and for a split second, rolled his eyes.

He saw a flicker in her face, a twitch stopped before it could become a smile. It was nothing much, but it was contact. It was a start.

While the minister raved on about the distractions of the flesh from perfect godliness, Max tuned him out and imagined wallowing in the sinfulness of Kate's flesh. He grinned inwardly when he thought how lucky he was that his dick couldn't give away his thoughts like it would if he were a cis male. *One advantage to being born with the "wrong" equipment.* He was careful not let the smile show on his face, and he turned his thoughts back to all the things he could do to Kate with his fingers and his tongue. Okay, he had almost no experience—but he had studied the subject extensively.

After chapel, Jagoff grabbed him by the shoulders and dragged him out, introducing him to his mentor in camp. "Chris is the only person you're allowed to talk to outside of bible therapy," Jagoff said. "He is your hope buddy." *My hope buddy looks pretty hopeless,* thought Max. He was a greasy, tall boy with shifty eyes and a big red zit nestling beside his nose.

"You're on level zero," Chris said. He handed Max a pin that said zero and motioned him to put it on his shirt over his heart. "That means you have no privileges at all. I'm level four, the highest. That's why I get to be a hope buddy. I get to talk to people without asking permission, and have dessert, and go into town on Sundays, and make a call home to my parents. If I can stay on level four for four weeks, I go home. Not that I want to go home," he said. "This place really straightened me out. I was lost before I got here."

Max thought Chris sounded like he was auditioning to be in a commercial. His voice was full of cheer, but he looked around furtively to see where the counselors were as he talked.

"Okay, well, chow time," said Chris. "Let's go eat." He led the way to the big barrack of a building labeled CAFETERIA. No air conditioning here, and it was hotter in than out now, with the heat of the day lifting outside. After the cool of the chapel it was like stepping into a kiln. Long tables stretched the length of the building, and Max and Chris found their places at the edge of the boys' side.

The girls were currently in line, loading their plates with food. Max assumed the boys' turn would come afterward, but when the girls had filled the plates, they turned and brought them directly to the boys' tables and placed the food in front of them. No one spoke. His hope buddy saw the surprise in Max's eyes and said, "The girls serve the boys before they eat, so that they learn proper womanly values of service and patience, putting others before themselves." He said this as if he had memorized it, but with pride, as if he wholeheartedly approved of this state of affairs. So Max internally dubbed him a prize asshole. In silence, the girls trooped back to fetch their own meals. Max had been warned that the campers did not speak without asking for permission first, but he had not believed that they would be able to command total obedience over 00 teenagers under the age of eighteen. Only terror could exert this much control. He had been warned that the camp directors believed unashamedly in frequent corporal punishment, but mere spankings alone could not produce silence this total

161

and frightened.

He looked down at the plate, where lukewarm lasagna squatted, and went to pick up his fork with a sigh of resignation. But there was no fork by his plate, and no knife either.

"Uh, they forgot to give me a fork," he told Chris.

"No, you don't get a fork. No one does. Some of the kids here would *stab* you with a fork if they got one. There are some bad kids here."

"So no knife either? We have to eat with…spoons? Just spoons?"

"You'll get used to it," Chris said. He picked up his and dug into the lasagna, which was a corner piece, crusty. The spoon pushed it down, but the lasagna held fast.

A laugh burst out of Max's mouth before he could stop it, and he coughed to hide it from the camp counselor who looked suspiciously his way. Then he picked up his spoon, carefully inserted it under some wilted iceberg lettuce, and balanced the food up to his mouth.

The girls, he noticed, had filled their plates and sat down. They looked utterly miserable. He looked down at his own plate, where the sad, cold food was scanty enough, and over to the girls' table next to his. The girls had significantly less food than he did, and once more Chris explained: "Girls don't need as much food, and they need to learn sacrifice more. They get half."

Outrage flashed through Max at that. *They're starving the girls. These assholes are starving girls, punishing them for being born female.* His heart beat fast, and he lowered his head to hide his fury. *This has to stop,* he thought. *We can't just get Kate out of here. We have to bring this motherfucking place down.* But that wasn't the plan. The mission was to save Kate, who wants to be saved. Who has asked to be saved. *What about the rest?* Max wondered. *How can we rescue everybody? How can we leave*

162

them behind?

He tried not to retch and forced himself to eat a few more bites, but he had eaten on the plane and couldn't force down more than a few small morsels, and besides, the spoon would not go through the hard edges of his lasagna either. So he distracted himself by studying the counselors and wondering which one was the mole. He gave them rude names in his head: Jagoff, the one who met them at the plane. GI Buttholes, four crew-cut musclemen who, to Max, looked identical in every way. June Cleaver, an inanely perky, fatuous blonde. His eyes lingered there a moment—she was sexy if you liked Doris Day. Oh, man—Blob for Jesus, a heavyset woman whose hanging arm flesh swung when she rebuked her charges. And the Dragon Lady—a thin, angry-looking woman in her sixties who looked like she could chew nails. Next to her, the Sad Sack, a miserable-looking man in his thirties who stared down into his plate. None of them looked like likely contenders. But then again, none of them should.

After the meal, the Dragon Lady, who Max guessed was the camp director's mother, Mrs. Madison, announced that the meal was not up to camp standards and had not been served with the right submissive spirit. The girls' cabin that had been in charge of preparing it would be physically rebuked. The group of girls who had been ladling out the food bent their faces down. They were led off while the rest of the camp finished the meal in silence.

After dinner came bible study/bible therapy, the only camp activity that allowed boys and girls to speak without expressly asking permission. Everyone shuffled over to find their name on a bible study list to see which group they had been assigned. Max was not in the same group as Kate. He grimaced and then picked up his bible and silently followed his hope buddy to the assigned room.

163

The Case of the Creepy Christian Camp

In his bunk later, after lights out, he assessed the situation: he had to make contact with Kate and let her know he was there to rescue her, and he had to contact his team and give them info to help make a plan. Tonight he would have to risk inciting a beating by testing their actual night security. he had been told he could not leave the cabin past lights out, no matter what. The team was out there somewhere, and if they did their jobs they should be able to smuggle in a cell phone or radio: he couldn't smuggle it in with his luggage. So he had to check under his bunk and in his things often to see if anything had materialized. He hadn't been told to, but he needed to get into the main camp director's office and try to copy the camp files onto a thumb drive; they needed enough info to decide how best to bring down the camp. Max's head spun a little bit, and he realized he was too tired to try anything tonight. It had been a long flight and a lot of information to absorb. Tomorrow. It would all have to wait for tomorrow. He fell asleep into a happy dream where he was James Bond seducing Kate as Pussy Galore.

Chapter 19: Kate

The next day dawned hot and gorgeous, and Max thought he would love the sunshine and the jungle—if he didn't have to wear the ugly and uncomfortable uniform of the camp. When no females were around, boys were allowed to roll up their sleeves, but that didn't help much when you wore dark pants broiling in the heat. For the boys, this was boot camp for Christ: surprise inspections, crew cuts, strenuous exercise, manly chores. They did the camp's grunt work—repairs and "animal husbandry"—but mostly, they built. Cabins, outhouses, barracks—all so that the camp could take more students. The hard work, they were told as they sweated in the humid heat, would make men of them: men men men. Max started to seriously question whether he even wanted to be a man after a few days—but then so were all the other boys.

As the days passed, Max watched and wondered and his temper grew. Most of the counselors were ex-military men, officers, part of the growing presence of evangelicals in the military. They treated the boys to military-style belittlement and verbal abuse. Max became "Maggot." Others suffered the same abuse. he shared his cabin with Worm, Fairy, and Turd. Boys were overworked and not allowed to speak unless spoken to;

the camp seriously courted heatstroke. But then, that was one reason to locate in the Dominican Republic, away from the litigious American courts. Boys who could not keep up, like Max himself, whose strength was not quite that of the cis boys, got extra abuse and scorn. The two things that made it even possible to go on were frequent stops to pray and the personal water bottles. When they stopped working after the first long day and entered the cool chapel, Max felt tears of gratitude come to his eyes and thought, *Heaven!* And then he realized what had just happened and thought, *wow, this is some serious brainwashing bullshit.*

On the third day he got lucky and was assigned to Kate's bible study group. They sat right under the eye of Mrs. Madison, the camp director's mother, but he was next to her, close enough to smell her, to reach out and touch her thigh. He flashed her a cocky grin and prepared to grab his opportunity. He took out a card and palmed it, the same card Kate had given to her brother, waited with it tucked right up his sleeve, and then when Kate placed her bible down on the table he did too. With a deceptively eager spirit, he asked a question about a chapter and verse and leaned forward to look it up, plucking Kate's bible off the table easy as pie, then slipped the card in as Mrs. Madison's eagle eyes momentarily fastened on her own book. He looked at the bible more closely, "realized" his mistake, and swapped bibles back with Kate. As the books changed hands, he whispered, "Hey, booger." Kate froze for a second and took a breath, and then a smile flickered over her mouth and a spark of rebellion flashed in her eyes; Max could see her struggle not to whoop and embrace him. *These shitheads can't take the spunk out of her,* he thought.

He didn't see her again till chapel the next day. Having served three weeks, she was released from the Sinner Wall, and as she climbed down she caught Max's eyes and winked—a quick, completely audacious wink. His heart flipped over, and before he could think it through he pursed his lips in a saucy kiss. Her eyebrows flew wide for a second and then glanced around to see if anyone had caught them, but all was well. Desire and fear pumped adrenaline into his system for a racing, sweaty high.

For the next two days, when they saw each other across the room, when they could, when other eyes weren't on them, there were sly winks, stolen air kisses, tiny shared winces of anger when the more fucked-up crap poured out of the mouths of the ministers. They were careful. with each meeting they risked one brief exchange, but in these lightning-quick communications they shared flirtation, friendship, and fierce camaraderie. A dangerous game played by headstrong teenagers in the face of danger. A reason to keep living.

On day seven, Max found the cell phone. When making his bunk he routinely checked under it, and in the pockets of his luggage. The counselors didn't keep rechecking their luggage: they combed through it on the way in and inspected the mail. How else would anything get smuggled in? The camp was a lonely compound down a bad road. The nearest store might as well be on the furthest moon of Jupiter. The campers were watched like pots that never boiled. Max had wondered how the holy hell anyone was ever going to communicate with him and get him the fuck out, much less Kate. Someone, somewhere among these counselors was a mole. He knew that. But he didn't know who—safer that way. So he waited, and hoped, through a whole week of sweat and bullshit and hellfire.

But on the seventh day—the Lord's day—he opened his toiletry case and found a small package. A phone, a thumb drive, and a few pills with a single word scribbled on a piece of paper: Ambien.

He wasted no time. He used his sleight-of-hand skills and

slipped the Ambien into his cabin counselor's water glass at dinner, and one hour after lights out, he risked punishment by slipping outside and making contact.

The moon was full and white, and as he slipped out of the cabin he took one long breath to appreciate how beautiful it was, how beautiful it could be here, if only…. In the jungle outside the camp, during the daytime, you could see lush beautiful red flowers, vines, luxuriant foliage. Even at night there was birdsong. Inside the camp everything but the largest palm trees had been uprooted: not a flower anywhere. *Probably flowers are whorish*, Max thought. *After all, they're pure sex, right?*

He moved through the night, trusting his camp counselor to remain in an Ambien stupor. He neither hurried nor stuck to the shadows; lessons from Felicity and Isobel told him how to move through the night without attracting attention. These lessons hadn't made much sense at the time, had sounded like hippie bullshit, but now he understood. You convinced the night to accept you; you walked easily and made no frantic sounds. Simple footsteps across the compound wouldn't alert anyone—it could always be some camp counselor using the facilities or patrolling. Scurrying, running, scampering in the bushes would alert the sleeping: someone is trying to sneak. So he walked straight but leisurely through the compound, making for the chicken coop. His heart hammered but his steps were soft and calm. The coop was at the far edge of the compound and would screen him from sight. The rustling and squawking of the chickens would offer a small sound screen for conversation.

Which was terse and to the point. "What's the plan?" he asked.

"How bad is it?" Felicity on the phone, on speaker. He imagined everyone listening.

"Bad. It's unrelenting gender crap and work and work

168

and work. You aren't allowed to talk to anyone or go to the bathroom at the wrong time without a beating. And I mean a beating. You hear the cries sometimes all over the compound. I want to burn this shithole to the ground. Can we do that?"

"I don't know. I think we have to settle for getting Kate out," Sequoia chimed in. "We need info—there's very little of it on this guy, this Victor Madison."

"He's a piece of work, but it's his mother running the show, I think. He doesn't say much, just hunches over his laptop like he's glued to it. But she seems to knows every possible bible quote to justify beating."

"Well, he owns the whole works on paper...if we're going to bring it all down, we need ammo. Can you get into the offices?"

"No, those offices are under guard 24/7. I can't just sneak in there. The only way in is to get punished, and then—well, you're being punished. Not exactly a good time to hack."

"Hmm. You contacted Kate yet?"

"Yeah, she knows why I'm here. She wants out and I don't blame her. Pull us out soon, guys!"

"Okay, we're working on an extraction plan. Hang in there."

Keith leaned in and spoke. "We have a plant inside the camp, but she's a new counselor. Getting this phone to you was hard as shit. I don't know if we can do it again. We need one day to finalize the plans and rehearse the mission. Day after tomorrow. All agreed?"

There was a rumble of agreement at the table. Max's heart sped up.

"Day after tomorrow it is, Max. Ditch this phone—I don't want it on you if you're caught going back to the cabin. Two days from now, at chapel, you throw a stink. Get yourself *and Kate* in trouble. Got it? The only way out is through. Has

169

to be both of you."

"Can do. Till tomorrow."

The connection broke; Max tossed the phone over the compound fence and started back to his cabin. His instincts told him to take the long way around this time and not go through the center of the compound, and Felicity and Isobel had hounded him: OBEY your instincts. They are messages from your liminal senses—something you're hearing, seeing, or smelling is whispering to you, and you listen. He saw the patrolling counselor as he slipped behind the neighboring cabin and then across one open space with no cover and into his own. "HEY!" the word broke the night open like a piñata. He dove into his cabin and into his bunk. A few of his fellow campers sat up awake, looking at him curiously. He signaled for silence, shrugged, and made rapid motions to indicate he had taken a wank break. Smiles cracked across their faces. The door slammed open.

"DID I SEE A CAMPER COME IN HERE JUST NOW?"

One of the big ex-Marine bruisers, a soldier for Christ, barreled in and the campers shook their heads but said nothing. A direct question was *not* the same as permission to speak: most campers had bruises from making that mistake. Mr. Davis, their resident counselor, woke with a tremendous, "WHAT'S HAPPENING HERE?" which came out with the same ferocious roar of an angry officer, a tone of utter authority that the Marine reacted to instinctively.

"Sir, I thought I saw a camper sneak in here just now!"

"Nonsense! I have been awake the whole time! No one has made a peep in here since lights out."

"Are you SURE, sir?"

Max held his breath. Was Davis lying for him? Was he the plant? He couldn't be—he was just too smarmy and repulsive.

"Of course I'm sure!" Davis yelled. "Get out of here and let us sleep!"

The Marine retreated and the boys waited in the cabin, as confused as Max—waited to see if Max was truly going to escape his wrath.

Mr. Davis got up out of bed and said, "God! Sometimes gorillas have no sense of smell! Boys, lock up your shoes before you sleep!"

He turned around twice, got back into bed, and fell immediately, entirely asleep.

Max said, "I will, sir!" Thinking, *Oh, Ambien, I love love love you.* And the boys began to laugh with relief, holding hands over head and muffling their laughter with the pillow, and one by one, signaling to Max a thumbs-up. They had done it! A small victory against the camp! Max put his hands behind his head and issued a small, low whistle of relief.

He woke the next morning with butterflies swarming in his stomach. He had gotten through this long, hard day by fantasizing about kissing his damsel in distress—but now he had to rescue her first.

Chapter 20: Dinner and a Discovery

T he night before Rescue, dinner was grim. Salisbury steak, turgid and grey, wallowed in a congealing pool of slightly browner grey. The steak was just barely soft enough to eat with a spoon, requiring a dig of pressure with each bite. Max fantasized about the delicious spread and tropical drinks that Leo would undoubtedly have waiting after the rescue and only took a token bite. Nausea was getting to him. Across the room he caught sight of red welts on Kate's hands. A rush of outrage intensified his nausea at the thought of them laying hands on her in "punishment." The salt taste of imminent sick filled his mouth and he looked away quickly, breathed deeply, and stared with great intensity at his "steak."

When dinner drew to a close, he walked over to check out his bible therapy assignment, hoping he could at least wink at Kate to keep her spirits up, but no. As he turned to find his group, he saw Mrs. Madison pull Miss Westlock, the sexy Doris Day counselor, aside and make an announcement: "Miss Westlock's group will merge with Mr. Buchman's tonight."

Because Max was watching, he saw the twitch of a muscle, a flash of fear on Miss Westlock's face before she replaced it with perky compliance. He knew he had found their mole.

And she was in trouble. Inwardly, he whistled. June Cleaver herself, Miss Pink Sprinkles, who always stressed a woman's downright *joy* in submission—that was their mole? She was good. Very good. How had she given herself away?

Chapter 21: Eve's Story

My Jesus doesn't give a fuck if I use bad language. That's something I'm sure of. That's my constant.

I was raised by people who had better things to do, and by the people they hired. When I was real little it was Rosita. I loved Rosita; she was cranky but kind, and she laid down the law with me.

But my parents? I guess I should have talked about them first. Okay, so…my parents. They were Hollywood hangers-on. My dad produced bad movies that had chainsaws or whatnot and big-breasted "teenage" girls. He had a lot of money. He started with a lot of money that his dad made in…office supplies? Pickles? Used cars? No one really ever talked to me about my grandfather, and he died of a heart attack before I was born. My dad was fifty when I came around; my mom was a big-breasted "teenage" girl. He'd had plenty of these girls before and he had plenty after, so I'm not sure what made my mom special, exactly. She was nice enough, and she played with me when I was really small, but realistically, she was a materialistic airhead. Maybe that's what he liked about her, actually. But those aren't rare traits in Hollywood.

Dad loved me in a bring-me-out-at-parties-and-brag-about-me kind of way, but he was…gross. He was drunk a lot. Used to say disgusting things like, "She's gonna get her mother's tits, and then she'll be unstoppable!" Well, he was half right; I did get those tits.

They threw parties, my mom and dad. Big Hollywood place, pool, people doing coke and whatever else was trendy at the time. A lot of ecstasy for a while. Which meant I did all the club drugs too—they didn't exactly keep an eye on me. But that was when I was a teenager. When I was really young I had Rosita, who kept me in my room during the parties, but even then I sometimes made a break for it and ran down to see all the pretty ladies and the craziness. I didn't know why I couldn't have fun too. Why was fun just for grownups? Why did they get all the brownies? Once when I told Rosita I was going to the bathroom I ran downstairs and grabbed a brownie off a tray and ate it. That was the first time I got high. I must have been seven.

When Rosita saw the chocolate around my mouth, she looked like she was going to pop something. She grabbed me and pulled me close and took a deep whiff of my breath, then burst into this long, blistering, passionate hate stream punctuated with "*Estupido! Estupido!*" She wasn't mad at me though, just my parents. She hugged me tight and ranted in Spanish, which I had gotten to speak pretty well by then. But I didn't understand why she was so mad at *them*—they didn't give me the brownie! I should have been the one in trouble! But then I started to feel it, and she told me, "*Hija*, you're going to feel strange for a while, but don't worry. You'll be okay."

Then she plunked me down with a tray full of snacks and let me watch cartoons until I got sleepy. I remember laughing and laughing because *Scooby Doo* suddenly made so much more *sense*. The whole thing was so much fun—fun the grownups got to have and I didn't!

175

The Case of the Creepy Christian Camp

Rosita got fired because of the brownie incident. Sort of. She confronted my parents about having that kind of stuff out where a kid could grab it, and they told her she was irresponsible for letting me out of her control. She yelled at them in Spanish. My mother got mad and told her, "No wetback illiterate is going to tell me how to raise my own daughter!" which was funny because my mother moved her lips when she read and Rosita had a bookcase full of stuff. The books were all in Spanish, which I think my parents thought of as monkey chatter. Rosita was much smarter than my mom, I knew even then. My dad knew this was trouble, but by then Rosita had stormed upstairs to pack and it was all over. I cried; Rosita cried; Dad shrugged; Mom went shopping.

After that my dad started hiring mostly wanna-be actress-models that seemed more like big sisters than grownups, and they didn't want to be stuck upstairs watching *The Little Mermaid* any more than I did. One of them warned me not to go down to the party and then snuck off herself: I went down ten minutes later and hung around drinking the half-empty cocktails people left all over the place. She got fired when my mother caught me puking in the pool. Another got fired when my mom caught her fucking my dad on their bed; Mom was supposed to be out having her mani-pedi. And so on. I knew about that because my mother yelled it at the top of her lungs while I was standing and staring ten feet away. If I'm not fucked up totally beyond redemption, believe me, it's because of Rosita.

She's also how I got to know Jesus. Rosita had a crucifix hanging up over her bed and made me pray at night to Jesus to give me strength and help me do well at school; she sometimes muttered something about giving me the strength to not turn out like my parents. She said it in Spanish, but I understood Spanish pretty well. I was working up the nerve to speak it back to her when she got fired. I thought of Jesus like sort of a Santa who could only give you stuff like strength and wisdom. I once prayed to him for some toy or other, but Rosita set me straight—"Jesus won't give you no dollies! He has better things to do!"

Ashley and Stephanie and Monica and Tiffany did not care about Jesus, and my mom told me how glad she was that they didn't have to deal with Rosita's "Jesus crap" anymore, so Jesus and I parted ways for a while, and I was alone. And then came Michael.

I met him at an acting camp my parents sent me to in the mountains so they could get me out of their hair. I went every summer. I had friends there, and friends at school, giggling girls who were lots of fun. Then one day at camp I was forced to be hiking buddies with the new guy, Michael, because I was fighting with my friend Libby, who had declared some other girl her new best friend. I got mad and yelled at her, and the camp counselors separated us and put me with the new guy. I was twelve. He was GORGEOUS. Melting brown eyes and black hair that fell in his eyes, and all of thirteen years old.

We didn't talk, me with my little nose out of joint and in the air. Then he said something rude to me, and I said something rude to him, and then he said something rude but hilarious and after that all I remember was a blur of laughter. And he became my new best friend. First to piss off Libby and then simply because he was Michael. I fell deeply, deeply in love with him—dizzying twelve-year-old love. He was my first kiss. We were so young. I didn't even realize, I didn't recognize that he stiffened a little bit, and leaned away for a moment, or I did but I thought it was just because he was a boy and that's what boys did maybe. Just like the girls used to run and kiss the boys when we were eight years old and they would shriek and run away.

177

The Case of the Creepy Christian Camp

Officially he was my boyfriend, but he always avoided being alone with me. Libby started hanging out with us too and batting her eyes at him and trying to steal him from me, which caused some big fights but he told me once that she was a dumb cow, so I shouldn't worry about it. It surprised me when I realized he was right: Libby was dumb. She was not as smart as me. That had never occurred to me before. That was the first time *anyone* told me I could be smart or wanted me to be smart. But Michael was the real smart one, super-smart in all ways: creative, good at school, funny, observant. All the girls loved him. He only hung out with girls though.

So you see where this is going, of course. Michael was gay. But no one saw it because he had me as a girlfriend and all the girls falling in love with him all the time. And he was athletic. He ran track and won races.

He turned out not to live too far from me, and pretty soon I was deemed old enough not to have a minder. Michael would come over and we would rove around my parents' parties together, dodging to keep out of their sight when we were little, stealing sips of booze, getting bombed, then running upstairs to watch silly movies and laughing and laughing. I laughed more with Michael than I ever have again in my whole life. Sometimes my girlfriends would come over too, and we would all have a slumber party, but Michael always had to go home at midnight. He was really good at covering up his breath with peppermint and pretending to his mom that he was just tired. His mom was "uptight," he told me.

When we were fourteen and fifteen we invented the lying game. That was where we went through the party and told people ridiculous stories about ourselves. Our favorite was that we had just come to California and were starring in an upcoming show about a brother and sister who used their psychic power to communicate with animals to solve crimes. Michael did

178

dogs and I did cats, of course. We could never really pass for siblings but no one cared—that wouldn't matter to TV execs anyway. That was also about when my parents gave up on chasing us out of the party. That's how old we were when I caught Michael kissing some hot young actor in a dark corner. I knew by then, and we had long since just stopped pretending that he was my boyfriend, but we had never said it out loud between us. So it was a shock to see him acting on it. It made it real. And it made me think it was time for me to "grow up" too. By which I meant graduate from alcohol and pot to a line of coke here and there, and to let guys feel me up. I had been groped plenty but always ran away when it happened before. But if Michael was doing it....

So you can guess what kind of path I was on: negligent parents, tons of access to booze and drugs, lots of morally dubious people around. I got deflowered in the pool house by a D-list movie star when I was sixteen, shortly after catching Michael kissing that guy. I was drunk; the actor was great looking and dumb as a brick; it was fast and painful. I'm lucky I didn't get pregnant.

Then—right before my seventeenth birthday—Michael disappeared. I called him one day, and his parents told me he ran away. I shouldn't bother to look for him, and it was all my fault for exposing him to my sick Hollywood lifestyle. My head swam, and I didn't know what to do. This wasn't supposed to happen. Michael and I were supposed to go to college together. He encouraged me to work hard in school despite the partying, just so we could go away to the same college and away from our awful parents. Michael was supposed to be a lawyer, and I was going to be an interior designer. But now Michael was gone. I didn't even know what really happened, but his parents must have found out he was gay, and he was gone.

That accelerated my slide into hell. I got defiant and slept

179

around and did drugs. When it was time to go to college I told my parents I wanted to "be an actress," and moved out with some other slutty young starlets to Melrose, where we partied. We kind of partied for a living. You can do that in LA if you're hot, and I was hot, let me tell you. I never had any trouble, even in Hollywood. I got some work as an actress too here and there—I had connections from my parents. I had no talent whatsoever, but I looked great in a bikini, blonde and tan and big titted, and I was loose and fuckable. Rock videos, small bit parts as arm candy, a little modeling. My parents subsidized. Believe it or not, they were *proud* of me. I couldn't act my way out of a paper bag, and I never was serious about it. mostly I just wanted to party. Oh, yeah, *and* I was a Playboy Playmate—my dad was REALLY proud of that. Which was very disturbing. I've been trying to forget about that. Ugh, it kind of makes me sick now. Basically I was living a life of quasi-prostitution. I would have slapped anyone silly who said so, but that's what it was.

And eventually, in that Hollywood scene, I ran back into Michael. He was partying and scraping by on his looks, just like I was. He told me his story: he ran away, lived by selling himself, got taken in for a while by some rich guy, then moved into this house where some real sleazeball gave underage boys speed and then filmed gay porn.

The next time I saw him, I was 21 and he was 22. We fell into each other's arms and cried and cried, then stayed up all night doing coke and telling each other everything. He didn't look so great. Five years of that kind of lifestyle will tell on anyone, and he had been living harder than me. A lot of stuff I had to drag out of him and I'm afraid I was more judgmental than I should have been. I was young and angry with him for leaving me. By morning we had had a lot of coke and got into a fight. He called me a dumb bimbo. I called him a whore.

He called me a stupid fucking useless big-titted cunt. He said he ran away so it was no wonder he never went to college and didn't get to live his dream, but I had no excuse at all. I yelled at him that he fucking LEFT me, he left me, and why would I do it without him? He was crying. He ran off. That was the last time I saw him alive. I don't even really know what happened to him, just the next time I ran into this guy we both knew, he told me Michael had died about a week after I saw him. I asked him how he died and he shrugged: drugs? Suicide? Something like that. "Who cares about that fag?" he said.

I was drunk and coked up, as per usual. I punched him. Then I punched him again, and again. I broke his nose, and they had to pull me off of him. So he called the cops and pressed charges. Asshole. I already had a DUI and a drunk and disorderly on my record so the cops said it was rehab for me, and off I went. And that's where I met Jesus again.

I know that sounds corny to a lot of people. If you told me Jesus would be that real to me when I was nineteen I would have laughed, then done a line of coke, then laughed a lot more. I mean, you know the story: I went to rehab. I saw the light. God called my name. I couldn't relate to a higher power of pure abstraction, and I saw, I did see, that I needed help. I thought about Michael, and I cried and cried and cried some more. And the people were great. I think what I liked best about them was that they all told me they had betrayed loved ones. They were terrible parents, terrible husbands and wives. And I thought of Michael and thought he was the only one in my life who had really loved me and didn't see me as tits and ass. Michael didn't give a damn about my tits or my ass. Even my parents just saw me, kind of vaguely, as good looking, and that's all that really mattered to them.

An old-timer came and talked to us, and she was fired up about the Lord. She was still sad, still sorry about the harm she had done, but she knew she was forgiven. I wanted that. I wanted to feel forgiven. And a higher power couldn't forgive me, so then I remembered Rosita and how she told me when I was little and I was naughty, that Jesus would forgive me if I was sorry. I *was* sorry, so I sat down one day in rehab under a tree and asked Jesus if he would forgive me…and he answered. We've been talking ever since. He forgave me. But he said I had to do whatever I could to save all the other Michaels who are out there, scared and suffering with nowhere to go.

I moved to the Bay Area right after that. Someone I was in rehab with had family up there and said they would take us in for a while. I needed to get out of LA and away from the coke whores and the bad boys. I came to love my new home. I got a job somewhere as a receptionist and started going to college and going to meetings and joined the Unitarian church. I also started working for every charity and nonprofit I could find that worked with gay youth, and that's how I met Sequoia, and we got to be friends. I told her about Michael, and she told me about her brother. And one day we were laughing and arguing about Jesus—she says faith is a way to inoculate yourself against thinking! I said thinking never got me anywhere good. She snorted and said I had never really tried it. Oh we tore each other to shreds and I loved her anyway, and she loved me. You can feel the love in her, and Jesus is love, so that's all right by me. My Jesus doesn't give a hoot about whether you believe in him or praise him because he's not vain. He just wants us to love each other.

So were in the middle of all this and she got a funny look on her face and said, "You know, we could maybe use someone like you." And she told me what they were up to.

It's hard. I won't say it's not hard. And I had to go through this whole "born again" conversion, and I lead a double life and listen to people say hateful stuff that turns my stomach. But I can do it. I do it because what I have in common with those people is we all love Jesus. I think so, anyway. They love someone named Jesus, but I'm not always sure we're talking about the same savior. At any rate, I can sing songs with them and break bread with them and worship with them, even though I don't agree with them. And thanks to the way I grew up, I've had a *lot* of practice lying. I thought I'd left my lying days behind me, but I talked to Jesus, and he says I'm lying for him now, so we're good. I know that I have done some good for the Michaels of the world, and I'm at peace.

Chapter 22: Eve Is Tested

M rs. Madison led the way out of the cafeteria and into her office. Other than the chapel, this was the single most luxurious place in camp: a bower of soft pink and tasteful blues, decorated with lush, framed landscape prints with graceful calligraphy that proclaimed the eternal power of Christ. The director motioned Eve to a chair across from a rosewood desk and leaned back, steepling her fingers in front of her as she gazed. In the flowery femininity of the room her eyes had the incongruous menace of a snake. Eve shuddered inwardly, prayed to Christ for protection, and smiled her widest and most fatuous smile.

"I'm so glad to have a chance to tell you just how wonderful I think this camp is and what tremendous work you are doing here. It's inspirational!" she gushed and bubbled. "You bring troubled children into the protection of the Lord! I can't imagine more important work!" She forced exclamation points to her sentences in her mind, reading from her internal script.

"That's so nice to hear, my dear," Mrs. Madison said. She did not smile. Her eyes did not waver in their cold, unblinking malice. "You know, when you first applied for this position, I had...doubts...about you. Your sins were considerable. Not to mince words: you were once a strumpet, lost on the path to hell."

"Yes," said Eve. She looked downward with modesty, paused, and produced a tear by thinking hard about the abuse the children suffered. She raised her eyes back to Mrs. Madison's and said, "I don't blame you. I was a terrible sinner, and at first I doubted that even Jesus would forgive me. But ours is a merciful and loving savior."

"Yes, of course," Mrs. Madison said coldly, without much conviction. "But sometimes to lead children to his path...unconventional forms of mercy must be applied. As Jesus said, 'I come not to bring the peace but the sword.'"

A chill rocked Eve, and she restrained a shudder but gave Mrs. Madison her wide-eyed-kitten look. "I'm not sure I understand," she said.

"Sometimes we need to show children the error of their ways...forcefully."

"Yes, of course! I understand *that*."

"But you are such a gentle creature, dear," she smiled a smile more frightening than any scowl. "Do you really understand? Would you be willing to wield the sword in the cause of righteousness? I think it is time to see how deep your commitment to these poor, unfortunate children really goes."

Eve's heart started beating violently. She was suspected. She knew it. There would be a test of her loyalty. Her prayer turned to a prayer for strength.

"Come with me, my dear," Mrs. Madison rose and led her to another small cabin. The one she had never been in, the place of screams.

A greater contrast between the carpeted soft pastel comfort of Mrs. Madison's office and the punishment hut could not be imagined. The floor was concrete and bare, and there were no windows. The hut was lit by a bare bulb hanging from the ceiling, a single chair in the middle of the room. Paddles and rods and implements of punishment hung from hooks on the walls. And on a small table sat an innocuous-looking box, in a white case, with a dial. Eve felt deep foreboding and realized her palms were damp with sweat and her heart was racing.

As she took in the room, one of the burly military guys burst in, dragging a camper behind him, a camper with a lavender bracelet, and pushed him down into the chair. The fear and misery on the kid's face was palpable.

"This is Michael," said Mrs. Madison. Eve's stomach lurched. *His name would be Michael. Did they know?* And looking at the box, she saw the electrodes, saw the guard forcing the boy into the chair, saw the camper's terror, and knew she had already lost.

"Come here, my dear," Mrs. Madison said. She motioned her to stand by the dial. Michael shook with terror, and the guard forced him into a chair, clamping the electrodes to his hands and feet with brisk impersonal motions.

"This camper's sins are egregious," she said. "He was caught *in bed* with another boy; that's why his parents sent him here. And he has not repented."

"I did! I do! I repent! I won't do it again!" The camper babbled, and tears ran down his face. His strapped in hands couldn't wipe them away.

"At this point, we know that that is not enough." Mrs. Madison said. "We aren't punishing you, dear, we are teaching your mind to hate your sin." She said this with the brisk tones of a nurse. If the nurse were Nurse Ratched.

She reached over and took a magazine from behind the torture device, a magazine called *Adult*, with a well-muscled topless man glistening and staring seductively off the cover. Michael averted his eyes.

"Look at it," said Mrs. Madison in a steely voice. His eyes reluctantly went to the magazine and as they did, Mrs. Madison turned the dial. He screamed and his body arched, and the smell of burning flesh filled the air. Eve averted her eyes now, unable to take in the sight. Mrs. Madison turned the dial back, and the sounds of the boy's racking sobs filled the air.

"That was mercy," she said, and Eve retched uncontrollably, making for the door of the cabin.

The guard grabbed her and brought her back.

"Now you," said Mrs. Madison, and the guard forced her hand on the dial. Eve snatched it away.

"The Lord doesn't want this," she said, her own tears rising. "Jesus doesn't want children tortured. He doesn't, he doesn't," she said.

"I see," said Mrs. Madison. "That's what I thought. You are weak and a sinner."

She reached for the dial herself and turned it. Michael screamed again, and when the dial was returned to normal he passed out, able to take no more.

"Take him out of here," she said to the guard. He hefted the slender boy to his shoulder, and Eve saw how small he was, this boy. Probably fourteen years old. She wanted to pass out herself and tried to rush out of the cabin as the guard opened the door, but he shoved her back easily with one hand. She stumbled, falling to her knees, which scraped on the bare floor.

"No, my dear. I think you need some time here to consider. Think hard on mercy, and the kindness we do by killing the sin inside the sinner. And perhaps later, we will burn your sins out too. For we are, after all," she smiled her cold smile, "merciful."

And they left, with Eve still on the floor, sobbing and breathing in the smell of her own sick mingled with the char of flesh that lingered in the air. She retched again miserably and then began a beseeching prayer to Jesus to save her, somehow, anyhow, to save her from her fate.

Chapter 23: The Rescue

The Skipper

Keith sits in front of Felicity and Isobel and goes over the plan one last time. The map of the compound drawn and smuggled out by Eve looked like it was drawn by a drunken toddler and was giving him a headache. He points out the routes, goes over the variables.

"More than any other mission, we're flying by the seat of our pants here. We have no way of syncing up the times with Max, and that means if he goes too early he could get beaten bad before we get in, and if he goes too late we could be fighting ex-military Christ drones for God knows how long before he shows up. It's a bad plan, compadres, but it's the best we could do. You ready?"

Felicity looks up and grins: Keith is grateful that fear is unknown to her and adrenalin her drug of choice. He wishes he had the spitfire's utter self-confidence, but he knows a cooler head is necessary for a leader. Isobel looks a little uncertain but Felicity grabs her hand and smiles at her. And she smiles back. Keith relaxes a little; his team is solid. They will win. They absolutely have to win.

Before he leaves the room, he heaves a deep sigh, picks

up a gun, and straps it to his ankle. And hopes he won't need to use it.

Gilligan

The drive there isn't a problem. The roads are bumpy, but Beto manages them, swerving to cross the ruts rather than sink into them. For all his fuckups, the driving at least has *never* been the problem. But his heart is pounding, and he seriously regrets for a moment ever getting involved in these crazy schemes. He loves cars; he loves drag; he loves Keith. But suicidal trips to the jungle to rescue teenagers from nutballs? It's a lot to ask of a girl. Still. He only has to wait with the car, out of sight around a corner, with a taser and tunes, and then haul ass back. And, yeah, he loves being one of this group. A family. A real fucking family.

Mary Ann

Felicity feels badly sometimes that she loves it so much: the danger, the fighting, the jungle, the cause. But would she be better at it if she hated it? She smiles to herself in anticipation. She knows she is going to kick *so much* ass. They drive up and park out of sight and hack and scramble through the jungle to the fence. They make Felicity go last through the jungle. She resents it, but sees the logic: she's small, and they can clear a path for her better than she can for them. Keith goes first, machete in hand, and Isobel after him. When they get there they scout along the wire fence until they find the place where the cabins have no windows to the back. Keith tosses the machete down, grabs a tool from his belt, and reaches up and cuts through the top of the fence with wire cutters, peeling the metal back with his bare hands. He turns to the women to help them over but they wave him off. Isobel hoists herself over the

189

fence with the sinuous grace that once made her a pole dancer extraordinaire and Keith smiles, shakes his head, and leaps over after her, all muscle and power. Felicity scrambles up like a cat and leaps down, but Isobel catches her and slides her down against her body. Felicity scowls; she hates help, but when Isobel holds the hug just a moment longer she squeezes her tight. For courage, for luck, for love.

The Professor

Chapel. that's the time. Kate's back up on the sinner table. As far as Max could tell, her crime is that no matter what she does or how she dresses, she is still the prettiest girl here, and the counselors—sour nasty bags—have labeled her a temptress. No matter. This is the night. Max shakes off his anger, walks by her, and whispers up: "Follow my lead tonight."

Kate looks down and her face lights up. Max looks around—they can't afford to be seen communicating. Not yet. He needs to be very, very bad and can't settle for a slap on the wrist. He shakes his head slightly, and she schools her face, then he takes his place in the chapel and sits back to hear the theme of today's sermon.

It could not have been more perfect. There's a guest speaker, and he launches into his topic: Why women should not be allowed to teach or preach. A theme dear to the heart of Victor Madison—or at least his mother, who manages to believe this heart and soul, then teaches it and preaches it whenever possible. Not for the first time, Max muses that faith seems to prevent the capacity to see irony.

"Women may imagine that they have the blessing of the LARD to speak because they feel the truth of his words," orates the smarmy bald man in a faint Southern accent, hitting the word LARD with a punch. Max imagines a giant tub of lard bathed in a lambent halo, and smiles. "But when they preach too publicly they bring terrible consequences. Look at Judy Brown, in prison for murder. Look how Becky Fischer had to back down and stop running her camp after her enormous hubris. She thought she was chosen by God and God brought disgrace upon her. And this will always happen to those who pretend they love the LARD while ignoring his commandments about the proper place of women." Mrs. Madison smiles and nods, eyes shining.

Max is waiting. He can taste it, his moment, it's coming.

"But that isn't the *real* problem, a few women getting their punishment from God for their sin in going against the bible's law and daring to preach to men. No, the reason for the rule in the first place, and why I am so glad to see this camp and the great work that it does, the real reason for women not to speak in public, is that this unlawful abrogation, this unholy theft of male authority, done without the blessing of the LARD, undermines the sacred distinction between male and female, and actually CAUSES, yes CAUSES, homosexuality. Yes, my friends, women speaking publicly defies the natural order, and men and women who don't know their correct places also no longer know their correct partners. And God has brought upon us a terrible punishment for this. These changes in the weather, that the godless think is caused by 'science'—the word spoken with scathing contempt—this is God's way of telling he will NOT tolerate the lawless godless ways of sin...."

"NOW WAIT A MINUTE!" Max yells, leaping to his feet. The silence of shock rocks the room. "If I know one thing in this world, it's that just because I'm transgender, that does NOT mean that I'm confused! YOU are the ones who are confused! Because what you just said right there, that is BULLSHIT! THAT! IS SOME BULLSHIT!!! RIGHT THERE!" He opens his throat to let out all his anger, screaming into the quiet.

Before he's done they run up to him to haul him to punishment, and he sees Kate whoop, sees her grin, and then yell: "Let go of him, you MOTHERFUCKING ASSWIPES!" She jumps down from the table, still holding the SINNERS banner, which the other startled "sinners" drop. She grabs it and runs to Max, reaching him a hair before the military guards, turning to tangle them in the banner, while she grabs Max and kisses him. A lone voice in the room cheers, but the rest sit in shock as Max grabs Kate's hand and pulls her into a run.

"Where are we going?" Kate gasps.

"Follow me," Max says. No breath to say more. It will make everything harder if they get caught.

Ginger

They're waiting behind a cabin and listening. There are birds in the jungle. Their song is strange, cheerful, but a little eerie. Isobel digs her fingers into the palms of her hands. She is, maybe a little, freaking out. They have never done anything quite like this. She looks at Felicity, who smiles reassuringly back.

A loud whoop rings out across the compound. It's time. Isobel heads out from behind the hut to face her fate.

Gilligan

Being left behind in the car is never easy but at least here, pulled over on a jungle road, he can play music. He hits the CD On button and promptly bursts out into profanity as the strains of "Wasted Away Again in Margaritaville" fills the SUV: "SHIT! Those fucking shitheads! Those stone cold mother fucking asshole dykes! I am going to *bitchslap* them into next Tuesday!"

They had replaced his dance mix. They had played pranks before. They thought that shit was funny, but they also thought he shouldn't be listening to music while waiting. Like he should just sit and freak and chew his nails. *No*, bitches, no. But this time he had anticipated their games. He fishes out the iPod and ear buds he has hidden under the seat and sits back to listen.

Another fuckup is in the making.

The Skipper

Max and the girl come screaming across the compound ten minutes after they arrived. They timed it well. *Thanks, Eve: your info on timing was better than your map.* He hates the need to use big dramatic tactics, but getting contact between Kate and Max was nigh impossible, and only in pell-mell confusion was it possible to run out and toward the fence. The team emerges as they hear the whooping to protect and guide the escapees, but he already sees his worst fear: the guards chasing the runaways are being joined by another guard racing to intercept. Action time.

He nods to the girls, and they spring into action. Three against three are not great odds when the guards are big and military trained. He prays, smiles at the irony of that, and surveys the situation. Here come the rescuees.

A flying and unexpected tackle from Keith takes down the intercepting guard, freeing the path of the runners, while Felicity and Isobel rush out calling to the guards to stop, that they need help. The guards, steeped in a sexist culture that underestimates women first and last, stop dead while the girls run up and waste no time: low, round kicks to the knees to give them an immediate advantage. The guards lose their footing, but before Felicity and Isobel can press their advantage they roar back onto their feet with animal bellows and charge.

193

Keith, on the ground and struggling with a brutally large opponent, yells for Max and Kate to get to the fence, but Max shakes his head on the run and books for the office, Kate following in his wake.

"Our mole! She's caught!" he yells to Keith as he passes. "We need to get to her and I don't know how or where! One of those huts, I think!" He gestures to the punishment huts, grim and windowless, flanking the office.

"Shit!" Keith says, and pulls himself up, smashing his fist down twice into the guard's face before leaping up to follow Max.

"Keep them busy! We have problems!" he yells over his shoulder to Felicity and Isobel. The guard with the now bloody face groans from the ground but starts to push himself shakily up as Keith runs.

"MAX! Stay with me!"

But as Keith turns to the huts Max is already veering off, making for the office. Keith grunts in frustration, runs to the first hut, inspects the lock and takes the gun out of its holster, smashing the lock of the first door he finds. He's thankful he brought it and even more thankful he's not shooting it.

Mary Ann

At first the guards go down, easy as pie. But they are big and tough and used to taking hits and they rise, leaving the girls battling fiercely to cover the rear escape. They hear Keith's cry that there's trouble and dig in, fight harder, unable even to look up to see what's happening or where the runners are until they see over their opponents' shoulders Max and Kate running back toward the chapel, a fresh guard on their tail, joined by the bloody and bruised behemoth. *Oh, oh, oh shit,* thinks Felicity. Four guards to fight, and Keith temporarily out of the fray.

The bloody guard is slow, though, and Felicity gathers herself for a burst of speed and power that sweeps a leg out to trip the running guard before landing with a satisfying crack on the already injured knee. She hopes it's broken, but it's futile. This fighter has an appetite for pain and keeps coming, and she battles on.

Mr. Howell and Lovey

Sequoia paces. "You're always so DAMN calm," she snaps at Leo.

He takes a deep drink of something fresh and fruity and served in a coconut. "And does it help one bit to chew on your lips and worry yourself into a stew?"

"No, but…how can I not worry?" She plops down into a deck chair, not seeing the blue ocean or the bluer sky in front of her.

"I know this is going to sound like the opposite of everything we do, my love," he said, sitting beside her and putting a drink in her hand. "But have faith. Our team is fierce and strong and smart. They have never failed. And that's the most important part of love I think. I believe in them. Like I believe in you."

She smiles at him gratefully. "I love you, you know."

"Then drink your drink, and have faith."

The Professor

Kate and Max hightail it back to the chapel with only a glimmer of a plan. Max feels the tugs of flagging energy, but digs into his fear and adrenalin, glad that Kate seems unflagging, even whooping from time to time with sheer pleasure at being, finally, free. As they veer away from the new guard on their path, Max sees the kids spilling out of chapel, gathering in front to watch the fight, their mouths agape as the terrifying omnipotent guards get kicked and pummeled—by *girls*. The counselors shout, and the Dragon Lady screams at the kids to go back into the chapel and behave themselves, but none do. They give a ragged cheer as Felicity lands her double-whammy kick, and Max feels the rush of inspiration. He runs closer to the chapel, dodging away from a grasping staff member and weaving back close to the kids he had pegged as most rebellious, and sure enough a foot comes out and sends the guard sailing, landing and skidding from his momentum as Max throws his head back and makes a large swooping turn and heads back, back to the office.

Ginger

The fight is going so damn well until that cockfuck guard, the one Max tricks into the dust, gets back to his feet with a roar and starts off after them again. He doesn't look where he's going. He barrels into Felicity from the back and bears her down, the other guard piling on. Isobel sees Felicity falling, her leg twisting underneath her as she falls; Isobel feels something pop and snap in her chest, fizzle in her head, and after that everything is a blur of red-hot motion. Isobel's fighting had been competent and smart before that, but with Felicity under threat she becomes a Valkyrie, Xena, Wonder Woman, and Kali combined. The previous goal, to tie the guards up and make escape possible, fades away under the desire to maim and tear, kill and destroy. She makes an unearthly cry and jumps the guards with legs flying and fists of steel. Five minutes later, all assailants are down, one clutching his lower abdomen, stain spreading on his pants—she kicked straight for the bladder and piss exploded out of him. Guard two spits out a tooth, while the third lies back groaning. Isobel reaches for Felicity's hand and they run, while Felicity gives a low whistle.

"Daaaaamn, girl. That was smoking, smoking hot." Isobel smiles as they run.

Gilligan

"If you like it then you should have put a RING on it! If you like then you should have put a RING on it. Whuh uh oh uh uh oh oh." He taps the taser he carries—just in case— against the steering wheel in time to the music.

The Skipper

Keith hears the swell of cheers as the campers trip the guards and wonders what the hell is happening and whose side the campers might be on: Are we winning? Or are we *seriously* fucked? But he has to do the job in front him: the second hut looms up and, gun already out, he clips the lock off with a single swift move.

Eve lies huddled in a corner. She's shaking and looks at him wild-eyed. She has never met him. He summons everything Isobel has ever taught him about calming down scared and mistreated people and hopes a big black man won't freak the woman out. He walks over to her and crouches right down. Hears Isobel's voice inside him: *Get on her level. Don't loom. Deep breaths and low voices.*

"Eve?" he whispers softly. She looks at him with terror, but manages to focus, close her eyes, and nod.

"Okay, honey. I'm the Skipper—you know what I mean?"

She takes a ragged breath and nods. She knows the code names, none of the real names. Better that way.

197

The Case of the Creepy Christian Camp

"Okay, so I'm getting you out of here. Okay? And I'm going to carry you, because you're shaky and we need to get out of here fast. So I'm going to pick you up. Are you ready for that?" She nods again, and he pulls her limp weight up.

He hoists her over his shoulder; she's nothing, a sack of feathers, but he won't be able to fight carrying her.

He swears and runs out the door.

The Professor

Max knows it isn't in the plan but he thinks *fuck the plan, fuck it fuck it,* because just maybe if he dodges and weaves and runs like hell, just maybe, maybe…and he runs into the office, Kate at his heels, to see the director himself, nervous, hunched over his laptop, listening to the sounds outside the hut. Max dives for his precious booty—the laptop, never out of Mr. Madison's reach, and he grabs it out of the director's astonished grasp. As Max turns to run, Madison tackles him and he goes down with a grunt, but throws the laptop to Kate as he falls, yelling, "RUN! RUN! RUN!"

Kate snatches it from the air and turns as Max twists and writhes and hits one sharp punch to the neck, and with one more heroic twist he is scrambling backward and running running running again, seeing Keith with Eve and booking for the fence.

Victor Madison

He emerges from his hut shaking and desperate—one minute too late to see them leap for the fence. His brain whirls. There is only one road out, one way to get any vehicle out. Could he be wrong? Could there be another way? Helicopter? No, no, he would have heard that. No, the road. They have to cut through the jungle but he…he runs toward the gates flat out. Desperation gives him wings.

He slams around a bend and the car looms up; he hears running feet behind him. What is he thinking? That he would fight them? He can't fight them. But maybe, just maybe. He puts on a last burst of speed. He needs leverage. He needs the car.

He throws himself at the closest door, passenger side, noticing a half second too late that he is not alone. A piercing shriek fills his ears, and the world goes black. His last thought was: *I really should have realized they would have a driver.*

The Skipper

And now they turn the bend and they're here, all of them, piling in, Isobel hauling Felicity in as they collapse into the seat and Max and Kate whooping like the children they are and Keith lowering Eve off his shoulder. She gives a huge shuddering sound of relief as the SUV tears off over bad roads, no time for anything but to go go GO. The SUV bounces and shakes, but roars over bad roads like a champ. They are okay. Keith takes a deep breath. They are going to be okay. No one, but no one, can outdrive his little buddy. But as a groan sounds from the front seat, he yells, "SHIT! What the fuck?!"

"*NO ME HACE CULPA DE MI*! Don't yell at me, Papi," Beto screams as he slams and cuts across the ruts.

Keith looks into the front seat, sees the director limp and twitching there, and realizes their trouble is very far from over.

Chapter 24: Beach Party

Victor Madison came back to consciousness in one confused rush, growling, "WHHAAAT?" and then slumped into his seat. Complete panic surged through him; he looked wildly around the car. No one seemed angry or scared or desperate. It was oddly comforting. An Asian woman leaned over and peered into his face; then she smiled.

"First off, you're okay, everything is okay. I'm Mary Ann, and *no one* is going to hurt you," she said. Her tones were crisp and competent. He found that he believed her.

"What the—what happened...HEY!" he yelled as memory flooded back. The chase. The desperate attempt to get back his laptop. The taser. And now he was in the palm of their hands, which was ironic, all things considered.

"We can't take you back just yet," said Mary Ann. "Some of your assholes—sorry, your guards—had guns! Guns! What was that for, to shoot the kids if they don't behave? Anyway, we won't hurt you. We're nonviolent."

He stared at her, remembering fists and kicks flying.

"In theory. Mostly. Anyway, we don't kill, we don't torture people who have different beliefs than we do, and we don't hit anyone unless we *really* have to. So relax; enjoy the ride.

When we get there, we'll talk about whatever it is you don't want us to see. But right now…there's six of us, one of you, and three of us are bad-ass."

"Hey!" Max interjected. "I'm bad-ass!"

Isobel smiled and patted his shoulder. "No, you're not, sweetie—but you will be. It takes time. Anyway, Victor. I'm Ginger; this is the Skipper; Gilligan is driving, and this—is the Professor. But you know him as Max." He stared at her in wide-eyed incomprehension. "Everyone, as you know, this is Eve."

"Come on, honey. Do you think we're going to tell you our real names?" She smiled. He saw her point. And the silly names made him feel, weirdly, a little safer, safe enough that he lay back and let the bouncy ride pass over him in numb, but no longer terrified, shock.

A long hour of driving on bad road later, they pulled onto a short, paved drive and into pure luxury.

Sequoia rushed out to meet them, hugging them as they piled out of the car. Hugs everywhere, and Max pulled Kate's hand and dragged her over to meet Sequoia. "She's kind of like my mom, sorta. This is my family."

"Lucky! Most of my family sucks—well, you know."

Then a huge voice yelled, "BOOGER!" and Kate was almost knocked off her feet as her brother stampeded out the front door and into her arms. The siblings began to cry. "Oh, God, you guys're so precious!" Beto said. "Oh, this shit always kills me! I'm glad I'm not wearing mascara!" he exclaimed as tears streamed from his eyes too.

Max tried to hold it back, but Beto punched him and said, "Don't be such a fucking boy!" and he started to cry too, and laugh. The birds sang, and Leo made his rather magnificent entrance with a tray of tall, frosty mojitos. Victor stared at them as they laughed, whooped, hugged, drank: Was this what it was like to be a satanic freak? Where were the goblets of blood, the strung-out junkies?

"I see we have an unexpected guest," Leo said. Not by one muscle of his face or note in his voice did he indicate that this was anything but a delightful surprise. "Mojito?"

Victor shook his head numbly. He had never had a drink of alcohol in his whole life.

"It was Gilligan's fault!" Max called over.

"It was not my fault, *muchacho*. My job is to drive the car. Not to beat off strangers who get into the car. That's the job of the lesbian karate twins. If a strange man gets in my car, I scream and taser. Honey, a lot of my best dates started that way."

Leo smiled, "Well, we will sort this all out soon enough," he said. "But for now, please. Accept this mojito. Don't say no—I muddled the mint myself. And the rum? I have to say Dominican rum is some of the best rum in the world. Delightful."

And such was the force of his charm that Victor reached out, as muddled as mint, and drank. An hour later he found himself sitting in a porch swing, finishing a second mojito and broaching the subject, his big subject, to Sequoia.

"You have my files—you *have* to give them back to me. I'll do anything, anything," he said as they looked out onto a warm, soft night.

"Well, that's something we can talk about tomorrow," replied Sequoia. "Tonight we're celebrating, you know."

"They'll miss me back at camp! They'll wonder where I am! I have to go back tonight, or you'll be arrested!"

"No no no. You won't *let* them arrest us—we have your laptop, remember?" She smiled at him so warmly it was hard to remember that that was a threat. "So I've been thinking. Tell me, do you have any money or credit cards with you?"

Victor clutched his middle reflexively. He was one of the

xenophobic American tribe with little trust, and he never went anywhere, not even around the camp, without his passport and a credit card strapped to an inside pouch. Sequoia saw and smiled.

"Excellent! Then it's easy enough. You call the camp and tell them we dumped you in the city. You're exhausted and you're going to stay at a hotel for the night. Then we can discuss this little...brouhaha...and come to an amicable agreement, I'm sure. In the meantime, you're our guest. We're feasting, dancing on the beach, drinking mojitos. The laptop is locked in a wall safe. Its secrets will keep. So let's just forget it until morning, shall we?"

And to his great surprise, he did. She took his hand and led him to a seat on the porch overlooking the beach. He sat on the porch in the warm night air and drank two more mojitos, liking each one better than the last. Going to a Christian college, living with his mother, no pleasure like this had come his way. The funny thing, he thought, was how it all worked together. The (devilish, evil, sinful) rum with lime and mint was a sensual, unfolding delight that left his mouth sweet and his temper sweeter. He tried to hate these people, who had spanked him in his own camp and abducted him—well, sort of. Who were freaks and weirdos and perverts and sinners. Who held his fate in their hands. But he couldn't summon the hatred; he couldn't feel the hatred, in the face of their happiness. All he felt was surprise: they delighted in each other, in the food that they ate—a traditional Caribbean barbecue, Dominican style. The food smelled luscious and tasted better than anything he had ever eaten. He saw the big black man feed the black woman a plantain off his own fork, and the look she gave him—were they a couple? The two gorgeous women ran on the beach and tackled each other, emerging laughing and dripping in the surf, and kissed in the moonlight. He averted his eyes and tried to feel revulsion. *Disgusting. Perverts. Evil*, he thought to himself. It didn't work. Disgust would not come. The affable host, who called himself Mr. Howell, moved between his guests urging them to eat, to drink, to laugh, to enjoy, and then cuddled up to the woman who called herself Lovey on a porch swing, and they just held each other silently for a while.

Victor watched the teens who had escaped from his own camp fill their plates, piling food on with abandon. Then they sat together on the beach a little ways off with the brother, and their voices carried quite far, all the way to his ears. He listened to them. He listened to them talk about his camp, the one his mother had planned and he, in theory, owned. About how awful it was. Their language shocked him. They kept saying the camp was FUCKED UP! He flinched from it. He could hear it, *everyone* could hear it, but no adult went down there to tell them to mind their manners or their language. He couldn't believe how free they were. How hard they laughed. How they drank mojitos with the adults, although Lovey, the black woman, said, "Just a few, honey! We need you in top shape tomorrow," as the boy—who was really a girl? —grabbed a tray to take to the young people.

Something hurt in his heart because he had never had this, ever, and he had never even known he had been missing something. He didn't even know what this *was*, this casual, loving, laughing way of being. The only word he had to describe it was "sin." And that didn't quite seem…right. But whatever it was, it wasn't his. He wasn't a part of it and couldn't be. Not too far away was *his* place, a grim little camp where everyone was in bed sleeping, even on a beautiful night like this, where no one ran or jumped or giggled or whooped or yelled "FUCKED UP." He remembered a minister he had once heard who had said that sin wasn't really that much fun. It was dirty and sordid and ugly. How being good, godly men and women was "deeply joyful." He thought he had known then was that meant, but he realized that deeply joyful was something he had never seen before tonight.

And he couldn't stand to see another minute of it.

He turned in to the house and found the room they had allotted him. The bed was softer and sweeter than any he had ever slept in, and noticing that was his last conscious thought before sleep claimed him.

Chapter 25: After the Rescue

The problem sat on their plates like a bad entrée made by an oversensitive cook. The decision to ignore it and concentrate on drinking was unanimous. Felicity and Isobel, Keith and Beto, Sequoia and Leo, all steamed up the night with each other, and the casa was filled with fuck moans.

Paul lay in bed listening to it and smiling, sometimes crying. He had listened for an hour and a half while Kate and Max talked and talked about what it had been like: the rules, the quiet, the terror. The two needed to talk, to chatter like monkeys, after their stint of enforced silence. Paul smiled thinking about it, thinking about the way Max looked at Kate, the way Kate flirted. Once when he went back up to the porch to grab a soda, he came back to find them just pulling back from a kiss. Well, okay, it bothered him a little—but if Kate could like both boys and girls why couldn't she like Max too? And he was a great guy. They had gone through trauma together. His sister could take people for themselves, just as they were. It was what was great about her. He wished he had her spirit.

Sequoia woke early the next morning to her alarm and bounced right out of bed, energized as she always was by sex and her chosen family. As tired as everyone was, the team would expect, and get, an early rousting from Sequoia, who barged into every bedroom with an exuberant, "Rise and shine, campers!" They groaned, but they rose. They even shone a lit-tle—it was a *beautiful* day.

They took their seats around the dining room table for the debriefing. Kate and Paul slept on—this meeting was for the team. And for the first time ever, Eve sat with them. The team took her in, and she smiled.

"Do we get to know her real name?" Max asked.

Sequoia smiled and shook her head. "Still better not, I think."

Eve smiled. "I like being Eve, anyway," she said. "It feels more real than my real name to me."

"Remind me again WHY we have to get up at the crack of ass for this?" griped a sleepy Isobel.

"Because we need to decide what we're going to do about our problem upstairs before he wakes us up and asks us, mak-ing us look like idiots," Sequoia smiled. "So explain to me one more time, troops: *why* are we kidnappers?"

"God, GUYS, I am so sorry. I mean, he just, jumped in, and I screamed, and everyone else jumped in, and there was gunfire, and then—shit. I fucked up. I'm really sorry," Beto had his head in his hands. "I guess from now on you *can* call me fucking Gilligan."

Max, as usual, was oblivious to his surroundings, with Victor's laptop out and humming, and then gave a bark of shock. "Shit! Shit shit shit!" Keith peeked over Max's shoulder at that and gave a long, low whistle of surprise. And then he laughed—a deep, rich, and hearty laugh—and kissed the top of Beto's head.

"Well, little buddy, looks like you might just have saved the day after all."

Max turned the computer around and everyone's eyes

207

popped as they took in the contents. Beautiful women filled the screen. No blondes to be seen—Asian, black, Latino. All with long, flowing black hair, gorgeous brown eyes, small rounded breasts. And big *hard* dicks. In the privacy of his porn world, Victor knew exactly what he liked.

Felicity whistled and then said, "I'm not going out on a limb when I say Mama doesn't know about THIS!"

Keith whooped a long, loud laugh. "This makes it just too fucking easy. Straight-up blackmail, my man—shut down the camp, or everyone's gonna know you like chicks with dicks."

"But *you* like chicks with dicks, don't you?" said Sequoia.

"Hell yeah I do! But I don't run a camp traumatizing children into thinking they're sick if *they* do."

"Okay, exactly—don't you see? This is what you want? To win by *shaming* him for his desires, outing him when he doesn't want to be outed? We don't do that shit! That is the *opposite* of what we do and what we stand for."

Keith looked at her with his mouth open. "You have got to be kidding me. You have GOT to be kidding me! You are telling me that we have here the ammo that can blow that whole fucking camp off the map and we aren't going to use it— for a principle?" His outrage ratcheted up. "We let them go on beating and…electrocuting people! Because we're too good to use a dirty weapon? NO! Sequoia, no. You didn't see that place. But you saw the state Eve was in. You have to know we do this by any means necessary."

Felicity spoke up: "We CAN out him! Fuck him! This man is a filthy hypocrite. His camp abuses children! It does it with their parents' consent, away from American law, and if we walk away and let it keep happening…no, we *stop* this. And we use what we have. And THIS—is what we have," Felicity pointed at the screen as she held forth. "We stop abuse. That's what we do. It's our prime directive."

"I love it when you get nerdy on me," Isobel whispered in her ear.

But Sequoia continued. "I'm not saying we let it continue. But let's say you blackmail him. You've seen what Christians do when they get caught. They apologize, the Lord forgives them, and on they go. At the best, he'll sell the camp. And some other asshole will take over. One we don't have any ammo on. Maybe the next asshole will be better. Maybe…worse."

"If he did, we'd out him! He wouldn't dare!"

"He just might, though," Max said thoughtfully. "The way it seemed to me in the camp—and here"—while they argued he had turned away from the chicks with dicks and had been plowing through more boring camp emails and documents—"it's his mother who really runs things. He owns everything on paper, but she calls the shots. She might throw him to the wolves, so that she can keep her little stalag alive. Especially if she thinks he's been seduced by Satan's perversions. She is as cuddly as a cobra, that one."

"Her own son?" Leo asked.

"Yes," said Eve. "You haven't seen her at her worst." She shivered. Keith put his hand over hers in a gesture of concern. "She's a monster. She's a crazy person, and I don't think people count as people to her once they break her insane rules. If she saw this, she would do her worst. And her worst is probably worse than what we can imagine."

"But what's the alternative? I mean, what are you thinking, girl? I know you have something going on in that beautiful brain of yours," Keith was watching Sequoia as she looked out to sea.

"We…we seduce him. We win him on our terms. We make him want to close down the camp himself: he owns it; it's his; and the only thing that's really going to stop it is if *he* chooses for it to stop."

209

The Case of the Creepy Christian Camp

"Oh, this is a *great* idea," Felicity piped up, all sarcasm and disbelief. "And then we'll get Rush Limbaugh to come out of the closet and he and Glenn Beck can get married and open a mini-cupcake store in the Castro. They can call it 'Neo-Confections!' I know, sweetheart, I know you really like to believe people can change—but are you *fucking* serious?"

"Look, I watched him last night, when you guys were feasting and making out and roughhousing on the beach. I watched him and talked to him. He was listening to the kids talk about the camp, and…I don't know. He seemed interested. Sad. Even a little confused. Not angry, like you'd expect."

"And even if it were possible, just remotely possible, that maybe there's someone in there you could convert, what are you going to do? Are we going to hold him against his will? We can't *do* that. We are in enough trouble as it is; we *kidnapped* someone. Our *only* hope of avoiding being arrested is blackmail. We need to get him back to their camp pronto, before they send out the troops."

"Actually—he called them last night and told them he was okay and that he wouldn't be able to get back today."

"Oh, Jesus. And what did he say when they asked why he wasn't coming back last night?!"

"He said he wanted to talk us into giving back Kate by warning us of the legal consequences. Since her parents didn't ask for her to be rescued, that's kidnapping too. But it also looks real bad for them; they lost a whole fucking kid. One reason parents send their kids here is because it's almost impossible to run away. The kids are trapped in a foreign country and the camp holds all the passports and money.

"Shit! Do we have Kate's passport?" Max piped up.

"Yes," said Eve. "Luckily, they didn't think to strip search me. I had it on me when they took me." She slid it over.

Sequoia shook her head in disbelief. "I have to admit I

210

never even thought of that. You are worth your weight in gold, girl."

Eve blushed and shook her head.

"Phew...we would have a bitch of a time getting her back in the country without her passport," said Leo.

"Back to the problem," said Sequoia. "This guy, he's hurting, and from what Max told me last night he can't even bring himself to dole out the physical punishment. And I saw his eyes last night. Let's just *ask* him if maybe he wants to stay with us one more night. Just...ask him. And give him a little taste of what life might be like. There's just an off chance that that's all he ever really needed. And if that doesn't work, well, we can always blackmail him later."

There was a lot of doubt in the room, but Sequoia's compassion and optimism were hard to say no to. They reluctantly nodded.

"Okay, then. I think what we *all* need is a really great night out. With drag queens!"

And Beto smiled ear to ear. "Oh, honeys, I know just the place."

Chapter 26: Club Night

Sequoia had often thought that people radically underestimate the true function of parties, marking them down to mere frivolity, irresponsibility. The American culture has a bizarre love-hate relationship with pleasure and fun. Pleasure is glamorized, but pleasure can be packaged and sold in an ad. Fun, though, is always homemade. Things that can be bought can help make fun, but they are never enough—fun is liberating, creative, inspirational. Great parties germinate great ideas. So whether this was a solution, a desperately stupid idea, or just a way to put off making a decision for one more day, the decision was made. They were out to hunt fun. Not just little fun. Big game. Wildness. Madness. Joy.

First, to sell Victor on the idea. She took him out on the veranda overlooking the beach and plied him with a breakfast so delicious and mimosas so sinful he folded like origami. The ease of that win gave her hope. He called back to the camp, told his mother he would be one more night, and hung up on her before she could work her evil magic. Giddy with freedom, he watched as everyone primped and preened and gussied up, and then he was fussed over himself, with Leo lending him clothes. Sequoia clucked and praised, and Beto *worked*, combing product in his hair, straightening his tie, tweezing his eyebrows—just a little, darling, just the manliest little bit—and then disappeared to dress herself.

Victor looked in the mirror, and a handsome stranger looked back and smiled. The tropical night breathed flowers.

The girl, Kate, spun around in clothes borrowed from Felicity, a vintage summer dress with yards of skirt to twirl in; Max slicked his hair back and put on his sharpest blazer, a rich bright blue that brought out the color of his eyes. They assembled downstairs and Victor thought, with that stab of envy, that he had never been with more beautiful or happier people. Isobel was in a sultry pin-up-girl sarong-style dress that looked like she had been poured into it, her hair flashing like fire. Felicity's dress was just as sexy but minimal, spare, showing off her tight body. Keith's light-blue Guayabera suited the easy elegance of his masculinity, while Leo edged more toward the dapper, white blazer and bow tie over a restrained Hawaiian print. Sequoia's billowing floral print in reds and yellows made her look like a tropical flower. Eve wore one of Isobel's dresses, which Beto had done an emergency hem and tuck to make fit: for once her movie star figure showed to advantage in a deep pink wiggle dress. They were all gorgeous, but when Beto walked in in full drag, she took Victor's breath away.

No, not Beto anymore: Miss Margarita, she introduced herself to him. Margarita in drag: dark, pretty eyes, fishy glamorous oomph. A big tropical flower in her hair. The aggression, the defensiveness, the chip on her shoulder seemed to melt away, and she played the ingénue to the hilt. Victor felt his heart give a loud, silly thump and then start beating faster. Skipper looked over at them and grinned.

At the club the girls and the kids clambered out of the car, leaving Leo to park—it's the prerogative of anyone wearing high heels not to have to look for parking. Margarita grabbed

213

Victor by the arm and pulled him out. He felt dazed. The world had just cracked open and revealed itself to be something completely other than he had thought. Live Latin jazz floated out to them, and when he entered the club he recognized it. How could that be? He stared around for a minute in disbelief until he saw a woman at the bar—Lucille Ball to a tee, with retro red wig, pouty red lips, red and white polka dot dress. The whole place—like walking into Ricky's club.

"Her?" Victor whispered to Margarita.

"Yes, Papi, of course," she whispered back. "She's part of the act."

With his typical swank, Leo ushered them to a large booth commanding a great view of the band. Champagne was already chilling at the table, but Leo pressed a mojito into Victor's hand. "I feel it's your drink," he said with a hint of a drawl and a wink. Victor felt drunk before he drank—the live music, the dancing, the excited chattering joy of the whole posse he was with. He marveled for a second and thought he had never had this, never just been out with a group of people who accepted him, who wanted nothing more than for him to have fun, with a beautiful woman on his arm and a drink in his hand. Last night at the beach he had felt his own loneliness and his envy at their casual joy, and now he felt like—one of them. They had simply reached out and folded him in. He marveled at how easy it had been. He tasted mint and rum, smelled Margarita's jasmine perfume, heard the exuberant beat of the band, felt the rhythm in his bones. This was *his* night, his one night of freedom from his life. Tomorrow—well, right now he couldn't imagine tomorrow. This couldn't last. This was a dream. But it was here now.

The houselights lowered a fraction from dim to dark, and the light came up on the stage. A dapper man burst into a torrent of Spanish, then repeated himself in accented English,

214

urging them to enjoy the night, the drinks, and the music. And to tip their waitresses. And then he yelled, "Hit it!"

The band swung into a dance version of Barry Manilow's "Copacabana," the lead singer hamming up his accent. Halfway through, "Lucy" sidled onto stage with a pair of maracas singing along in a grating, off-key, two-packs-a-day voice. The audience giggled and sniggered at Lucy's dancing, all elbows and wild graceless joy. The singer stopped, stared, letting the audience soak up the fun of the gyrating singing comedy and then bellowed the inevitable, "LUUUUUCCCCCY!"

The audience broke up, as Lucy began to cry and then ran off stage, yelling, "Aw, Ricky!" in the deepest rumble imaginable. The final chorus wound down with Lucy sneaking back on stage for the final "Don't Fall in Love," sung in her off-key bass voice before she was hustled off stage again.

"Ricky" came back and urged the customers to take advantage of the Latin dance lessons on offer from a bevy of drag queens ranging from showgirl gorgeous to a comically bearded queen who went from table to table teasing and taunting and complimenting and coaxing until she got a taker. The lights came back up a fraction as the music started again and the dance floor filled up. Victor felt a rush to his toes as Margarita whispered with hot breath in his ear, "Papi, I am going to teach you to samba," and then he was lurching, protesting, to the dance floor. He had never danced. Not ever. But found himself moving to the music with Margarita complimenting every step. "You have natural rhythm, Papi! Never doubt it!"

Time stopped *meaning* anything, and he stopped counting minutes or drinks or dances or laughs. Dancing danced and shows showed; rum and mint and music and laughter were all mixed up in that. Margarita stayed with him—almost the whole time, yet once passing him off to another very pretty queen who danced him dizzy and handed him back. But at

215

some point, tired, he made his way back to the table. The world spun around and righted itself and into that moment Margarita looked deep in his eyes and asked a question: how did a man who could dance like that and laugh like that end up running that camp?

And he was loose with mojitos and the night, and he told her…everything. More mojitos came and went while he told his story, and she listened.

He expected condemnation, disapproval, but all he got was sugar. Margarita told him in the dark about running away from home, about being called trash and garbage by his mother, and taking off. So she knew about mothers.

Victor whispered, "I'm not as brave as you."

"You could be. No one's brave on their own, Papi. Not anyone," and she leaned her head back against his shoulder and their hands met and held and they stayed like that, quiet and thoughtful, until Margarita said, "You know what, Victor? When she met us, Lovey had us all write everything down. Everything we could remember about why we were who we were, why we did what we did. Do that, okay? It helps. You figure out who you are, and who maybe you want to be."

"Yeah," he said. "I will, I'll do that. I think I have always been afraid to write it down before—I hated what was inside me. I was taught to hate it. But maybe it's time to look."

She squeezed his hand in answer.

And then the kids came laughing back to the table and soon after that the club closed, everyone taking a final shot from the bar and piling back into the cars, where the sober designated driver—of course, Eve—drove them, giggling and chattering and talking over how fun the evening had been, until they were home.

At the door to her room, Margarita kissed Victor one last time. "Don't go tomorrow, Papi. Stay with us and think things over for a while. Get your head together. Write it down."

"Maybe," he said. "We'll see." He sounded thoughtful. Margarita felt a sinking in her stomach—they gambled. Would it work? Or was it just a great night out? Their last? She had an image of herself in a prison jumpsuit and shivered from head to toe.

Chapter 27: Vic's Story

Victor's story, written three months later

I was always a Good Boy. And I always hated it. My mother named me Victor Timothy after my two grandfathers—with her father first, of course. I go by Tim now—I've been a victim long enough. A Vic Tim. Thanks, Mom. Scarily prescient. But not anymore.

I *had* to be a Good Boy, because my father was a Bad Boy. My dad, Chet Madison, made ridiculous amounts of money publishing a line of Christian romances in which women converted Bad Boys with the strength of their faith. You wouldn't believe how much money there is in that. I read a few of these, just curious to know how my parents made their living. The heroines flutter around with no makeup, but they don't need it because they glow with the light of the Lord. That might be an actual quote. My mother wrote the first five and then quietly farmed out the pseudonym, Christine Angel (she really had a way with names, my mother—maybe mine was no accident after all), and turned editor, enforcing the guidelines, which went something like this: Bad Boy meets girl when some relative or friend drags him to a church picnic or potluck. He's drawn to her strange, radiant light like a moth to a Christian flame, but resists his attraction because he knows she is too good for him. That's the first step to his redemption. Then he is thrown together with her by circumstances beyond either of their control (oh, those mysterious ways of the Lord, aka Christine Angel) until he realizes she has given him the inner faith to conquer his demons and walk the straight path. He asks her to marry him, chaste kiss, wedding bells, Jesus Christ. Tons and tons of Jesus Christ. In every sense.

My mother wrote them, but my dad promoted them, and when they expanded their line, he promoted that too. He was a charmer. The kind of guy who always had a lopsided smile and a shit-eating grin. A Christian Harrison Ford. He would go on interviews and confess that he himself had been saved by his lovely wife. One Christian magazine actually said he had a roguish twinkle in his eye. I felt a wave of nausea when I read it.

I am pretty sure my father cheated on my mother going back a long, long way. He was gone a lot, at conferences and meetings with Christian bookstores, so he had plenty of opportunity. Back in the bad old days before cell phones, the phone would often ring, mother would pick it up, and whoever it was would hang up. And she would say, "Someone hung up again" in this funny, pointed way. When I was a kid, I knew something was off, but I didn't get it. Then once, when I was fifteen and my voice had broken, someone rang up and called me darling before she realized I wasn't my dad. So that's when I knew, and then I understood why my mother was always saying that bad women were temptresses. Sometimes I wondered why my father didn't leave, but that was before I realized that my mother ran the business. She hid that from me when I was growing up, because women aren't supposed to be the boss—so it wasn't until he died that I realized she had been running the show the whole time. He was a charming glad-handing front man. She was a ruler with an iron fist.

Mother was always heaping the coals of her goodness on his head—on both of us. She never criticized him openly: she quoted the bible about a woman's duty to her husband. Relentlessly. After I was about ten I never remember her speaking to him about anything but business of one kind or another, unless it was bible quotes. To me, she talked *all* the time about prostitutes and adulteresses, and we all know what the bible has to say about them. So I got the message. She told me over and over that my father wasn't to blame; the women were. She probably hated him, but she definitely hated women. I could see that she was miserable, and I felt helpless. She was my mom. I loved her, and he was hurting her. He never paid much attention to me—he was the kind of dad who breezed home when he felt like it, rumpled your hair and called you "sport," and then was gone.

So I felt this tremendous pressure to make this up to my mother, to be the wise and steadfast son who would cause his mother to rejoice. I even thought in bible quotes—they were all I knew. That's what she would say I was, so I had to be that. And I did. Schoolwork did *not* come easily to me, but Mother made me do it, and I plugged away at it. I managed to consistently get As and Bs. She was disappointed with the Bs. She had been valedictorian of her high school, attended two years of college on scholarship, and then quit to marry my father. I did not inherit her brains. Or her ambition. Or her force of character. I didn't like school much. I did like sports, but I liked the *wrong* sports. Baseball was boring, and I wasn't big or strong or brave enough for football. I liked soccer and basketball, but there were no soccer teams in schools back then, and my mother wouldn't let me play basketball because she thought it was for black people. The wrong kind of black people. She only liked black people when they were singing hallelujah, and not much then. She thought they sang it wrong.

When I was sixteen my dad was diagnosed with stomach cancer, which is one of the worst kinds. Almost always fatal. He hated doctors and hospitals and all the external signs of illness, so my mother sighed her martyr smile, converted the living room to a hospital room, and hired an agency to provide round-the-clock in-home nursing. Who knew that that would change my life?

My dad was hell on the nurses. He pinched the first day nurse's ass when he was happy and threw things at her when he wasn't, so she naturally quit. The next three did too. Finally we got a mousy little thing whose ass was so flat it was unpinchable and didn't mind having things thrown at her. Then there was the night nurse: the first one was sixty years old and spoke to him like he was a special-needs child, so he told her hair-raisingly misogynist jokes and she quit within twenty-four hours.

So there we were at home, and I was taking care of my father, making him a meal. My mother was making a rare visit to the sickroom.

"Why's the boy bringing me food, Margaret? Isn't this a woman's work? Do you want the boy to be a fag?"

"He's honoring his father, Chet. And I would very much appreciate if you could moderate your language," her tone had the acid sweetness of a lemon drop, her mouth pursed with the sour taste of her words. "The agency says they can't keep sending more nurses. So if you want your son to be relieved of women's work, try to speak like a Christian."

I was standing by the door to the kitchen, edging my way out of the room. My father's temper was increasingly volatile, and he was capable of hurling obscene invective at my mother: why should he care anymore what she thought?

I saw my father's hand start to curl around the cup of tomato soup in his hand and breathlessly waited to see my moth-

221

er splashed. The truth was, right at that moment, I wanted him to do it. I thought I loved her, but it was exciting, and I...I wanted it.

But in that moment the doorbell rang, and my mother strode across the door and let in...the night nurse.

In walked the most beautiful woman I have ever seen. An Amazon. A goddess. Six foot two in her practical nurse shoes. And black. Wearing one of those white nurse dresses they still wore in the '80s, before everyone started wearing ugly scrubs. Time stopped in its tracks, and the whole world held its breath. My jaw dropped. She said her name. Morgan Dumont. After a pause to gather herself, my mother greeted her with cool politeness, but I could see the shock behind it. She excused herself abruptly and left the room.

My dad had no hesitation and no filters: "Well look at YOU! God sent me a sexy, sexy angel. How are you, darlin'? Come to cheer up a dying man?" She walked over to his bedside, and he promptly smacked her on the ass.

But she just put her hands on her hips and said, "Well *thank* you, honey. Now let's see what we can do to make you more comfortable." And she left the room with a swish of her hips and came back with his drugs.

My mother did everything she could to get her fired or make her quit. But Morgan was stubborn. She *liked* my dad. She told him he could pinch her ass exactly once a day, because any more than that and she started feeling like fruit at the supermarket. She made him laugh. He told her stories about what wild times he'd had when he was supposed to be at Christian conferences: I know because while my mother was out taking care of business she made me go sit with my dad. She wanted me to keep an eye on that nurse. "I don't trust her," she muttered. "Make sure she doesn't steal anything."

Morgan was nice to me. Not flirtatious, just...kind.

Made me a sandwich from time to time. Asked how I was doing. Then one day she looked over at me and I was torn up, my father dying, my mother not even actually talking to him, not even then. And it felt like everything inside me was knotted and confused and…I don't know. Like there wasn't a person on earth I could trust.

I was standing in the kitchen, and she was at the sink. I was just standing there, I didn't have anything to do, I wasn't eating or getting food—I barely ate in those days. A growing boy, just long bones and not much else. And Morgan looked at me and gave me the funniest look, like she was weighing things in her mind. And then she smiled. She put down what she was working on and walked into the pantry. And called me in.

I walked over to the door, and she grabbed my arm and pulled me close, and she murmured something in my ear. I didn't even catch what it was, just that the tone was sweeter than anything I had ever heard and the heat of her breath on my ear sent chills up and down my spine. Now I was a teenage boy, so I was horny all the time. All the time. But I barely ever even masturbated. Partly because my mother warned me it was a sin, and it's hard to masturbate when you imagine your mother and Jesus both frowning in disapproval. And also, it was like, I didn't know what to fantasize about. I would try to block out Jesus and imagine pretty girls but they kind of turned into Jesus and then I started beating off *to* Jesus, but he would be this very feminine-looking Jesus with pretty brown eyes and that would freak me out and I would stop. I had a lot of wet dreams. Mother told me one day that I had to do my own laundry from now on. I was mortified. I still have problems with laundry, this sense of shame about just the simple act of doing the wash.

But when Morgan whispered in my ear there was no Jesus. Just her. And she was warm and solid and big, and she smelled like perfume and this other smell I couldn't identify but I liked it. And she sank to her knees and I felt her breath there, against my penis, through my pants and I was getting harder and harder. When she zipped down my pants and took it into her mouth I thought, *God, I should run, I am being sinful*, but I knew I wanted sin right then and when I came I moaned Jesus but I meant Morgan. I almost cried. I whispered thank you, thank you.

She kissed my cheek and wiped her mouth off with the back of her hand and stepped out of the pantry with no trace of guilt. I staggered upstairs and lay down on my bed. I thought that, yes, the mouth of an adulteress WAS like a deep pit, just like Mother always said, and then I fell asleep, the first sleep without bad dreams since my father came home to die.

And maybe if we had left it at that, it might have just been one sweet memory, but I was young and horny and she was generous and greedy, and we tempted fate until we lost. One day just three weeks before my father died Mother came home and we didn't hear her, but she heard us. She opened the pantry door, and then she just started screaming.

Then she collapsed on the floor. I rushed over to her, tucking myself away, saying, "Mother, mother, wake up. I'm sorry. I am so sorry."

Morgan just gathered her things with this stony flinty look on her face. Mother came to and just started yelling at her, "Whore! WHORE! You filthy, filthy BLACK whore." She was screaming. She said the word "black" like it was the worst thing in the world. Her face was contorted and gruesome with hate.

And Morgan just looked at me and said softly, "Don't let her bully you, honey."

I was confused. I said, "She doesn't bully me."

And she said, "Doesn't she?" and she walked out. I never saw her again.

My mother called the service to have another nurse sent, then staggered to the living room to calm Dad down. The screaming had woken him up and we could hear him calling out, "What's happening? What the HELL is happening?"

Mother wouldn't talk to me. She wouldn't look at me. I was thanking God she hadn't told the service what happened. She could have had Morgan fired, no problem. But even more, I was just stewing in guilt and shame, just an ocean of guilt and shame. I thought I would drown in it. I couldn't breathe.

That night she beat me. She called me into the kitchen, after Dad had his painkiller and was out for the night. She picked up a broom right above the bristles, and she quoted the Bible: "Rod and reprimand impart wisdom, but a boy who runs wild brings shame on his mother. Correct your son, and he will be a comfort to you and bring delights of every kind."

And I just sank to my knees and let her beat me. Over the back, on the ass, across the shoulders, on my arms and legs. She went a little wild. I had welts. She kept me home from school until the evidence healed. I am just lucky she didn't hit the kidneys because she wasn't doing a great job of aiming. And I didn't stop her. I knelt there crying and trying not to scream too hard because I didn't want to wake up my dad, and I kept thinking that I was *disgusting*, and I deserved this, and she was right to beat me. I was garbage.

After that, my mother sat me down at the kitchen table and made me a cup of cocoa. I sat there still shaking and drinking this cocoa, and she said, "I beat you so you would know not to ever, ever do that again. But I know it wasn't your fault. She tempted you. She was a…" her mother pursed up like she had just drunk vinegar straight. "Well, you know now what they look like, what they can do. And you'll do better now, right? I need you to be a comfort to me. Not like…"

It was the closest she ever came to saying what my father

was like, the womanizing. I looked down into my cocoa and promised. That I would never, not ever. And I meant it. At that moment, I hated Morgan. I hated her for bringing this shame on me, for tempting me. I blamed her, when I should have been thanking her.

I hated her more because I couldn't stop. I would masturbate and imagine how hot and wet her mouth had been and how she could take all of me in, all my dick but also, all of me, and hating her made me want her more and I would come and come in this horrible confusion of shame and guilt and desire. I finally decided that, hey, I needed to choose the lesser of two evils and I went to find some porn. It was before the Internet, so that meant magazines. I wanted some girl to beat off to that would replace her in my mind. And then I would know I was normal. A nice, normal white girl, just to show I was normal. I knew porn was wrong, but my fantasies were wrong too, and my wet dreams were nightmares. And I just wanted it not to be Morgan because sometimes I would masturbate and then cry in confusion and it felt…just horrible.

It didn't work great. Most of the girls, they seemed too round, too soft. But every once in a while there would be a girl, with a very tight muscular body, and then…then it worked. I developed a collection. Then one day I was in this porn shop, and there was a magazine called *Shemale*. I was so dumb I didn't even know what that meant, but I picked it up and looked at it. And there they were: chicks with dicks. And I looked at them and it all just suddenly clicked. The height. The half remembered smell. The hard slim muscular body. How hard her breasts were the one time she let me feel them. And I thought, oh God, no. Oh no no no no. But there was my goddamn dick, rock hard, perking up like a dog who smelled steak.

I think my mother knew, guessed, something. She had always been a little crazy on the idea of gender roles, the importance of keeping them absolutely clear and crisp and separate. But she became *obsessed* after my father died, and when the insurance money came in she bought this land in the Dominican Republic and started the camp. And put it all in my name because I was the "man." And I went along with it. Maybe I was hoping the camp would work for me too. She thought all children's problems could be solved through Jesus Christ and very strict gender-role training. I hoped somehow it would work.

I didn't know then the lengths she would go to. I was still sick and confused when she started hiring people and outlining what she wanted and how it would work. I tried to speak out now and then, and she would rationally explain why it was all necessary. The beatings. The rules, the control. And she would give me this look that told me that of course I knew, *really*, why she had to do all this, and when she gave me that look I would bow down and acquiesce.

What I wanted, honestly, was for it to just end. I would have burned it down if I could have figured out how to do it without hurting people. And then they came along. And I wasn't who they meant to rescue, but they rescued me anyway. Now I apologize to Morgan in my heart for all of the terrible things I thought about her. I still feel shame; you can't just dump out the shame and not feel it after you were raised like I was. But I am working with it. I am working on it. I don't have to be imprisoned by it anymore. I was set free.

We closed down the camp, and my mother couldn't do a thing about it because on paper I owned everything. We sent the kids back to their parents—that was hard. Max screamed that we should keep them all, because parents who would send their kids here were *for sure* abusive. But we made sure they got cards and we told them to call if they needed help. They wanted to go home—most of them, anyway. I sold the land to a couple of guys who wanted to build a gay resort—perfect, right? And, well, I moved on. I came back to San Francisco with Beto and Keith—I get to know their real names now—and I bought a place and met some people, and I have a social life now, friends, sometimes even lovers. They have to be patient with me. I get…triggered. One minute hot and turned on the next moment quivering and waiting for the broom to descend. But I'm getting better. I'm getting better.

Epilogue: Lovey in the Rose Garden, in Her Journal

In between the big exciting times, there is always work to do. The work is always big and small, frustrating, rewarding, endless, composed of a thousand different details. Do you know who to talk to to discuss housing arrangements for a transgender freshman at UC Berkeley? I do. I have a thousand different numbers like that one, and I've had thousands of conversations just trying to open people's eyes one little damn peep at a time. That's why I like to walk in the rose gardens. The roses know who they are, exactly, and the gardeners never spend any time telling them they shouldn't be what they are. They just help them bloom. Sometimes I think about what we do that way: just transplanting flowers to somewhere they can bloom.

I'm about to go on vacation—maybe. A real one, not one with rescued children to cluck over and mother. I almost don't see the point. But Leo wants to take me somewhere, and he is probably right. He usually is. I packed Max up and drove him to his dorm, and now he's at college. I had to fight him to go, but he's there, and even though he's all of ten minutes away from me up in the Berkeley Hills, I still miss the little shit. It's weird how he became mine so fast and then grew up so fast and left me. So I'll go away for a while and let him be his own man.

The Case of the Creepy Christian Camp

Kate is with her grandparents. She and Max skyped for a while, and then I think Kate met someone else. Max took it hard, I think, which is to say he wouldn't say a damn thing to me about it. Someday I'll convince him he really doesn't have to be this much of a boy about everything.

I started thinking now that it's been a while since we've started doing this, and life is changing all the time. Maybe twenty years from now what we do won't even be necessary: won't that be nice? And then what will old warhorses like us do? I imagine we'll find something, but until then...until then there is still plenty for us to do. I'll just check my email here in the rose garden before heading home to cook dinner. Fish, I think. With hush puppies.

Shit! I got an email I was hoping never to get...the very first kid we rescued, an MTF trans kid named Carol (nee Carl). Sweet girl, married a nice young man, and they had a kid, a boy. Carol let her parents back into their lives after a big crying reconciliation—and they have kidnapped the boy. I've been expecting it for a while, and now it's here: rescue the next generation.

Well. I think my vacation is going to have to wait.